D1521095

BETHLEHEM BOYS

BETHLEHEM BOYS

A Novel

by Jeffrey Briskin

THE PARKAV PRESS

BOSTON   2019

www.bethlehemboys.com

This is a work of fiction. While some elements loosely follow events depicted in the Bible and in the works of ancient historians, the narrative and characterizations are purely speculative and are not intended to depict the life story or actions of any actual person.

ISBN: 9781793939197

Cover design: Noel Sellon.

The Parkav Press, Boston, MA.

DEDICATED TO:

The late Sir Terry Pratchett, creator of
Sam Vimes, the very model of a premodern copper

and

Esther, my wife and inspiration.

AUTHOR'S NOTE

As *Bethlehem Boys* is narrated by a Jewish man living in a Jewish village more than thirty years before Christianity began, transliterated Hebrew is used for names and places and religious ideas and concepts to create a more authentic feel for its time and setting. To aid in comprehension, English translations for many of these Hebrew words—and a few locales in Latin named by the Romans who occupied Judea at the time—appear in footnotes.[1]

---

[1]Actually, Aramaic was the everyday language of ancient Judea, but most Jews had Hebrew names and most towns, mountains and bodies of water were still referred to by their Hebrew names.

CHAPTER 1

Wake up! The Messiah has been robbed!"

Over the years I've been shaken from sleep many times by people shouting through the door of my house in the middle of the night. Normally I ignore them, or, if they persist, I respond, in a voice that is anything but helpful, that I am off duty.

But this unusual plea piqued my interest. Trying not to disturb Naomi, my wife, I navigated gingerly through the darkness, stubbing my bad left knee against the leg of a table along the way. By the time I opened the door I was ready to release a stream of curses at the drunkard, beggar or fool who had dared to interrupt my precious slumber.

Moonlight blinded me for a moment, until my night vision adjusted to reveal an old man holding an oil lamp.

"I'm off duty. Constable Elihu is on night patrol."

He shook his head. "I will not seek the aid of that pompous fanatic. He sneers at me whenever he passes, as if I were a leper."

It took a moment for my sluggish memory to identify him. "You're the saltseller, right?"

"I'm Uriel ben Teman. I was once Yehud's[1] leading purveyor of the life-giving mineral, but I am retired." His free hand grabbed my arm. "Now come!"

From across the room I heard a sleepy murmur. "Who's here, Gidon?"

"Uriel the saltseller," I replied.

"Retired!" chirped Uriel.

"Oh. Tell him we're all stocked up for the week," murmured Naomi before falling back to sleep.

Once again, Uriel pulled my arm. "Come! We must find the thieves before they make off with the Messiah's treasures!"

---

[1] Judea.

JEFFREY BRISKIN

Sighing, I threw on my cloak and skullcap, grabbed my blue sash and
truncheon, closed the door and followed the old man. Even though it was
spring it was unusually cold and I cursed myself for not bringing gloves. As we
walked along the road that encircled the city, past small stone homes abutting
tiny huts with thatched roofs on one side and three-story apartment buildings
on the other, I was reminded of Bethlehem's unwritten rule of home
ownership: *If you can afford the land, build whatever you want on it.*

Trying to make conversation, I said, "So. This messiah. Someone we
know? Ariah ben Rani? Or Yehudah the Magician, perhaps?"

"No, no, no!" Uriel snapped. "Imposters, all of them! He is the true
Chosen One."

Uriel was a relative newcomer to our small village. A widower who had
lived most of his life in the coastal town of Ashdod where he had made a
fortune harvesting salt from the shores of the Mare Nostrum[1] and selling it to
our Roman occupiers. For reasons no one understood he decided to retire in
Bethlehem. There were rumors that he was a spy for the Kumran Isiyim,[2] that
strange tribe of religious ascetics who lived in caves in the desert surrounding
the large, foul-smelling body of water we Yehudim[3] called Yam ha-Melah,[4] the
Sea of Salt.

For an old man Uriel walked very fast. Then again, he wasn't hampered by
a limp, as I was, the legacy of a war wound that had never healed properly.
When he was nearly twenty feet ahead of me I shouted, "Slow down!"

He stopped and waved at me with a bony hand. "Hurry! Hurry!"

Hoping that conversation might slow his pace, I asked, "So, what makes
you think this messiah is the real thing?"

---

[1] The Mediterranean Sea.
[2] The Essenes of Qumran.
[3] Jews.
[4] The Dead Sea.

He pointed to the sky. "Do you not see the star that journeys here from the East? Two hundred years ago the Prophet Tuvya of Adhasa said that the appearance of such a star would mean that the time of the Messiah is here!"

I had never heard of this particular Prophet, but the "galloping star" had been the talk of the town ever since it had appeared in the eastern horizon last month and slowly began making its way westward across the sky. Doomsayers interpreted it as a sign that the end of the world was near. Optimists like Uriel apparently believed that it signaled the arrival of the long-awaited savior of the Yehudim. And what about the rest of us—the farmers, carpenters, masons, butchers, fishermen, birdsellers, merchants and laborers who didn't have the luxury of spending our days sitting around tables in the synagogue debating the significance of stellar portents? Well, we just hoped it didn't fall from the sky and kill us.

"I studied the Torah[1] and the Prophets and Judges for many years and I never encountered the name of Tuvya of Adhasa," I said.

Uriel shook his head in contempt. "Of course you didn't. Your Sedukim[2] masters would never include in their canon the words of a Prophet championed by the Isiyim."

Ahhh, I thought. "So what they say about you and the Isiyim is true."

He scoffed. "Do I look like a wild-haired, cave-dwelling hermit who lives on nuts and berries? I am not an Isiyim. But that doesn't mean I don't share many of their beliefs."

I was too tired to discuss theology so I silently followed him until we reached a large stone building surrounded by a wooden fence. At the gate six men were yelling at a short fat man clad in a tunic.

"How could you let this happen, Sagiv?"

"A plague upon your inn!"

"May Elohim[3] strike you dead!"

---

[1] The first five books of the Old Testament.
[2] Sadducees, the most traditionalist sect of Judaism.
[3] One of many Hebrew names for God.

Wielding my truncheon, I pushed through the crowd. The fat man's panicked expression changed to relief. "Ahhh! Praise Elyon[1] the Watch is here! Can you please ask these hooligans to leave me alone? They're disturbing my guests!"

Sagiv ben Dan was the owner of Bethlehem's largest inn and a respected member of our little village. He was the last person you'd expect to be the target of a mob.

"What's going on here?" I demanded, scanning their familiar faces. They were all merchants and tradesmen. Some of them I had known my entire life.

"Arrest the innkeeper, Gidon!" demanded Erez, a flower seller.

"That's Senior Constable Gidon to you," I replied, fingering my sash.

"Why should we trust a puppet of the filthy Roman heathen?" shouted Raz, the teenage son of Meir the candlemaker.

The other men backed away from the boy. Insulting the Watch was foolish. But publicly cursing our hot-tempered occupiers was suicidal.

Stepping closer to Raz, I replied, "I am employed by the Bethlehem Town Watch, which reports directly to the Sanhedrin[2] in Yerushalayim.[3] They're my puppetmasters. Who are yours?"

The boy started to approach me but stopped when I waved the truncheon menacingly. "You recognize my official weapon, don't you? You were there when I used it to knock some sense into your older brother Nachum when he got drunk and tried to steal a donkey from Dov the blacksmith."

This seemed to quell his anger. He spat on the ground and stalked off. Turning to Uriel, I said, "You brought me out here in the middle of the night to report a theft. Tell me what happened."

Waving a finger at Sagiv, Uriel said, "This man failed to protect the Messiah!"

---

[1] One of the many Hebrew names for God.

[2] A council of learned community leaders responsible for managing all aspects of judicial, ecclesiastical and administrative life in Judea. Most larger towns had their own Sanhedrin. Smaller villages, like Bethlehem, fell under the authority of regional councils.

[3] Jerusalem.

The innkeeper shook his head. "This is not true, Senior Constable!"

"Yes it is! The theft took place here, at your inn! Do you deny it?"

"I don't deny the theft but it didn't happen in the inn."

"But the victims were your lodgers, nonetheless, and that makes you—"

"Quiet!" I snapped. My leg was hurting and I wanted to sit down. Even more, I wanted to go back to sleep. I wasn't even supposed to be here right now. Turning to Sagiv, I said, "Did a theft take place on this property?"

Sagiv shrugged. "Such a claim has been made although there is no proof."

"No proof?" Uriel exploded. "There's plenty of—"

Waving my hands, I said, "Enough! Sagiv, take me to the room where the theft took place."

"Allegedly took place," Sagiv weakly protested.

After warning the mob to stay outside the gate I followed Sagiv and Uriel to a large fenced-in area behind the inn. There was a small plot of winter wheat, a well, and a barn with a sliding door. A wooden mezuzah[1] had been nailed to the doorpost.

Uriel knocked on the door. "We wish to come in."

From within I heard a muffled voice. "Yes."

Uriel slid open the door. My nostrils filled with the odors of hay, manure and animal sweat. A scrawny mule watched us from a narrow stall. Three goats and a ram were lazily chewing their cud in a small pen. In another half a dozen chickens gazed at us from their roosts.

In the middle of the barn was a large blanket upon which sat a middle-aged man and a young girl. He was thin and gangly, with a wild mane of gray hair and an unkempt beard that extended halfway down his chest. His cloak and skullcap were frayed and caked with dust and his long fingers twirled one of the four blue tzitzit[2] that trailed from the corners of his undergarment. His brown eyes stared into the distance, barely registering our presence.

---

[1] A decorative case holding a parchment with prayers. One was mounted on the doorpost of a Jewish dwelling, as mandated in Deuteronomy 6:9.

[2] Tassels of blue thread that hung from the corners of a garment, as mandated in Numbers 15:37.

The mother was a tiny teenage girl dressed in a dusty brown frock with a long blue shawl. She was clasping something in a blanket. Unlike her husband, her expression was alert and peaceful. She acknowledged our presence with a nod.

I approached the man and said, "I am Senior Constable Gidon ben Einan of the Bethlehem Town Watch."

The man looked up at me and said, "I am Yosef ben Yaakov of Notseret."[1]

Pursing my lips, I said, "You are a long way from home."

He nodded. "We are here for the census."

"You were born in Bethlehem?"

"No, but I am a descendant of King Dovid."[2]

I sighed. Yet another "census pilgrim" coming home to be counted in the census of Publius Sulpicius Quirinius, the Roman governor of Assyria[3] and Yehud. What was supposed to be a straightforward way of counting the Yehudi[4] population to justify increasing our crippling taxes had been transformed by rumor and chicanery into a clarion call for all Yehudim to return to their ancestral towns and villages to be documented as official residents.

Most Yehudim stayed put since there was no real incentive to leave your home and pottery business in Yericho[5] just to be counted as a resident of your father's village of Yaffa.[6] Unless, of course, you claimed to a descendant of Dovid. The second king of Yisroel[7] had been born right here in Bethlehem, although once he took over the throne he never returned to his hometown. Our little community might have forever remained a backwater were it not for the epidemic of messiah fever that had infected so many Yehudim in recent years. Its main symptom was a fervent belief that somewhere out there a righteous

---

[1] Nazareth.
[2] David.
[3] A general name Jews would have used for the lands north of ancient Judea that at one time encompassed parts of modern-day Syria, Lebanon, Iraq and Turkey.
[4] A Jew (proper noun) or Jewish (adjective).
[5] Jericho.
[6] Jaffa.
[7] Israel.

man, anointed by Adonai,[1] would emerge from humble origins and lead a mass uprising that would drive the gentiles out of our ancient land and re-establish the true kingdom of Yisroel. Supposedly, the coming of the Messiah was foretold by the Prophets, who predicted that this savior would be born in Bethlehem and a direct descendant of King Dovid.

Well, we Yehudim had been waiting for the Messiah for many generations and over the years there had been no shortage of candidates. It seemed as if after every drought, plague or earthquake some filthy, wild-eyed man would wander into town from the desert and proclaim himself the true king of Adonai's chosen people. If his ancestral credentials checked out, he'd garner a small group of followers who'd stick around until they discovered that he was either a fraud or simply insane and then cast him aside like an olive pit.

A village like Bethlehem could take in and spit out one or two of these charlatans a year without incident. But the census had really turned up the heat. Hundreds of fathers who claimed patrilineal descent from King Dovid had brought their pregnant wives from every corner of Yehud, Someron[2] and the Galil[3] to be counted by the census and to make sure that their unborn son –who after all, might one day grow up to be the actual Messiah–would be born here. These census pilgrims now occupied every available room at our inns and apartment buildings. Those who couldn't find rooms leased small plots of land where they could pitch their tents.

Then there were the Yosefs of the world. "Why are you lodging in a barn? This isn't a healthy place for a child."

I knew what his answer would be even as I asked the question. "We are poor. We don't own a tent and can't afford to stay at an inn."

I turned to Sagiv. "You couldn't spare a room for a woman with child?"

"Every woman staying at my inn is pregnant," he answered. "This is the only sheltered space I had left."

---

[1] One of many Hebrew names for God.
[2] Samaria.
[3] Galilee.

"And how much are you charging them?" I asked.

"One shekel a week."

"For a filthy, unheated barn? If any member of this family dies I will bring you before the Sanhedrin to face charges of negligence!"

Sagiv's face paled. Pointing at the girl, he replied, "The mother says they will not be harmed because Elyon watches over the child."

I sighed. Elyon. Elohim. Adonai. How could we Yehudim ever hope to re-conquer our ancient land when we couldn't even agree on a single name for our God?

"Perhaps," I said. "But I would like to see for myself." Turning to Yosef, I said, "May I view the child?"

Yosef nodded. "Miryam, show our son to the constable."

The girl pulled aside the blanket. A baby boy wrapped in a swaddling cloth was suckling at her breast. "His name is Yeshua ben Yosef."

I raised an eyebrow. Most Yehudim didn't publicly reveal the names of their sons until they were circumcised on their eighth day of life. But maybe they did things differently in backwater villages like Notseret.

Leaning in closer to take a look at the child, I was surprised at his appearance. I had seen enough newborn children to know what they should look like. This one didn't bear the wrinkles, baldness and swarthy pallor of recent childbirth. His skin was smooth and his head sported a thick mane of curly brown hair. "He was born when?"

"Two nights ago," said Yosef. "In this barn."

The baby detached himself from his mother and gazed at me with large brown eyes. Maybe it was my imagination, but his facial expression seemed to convey the wisdom of a grown man. Instinctively, I reached down to pat his hair.

"Do not touch him!" screamed Uriel. "He has been chosen by The Almighty!"

I told Sagiv to wait for us at the gate and gently guided Uriel by the elbow outside the barn where we could speak without being overheard.

"Uriel, King Dovid had twenty sons. By now there must be thousands of his descendants alive in Yehud today. Half of them are probably right here in Bethlehem and the other half are on their way. What makes this infant any different than the dozens of other boys who will be born here?"

"Because he is the Chosen One!" Uriel snapped.

I rolled my eyes. *Oh well, that explains everything.*

Sensing my skepticism, he added, "The scholars said so, too."

I raised an eyebrow. "Scholars? What scholars?"

"That's why you're here. Earlier this evening three of them came to pray to the child and give him precious treasures."

"Were they from Yerushalayim?"

He spat on the ground. "Ha! Those ignorant Sedukim wouldn't know the Messiah if He rode in on the angel Gavriel's[1] wings. These scholars were foreigners."

"And what kinds of gifts did they bring?"

"Gold and precious ointments and scents."

"Did you meet these scholars?"

He paused. "No. But Yosef told me about their visit. And he showed me the chests. Before they were stolen."

"Did you see the actual treasures inside the chests?"

"Of course not! They didn't belong to me."

"And were you with the family when the theft took place?"

He shook his head. "No. I went home to rest. Several hours later, Yosef came to my door telling me that the treasures had been stolen while they slept. After I returned here to confirm that they were gone I came to get you."

"Did anyone witness the theft?"

"I don't know. That's your job to find out."

I sighed. It was going to be a long night. "I need to talk to the father. Bring him out, please."

---

[1] Gabriel.

While Uriel went inside, I leaned against a wall and gazed at the inn. It was a large stone structure with two floors. On each corner of the roof was a small chimney. Wisps of smoke were billowing from three of them.

I heard a rustling noise and turned. A rat was squeezing through a hole in the barn wall.

Yosef emerged, followed by the saltseller.

"Uriel, go back inside," I ordered.

"I must be here to witness your—"

"The mother needs protection. And company. Go."

I closed the door and motioned for Yosef to follow me to the well. "Uriel has told me his version of what happened earlier this evening. I want to hear yours. The full story, starting with the day you decided to come to Bethlehem."

He nodded. "My wife was seven months' pregnant when we first heard about the census. I didn't want to come here but she insisted."

"Why?"

"I am a descendant of King Dovid. For this reason she insisted that our son be born in Bethlehem."

"Do you always do everything your wife demands?"

He lowered his head. "I am a poor carpenter who lives in a tiny hut with a dirt floor and a grass roof. It's a miracle that Miryam's father agreed to let her marry me at all. I will do anything for her, even if I must journey a thousand miles and share a barn with goats and fowl."

"So, when did you leave Notseret?"

"Two weeks ago. We walked the entire way, carrying our few possessions on our backs."

"When did you arrive in Bethlehem?"

"Two days ago. I had spent nearly all of what little money I had on food for Miryam. She was in the grip of childbirth and I begged the innkeeper to let us have a room, but he said the only space he had left was in his barn. Yeshua was born the first night we arrived."

"Did a midwife help with the birth?"

"Yes, one arrived just as he was emerging from my wife's womb. She cut the cord and bathed and swaddled him and guided him to Miryam's breast."

I didn't even want to guess where the bathwater came from. "After the child was born did anyone visit you?"

"The innkeeper gave us some stale bread and shriveled dates."

I reminded myself to have a stern word with Sagiv later. "And these scholars. Tell me about them. When did they come?"

"Shortly after sundown."

"What were their names?"

"I don't remember."

"How did they arrive?"

"On asses."

"Describe them."

"They had long gray hair on the back and white hair on their bellies and large ears—"

I rolled my eyes. "The scholars, not the asses."

He blushed. "Oh. They had long beards and wore colorful robes."

"What kind of scholars were they?"

He thought for a minute. "The kind that tell the future by looking at the stars."

"Astrologers."

"Yes. They said they found us by following the trail of the roaming angel."

"That what?"

He pointed upward. Right, right, the roving star. It did seem to be hovering in the center of the sky above our heads. But I was a watchman. We didn't deal with angels in the sky. We dealt with facts on the ground. "Tell me about the gifts."

"They brought three wooden chests."

"What did they contain?"

"One had many gold coins. Another was filled with pieces of a yellow ointment one of them called myrrh. The other had sticks of incense they called—uhm, let me think—fren—frin—"

"Frankincense."

"Yes, frankincense! I had never heard of such wondrous things."

"And these scholars said they were gifts. For your son."

He nodded, vigorously. "Yes! They said they had come from Persia and Ethiopia and the Hindoo lands to pay homage to him."

"How long were they here?"

"Only for a short time. I invited them to stay but they said they needed to return home. I think they just didn't want to spend the night in a barn. Who could blame them? It's dirty and stinks of manure and with all the bleating and clucking I barely get any sleep."

"Did anyone else besides you and your wife see these men?"

"No."

"I find it hard to believe that neither Sagiv nor anyone else staying at the inn saw or heard these visitors."

He shrugged. "I do not know. Perhaps they were very quiet?"

"Did anyone else besides you and your wife see these chests?"

"Yes. Uriel ben Teman did."

"When did he see them?"

"Not long after the scholars left."

"Had he visited you before?"

"No. Miryam was feeling faint and asked for some salt. The innkeeper told me that Uriel ben Teman was a saltseller. I went to his house to ask for his help and he brought some salt, bread and wine. That's when he saw the chests."

"Were they still here when he left?"

"Yes. We went to sleep after that. When I woke up the chests were gone."

I rubbed my chin. "You didn't hear anyone enter the barn?"

"No. We were all very tired."

I stared at him for a long moment. I am a cynical man but I couldn't detect anything but naiveté in his demeanor. "I want to take a closer look."

Yosef followed me into the barn. Uriel was standing next to the goat pen. "Now do you see? A great crime—"

"Shh!" I snapped. Turning to Yosef, I said, "Show me where the chests were located."

He walked over to a wall. "We placed them here so no one would trip over them."

As Uriel watched me suspiciously, I lit a candle and knelt down to examine the area, wincing at a stab of pain in my knee. I looked for impressions the edges of a wooden box would have made in the soil and for wood shavings and sawdust. I sniffed the air, trying to identify the lingering scent of myrrh and frankincense. I had no idea what they smelled like but I figured that they'd leave some kind of aroma that stood out from the stench of the livestock.

After nearly ten minutes, I found nothing. No marks. No slivers. No smells.

I stood up and gazed at the mother who was resting on the blanket. She had moved the baby to an ancient wooden cradle.

"Is that cradle yours?"

Yosef shook his head. "A man gave it to us."

"Hebel the parchment maker," added Uriel. "Once he knew the Messiah was here he wanted to help him. His children are grown so he no longer needed it."

To both Yosef and Uriel I said, "Chests of gold and expensive ointments. Why didn't you place them in storage at the inn?"

Yosef shrugged. "I never thought that anyone would steal an offering to the Messiah."

Simpleton! I wanted to scream. *What do you think happens when three thousand census pilgrims swarm into a town with storage chests full of clothes, household utensils, food and wine? That's why we've barely heard any reports of*

bandits attacking people on the road—they all lurk in the shadows and wait to rob
them here while they sleep.

I sighed. The chests were probably halfway to Perea[1] right now. Still, I had
to go through the motions. "Do you have any idea who might have stolen
them?"

"No. We don't know anyone here."

I turned to Uriel. "How about you?"

The saltseller grimaced. "Obviously, it must have been a Roman, Arab or
some other heathen. No Yehudi would dare steal from the Chosen One!"

The old man was beginning to get on my nerves. "How long will you be
staying here?" I asked Yosef.

"Until we have been counted in the census."

With more than a million Yehudim living in hundreds of towns and
villages in the Holy Land, it might be months before the Romans finally got
around to Bethlehem. This family couldn't stay in a barn all that time.

I left to find Sagiv. More than twenty men now stood by the gate. Several
carried loaves of bread. One held two roasted turtledoves. My stomach gurgled
in hunger. A man clutching a bushel of grapes approached me and said, "Are
you done speaking to the Messiah's father? We wish to pay homage as well."

Hmmm, I smirked. *Where were all of you when these poor wretches couldn't*
find anyone to take them in? And why are you just offering them food, instead of
giving them shelter in your homes?

Sagiv was sitting on the inn's doorstep. "Move the Notsrim[2] into a room.
One with a fireplace. And make sure all of them are fed."

He stood up in protest. "I told you, I have no rooms—"

"Oh, yes you do," I replied. "Every innkeeper keeps his best room
unoccupied, just in case a king or Roman general happens to drop in
unexpectedly. I know that yours is on the second floor. There's no smoke
flowing from its chimney."

---

[1] A region east of the Jordan River that at one time was under the rule of King Herod.
[2] Nazarenes.

He sighed. "Fine. They can stay. And who will pay for their lodging and food?"

Motioning to the crowd, I said, "Ask them. If they really care about the family they'll be willing to donate more than a few loaves of stale bread."

"And if they don't?"

"Then you will shoulder the costs yourself. Unless you'd rather have me take you to the magistrate."

He frowned. "I will lose a fortune lodging these Galilim."[1]

Placing a hand on his shoulder, I smiled and replied, "Look on the bright side. If Uriel turns out to be right about this boy, imagine how much people will pay to stay at the inn where the Messiah was born?"

---

[1]Galileans.

CHAPTER 2

The next morning, I dragged myself out of bed two hours after sunrise. Naomi had thoughtfully left a plate of dates and a cup of fresh goat's milk before heading out to her stall in the market. As I sat at our table gazing around the spare interior of the house my father, a tanner, had built more than fifty years ago, I wondered, as I often did, why my wife had ever agreed to marry me.

Being a watchman's wife offered no status for a woman like Naomi, who had been born into a family of wealthy Yehudim who lived in the village of Oxyrhynchus in Egypt. After Naomi's mother died when she was eleven she and her father immigrated to Bethlehem, where he became a successful goldsmith. For most of her life she had lived in luxury, but she moved down several social ranks when she married me. I was still a soldier back then and my pay was marginal. This didn't change when I retired from the army and became a watchman. My hours were long and the chances were high that any given scuffle with a knife-wielding bandit would leave her a widow. The one thing she did have was security. Every criminal knew that if he tried to burgle a watchman's home or attack his family the entire force would band together to hunt him down like an animal.

After breakfast I slipped the leather battle armor my father had crafted for me under my cloak and wrapped the blue sash, my official mark of office, over my shoulder. The truncheon went into my left pocket and I slipped my real weapon, an eight-inch long war dagger, into a sheath on a belt around my waist.

The morning sun was low in the sky but the weather was beginning to warm up. Within a few weeks the cooler temperatures and gentle spring winds would give way to the stifling heat and humidity that made Yehud a sweat bath eight months of the year.

My bad knee was hurting more than usual and anyone who watched me limp by as I headed for the center of town would have thought I looked like an old soldier. They would have been right.

My journey ended at the headquarters of the Bethlehem Town Watch, a large stone building set off from the main road. Above the doorway was the Ivrit[1] word "Tzedakah," meaning justice. The letters had been installed by the Sanhedrin of Yerushalayim, who oversaw nearly aspect of Yehudi life, from establishing and enforcing religious laws to settling legal disputes and conducting trials. The letters were there partly to identify the Watch house as a legal entity, but mostly to remind us watchmen that anyone we brought into the building against their will had a right to live long enough to receive justice as defined in the Torah, the book of Laws given by Adonai to the Prophet Moshe[2] on Mount Sinai. There was also an unwritten understanding that a criminal's organs and extremities would remain intact while they were in our custody. It was the kind of reminder you often needed when you were tempted to administer your own lethal kind of justice, especially after you emerged victorious from a skirmish with a half-crazed, three-hundred-pound berserker who had landed some very painful blows on your rib cage.

I entered the Watch house and felt waves of warmth emanating from a stove in the center of the room.

"Good morning, Senior Constable!" chirped Junior Constable Amos ben Malakhi, our newest member. He was 19 years old, well over six feet tall and built like a tree trunk. With his long mane of curly black hair, bushy beard and enormous hands, his appearance would be enough to convince people to cross to the other side of the road if it weren't for his perpetually cheerful disposition.

"Good morning, Junior Constable," I replied, sniffing the air, which was filled with the aroma of boiling leaves.

"Tea will be ready in a few minutes."

---

[1]Hebrew.
[2]Moses.

"Wonderful," I said, sitting down at my desk, a small table with a wobbly chair.

A moment later, a thin man with short gray hair and a close-cropped beard entered. He saw me and frowned. "You're late, Senior Constable."

"I apologize, Commander. Although in my defense, I was called out in the middle of the night to handle a complaint."

Commander Shaul ben Yoav sat down at his own desk, which was located across the room next to an iron door that led to a small holding cell. "I heard. A theft from a barn behind the inn?"

"Yes," I replied. "I'll write up a report this morning."

Junior Constable Amos brought over a steaming mug of tea and whispered, "Is it true that the thieves stole chests of gold and silver and honeycomb from a baby?"

I sighed. Word got around. "Something like that."

"And how do you intend to proceed with this investigation?" asked Commander Shaul. We had known each other for more than twenty years, and even after all this time I was still astonished at how intact his hearing had remained. If he was in the room there was no such thing as a private conversation.

"I plan to canvass the area around the inn to see if anyone might have witnessed the crime."

"Alleged crime," Commander Shaul replied. "From my understanding, there is no proof that these so-called 'treasures' ever existed."

"The Notsrim said they were given by three foreigners who visited them in the middle of the night."

He scoffed. "And no one saw them coming or going."

"Uriel ben Teman said he saw the chests."

"Did he see what was inside them?"

I hesitated. "No."

"Ha! For all we know, these Galilim may have brought empty chests with them and made up a story about strangers bearing gifts. Then, when no one was watching, they buried them in the hills and claimed they were stolen."

"Why would they do that?"

"To earn the sympathy and charity of gullible people like the saltseller."

He had a point. Hadn't I forced Sagiv to move the family into his inn on his own shekel? Would I have done that if the crime—or the claim of a crime—hadn't occurred? Then again, I had met the Notsrim, and he hadn't.

"If you had seen them you wouldn't have such suspicions. The father looked like a lost lamb and the mother was no older than a child. They actually paid Sagiv a whole shekel to stay in his vermin-infested barn."

"All right, so let's say their story is true. Why would anyone give them such priceless treasures?"

I shrugged. "Didn't you hear? Their newborn son is the Messiah."

Junior Constable Amos flashed a grin of rotting teeth. The commander rolled his eyes. "Yet another messiah candidate. That's three in the past two weeks. I will be so happy once this census is over and all these—transients—return home."

Wagging a finger, I said, "Careful, Commander. One of them might be the real thing."

Grabbing his helmet, Commander Shaul headed for the door. "Well, if one of them is the Messiah I most certainly will be dead long before he restores the kingdom of Yisroel to its former glory. Meanwhile, I'm going to give my weekly report to the magistrate. Spend a few more hours on this so-called theft and then drop it. Reb Lemuel doesn't like us wasting time on wild goose chases."

I nodded. Reb Lemuel ben Kfir was Bethlehem's town magistrate and a member of the Sanhedrin. He was also the supervisor of the Watch. And he didn't like drawn-out investigations. Whenever he could he reminded us that our job was to prevent crimes from happening or to catch the sinner in the act. I would be a rich man if I received a shekel every time he wagged a finger at us and said, "If the identity of the lawbreaker is unknown do not waste time trying to find him. If Adonai wants him brought to justice He will deliver him with His own hand." Since I was the Watch's chief investigator of unsolved crimes I was nearly always the main target of this particular admonishment.

After the commander had gone, Junior Constable Amos sat down across from me. "The commander had better watch his words. The Messiah may proclaim himself sooner than he thinks."

"He certainly will if you Apocalypts have anything to do with it. You people are the chief spreaders of messiah fever."

He smiled. "We're only confirming what the Prophets foretold. The Messiah is coming whether Sedukim like Reb Lemuel and Commander Shaul accept him or not."

"Commander Shaul is not a Sedukim," I replied. "He is a Levite,[1] but he chose not to join the priesthood. And he doesn't embrace the Sedukim's belief in the literal interpretation of the Laws as written in the Torah or the ecclesiastical supremacy of the priests in Yerushalayim. If he had he never would have served along with me in King Herod's army."

"Why not? King Herod was a Yehudi."

"No, he wasn't. He was a pretender."

"He rebuilt the Temple!"

"That doesn't negate the fact that he was an Idomite.[2] A descendant of the Patriarch Yaakov's[3] brother Esav.[4] His family was forcibly converted to the Yehudi faith after they were conquered by the Hashmunayim.[5] His father, Antipater the Idomite, was a Roman puppet who convinced them to install him as ruler of Yehud against the wishes of the priests and just about everyone else. When King Herod took over the throne, he rebuilt the Temple mainly as a way

---

[1] A member of the hereditary priestly class in Judea.
[2] Edomites, a tribe of gentiles (non-Jews) whose leaders converted to Judaism after the Hasmoneans (see below) regained control of Judea.
[3] Jacob.
[4] Esau.
[5] Hasmoneans, the descendants of the Maccabees who wrested control of Judea from the Seleucids in the second century BC, as recounted in 1 and 2 Maccabees.

to win the support of the priests, but he himself worshipped both Adonai and the Roman gods."

The watchman's eyes widened. "I never knew this."

"He did a good job of hiding the truth. But I served in his army for fifteen years. Whenever we won a battle, our Idomite commanders sacrificed a goat to Adonai and a boar to Jove."

He rubbed his beard. "Wow. I have so much to learn."

I nodded. Junior Constable Amos was the illiterate fourth son of a family of prosperous wine merchants. As a member of the Apocalypts, he believed that it was just a matter of a time before the genuine Messiah proclaimed himself. It was a sect that had grown increasingly popular in recent years, particularly among the young and restless who were tired of being vassals to the Romans. But Amos was large and strong and good-natured and willing to put in long hours for little pay and even less respect, which made him a perfect candidate for the Watch.

Many visitors to Bethlehem thought that we watchmen were an elite group. How wrong they were. First of all, there were only four of us. Four men charged with keeping the peace in a sleepy town that in recent weeks had swelled from a population of six hundred to more than three thousand men, women and children, plus hundreds of sheep, goats and a few dozen camels. Four men were responsible for preserving law and order amidst a growing scourge of bandits, swindlers, thieves, murderers, apostates, magicians, swindlers, heretics and other assorted rabble-rousers.

We should have had twenty men. But our Sanhedrin masters weren't willing to hire any more. And even if they were we'd have trouble filling the ranks. Not that the job required any special skills. If you could squeeze into one of our old, ill-fitting leather armors you met nearly all of the qualifications. It also helped if you forgot that most of our equipment had been harvested from the corpses of long-dead soldiers and the occasional watchman who had wandered into the wrong alleyway and never made it out. On two feet, anyway.

But there were plenty of other reasons why you wouldn't want to be a watchman. If you were concerned about purity, for example. The chances were high that at least once a week you'd end up rolling in the mud fending off an attack from a vicious thug, and you couldn't worry about staining your limbs and clothes with blood because if you did you might hesitate for a moment, giving him the time he needed to bash your head in with a brick.

You also had to accept the fact that your Watch-issued armor wouldn't provide that much protection if you weren't particularly adept at dodging blows. That's why on patrol I always wore my old battle armor. My father had made it for me because he rightly mistrusted the armor supplied by King Herod. While that cheap Idomite leather mail split into shreds at the slightest thrust of a blade, my father's armor held sturdy and true for more than forty battles. Unfortunately, my father hadn't thought of creating armor for my legs, which were left unprotected when a Nabataean's arrow pierced my left knee during a pitched skirmish. By the grace of Adonai, I neither bled to death nor lost my leg but to this day I still walk with a limp. This disability made me rather useless in chasing criminals who ran faster than a tortoise. Which is why when I wasn't out on patrol my primary role was to investigate crimes whose perpetrators were unknown.

The word "Tzedakah" had also been branded into our truncheons, and it was often the last thing a criminal saw before he woke up in our cell. You could also carry your own dagger, club or knuckle band but never a pike or crossbow, as the use of such weapons was restricted to our Roman overseers.

Being a watchman wasn't the best career for those keen on living long enough to bounce grandchildren on their knees. I was the only married man. Commander Shaul's wife had died of the plague many years ago and he had no children. Junior Constable Amos was certainly old enough to settle down. His parents were actively interviewing numerous families in Bethlehem and beyond to find a young daughter who would make an ideal match–and bring a sizeable dowry–for their son. And then there was our fourth member–

"In here, sinner!"

—Who entered just as I was closing my eyes for a short nap. "What is it this time, Constable Elihu?"

"This man is guilty of coveting his neighbor's wife!"

I sighed. Constable Elihu ben Hoshea was the fanatic of our little squad. He was 22 years old, six feet tall and so thin he could hide behind a spear. His bulging, wide-set eyes dominated a thin, hawk-like face that ended in a pointed chin and close-cropped beard. With that severe appearance, it wasn't surprising that he was also a member of the Sedukim. Since, unlike Commander Shaul, he came from a poor family whose ancestors were neither Levites or Cohenim,[1] he could never fulfill his desire to become a priest or a member of the Sanhedrin. Denied the justice-dispensing powers of these exalted roles, he compensated by arresting anyone who didn't live up to his austere moral code. This caused endless headaches for those of us with a higher tolerance for petty sins.

Yet, in spite of his annoying personality, he more than made up for it with his skill and bravery as a fighter. You might not want to break bread with him, but if you were ever confronted by a gang of thugs you definitely wanted him at your side. Any would-be miscreant who felt the glare of Elihu's eyes upon him would think twice about committing mayhem in our little town.

With the commander on patrol I was the acting senior watchman, and so it fell to me to handle Comrade Elihu's arrest. I gave his arrestee a quick once-over. An old man with leathery skin dressed in rags and leaning on a cane. "What did he do, Constable?"

"I discovered him gazing through a crack in the wall of the women's mikveh!"[2]

"Was anyone in there?"

He blushed. "How would I know such a thing? It is forbidden for men to enter such a sacred place!"

---

[1] The other hereditary priestly class.
[2] The Jewish ritual bath used to cleanse spiritual impurities. Women visited the mikveh at the end of their menstrual cycle.

"Did you ask the attendant?" I asked, fully aware that the young watchman believed that, other than his mother and sisters, all women were the sinful descendants of Chavah,[1] the first woman, and should be avoided whenever possible.

"Of course not!"

"Then how do you know he was actually coveting?"

His face contorted into the smugness of the righteous. "Rabbi Shammai said, 'He whose actions demonstrate unlawful intentions are sinners, even if the Law itself hasn't been violated.'"

No one could hold a candle to Constable Elihu when it came to knowledge of the Laws. Many who encountered him—not often voluntarily—asked me why he hadn't become a rabbi himself. What I didn't tell them was that so much of his mind was devoted to memorizing punishments for violations of the Laws that there was no room left for original thought. Or mercy and compassion, for that matter. In Rome he would have made the perfect bureaucrat or executioner. Here, he needed close supervision.

I turned to the old man. "What were you doing looking through the hole of the mikveh?"

He shook his head. "I did not know it was a sacred place. I am a traveler from Gezara on my way to Yericho. I was looking for a tailor to mend my ripped cloak. I am nearly blind, so I did not know the purpose of the building and was looking through the hole to try to identify what kind of establishment it was."

I looked at the old man and then swung my truncheon toward his face, stopping it within a foot of his nose. He didn't flinch.

Turning to Constable Elihu, I said, "Let him go, Constable. Even if he had sinful intentions, his blindness would deny him the satisfaction of fulfilling them."

"But Senior Constable—"

---

[1] Eve.

"We don't have enough men or room in our cell to handle anything other than major lawbreakers. For the minor offenses, Adonai will mete out justice in the afterlife."

His face darkened. "Yes, Senior Constable."

"You mean I'm not going to be stoned?" asked the old man.

"Not unless you want to be," I replied.

He rose to his feet and grabbed his cane. "May Elohim bestow a hundred blessings upon your house!"

"Go in peace, old man. And stay away from mikvehs!"

Comrade Elihu hadn't agreed with my decision. But his compulsive need to obey authority outweighed his personal considerations. Since the Watch ultimately fell under the jurisdiction of the Sanhedrin, our hierarchy and actions were ultimately sanctioned by Adonai. As senior constable, I held both legal and ecclesiastical authority over both him and Junior Constable Amos when Commander Shaul wasn't here. If and when Elihu was promoted to my rank he would no longer have to obey me unless I were promoted to commander. Which would never happen because I wasn't a Sedukim. Since Elihu was he might very well assume the role someday. Adonai willing, I would be retired or dead by that time.

Constable Elihu left to find other sinners to arrest. Junior Constable Amos went out to monitor the volume of new census pilgrims entering town. The Watch house was empty. On my desk was a blank piece of parchment, awaiting my written description of last night's events. But I was still so tired! A few minutes of rest wouldn't hurt…

A sharp rap on the desk awakened me from my sleep. "What? What?"

"Senior Constable!"

My bleary eyes looked up into the unsmiling face of my superior officer. "Yes, Commander?"

"Is your shift over?"

"No, Commander."

"Are you paid to sleep on the job?"

"No, Commander."

"Shall I bring you before the magistrate for stealing the value of your labor?"

"If you believe that is appropriate, Commander."

"Or perhaps I should simply fire you?"

"Never would I dream of trying to influence your judgment on a matter of regimental discipline, Commander."

"Or I could just demote you and elevate Constable Elihu to your rank."

I shrugged. "If that is your wish, Commander."

He paused. We stared at each other. He expected me to get up. I didn't.

"I'm going to give you one last chance, Senior Constable. Don't let me catch you sleeping on your shift again."

I rubbed my leg and winced. "Your mercy is always appreciated by this slothful old watchman, Commander."

He nodded. And that was that. The end of our daily ritual of superior-subordinate banter. We both knew his threats were as empty as the deserts that surrounded us. Shaul had formed the Watch ten years ago and I was his first hire. It took him nearly three years to build up the force to its maximum four-man squad. There wasn't exactly a huge line of men waiting to join and few stayed longer than a year. In fact, there were more former watchmen in Bethlehem than active members. For a measly starting salary of five shekels a month there were easier ways of earning a living that didn't involve the risk of injury or death on every patrol.

Commander Shaul knew he couldn't afford to lose his most experienced officer. And one of his oldest friends. We had served together in King Herod's army, where he had been the leader of our squad. On several occasions, I had saved his life, including the battle in which I lost the usefulness of my knee.

"Where are you in your investigation of the stolen gifts?"

"I've asked my informants to poke around for information," I lied.

"Get your answers quickly, then. Reb Lemuel has taken a personal interest in this case."

"Why?"

"Because he doesn't want Bethlehem to become known as a place where people can steal from messiahs and get away with it."

My jaw dropped. "Are you saying that our learned magistrate is taking the Notsrim's claim seriously?"

"Of course not!" He pulled up a chair and leaned in to speak in a near-whisper. "But there are plenty of people here who do."

"I've noticed that."

He shook his head. "These Apocalypts, and even some Sedukim, say it's no accident that Publius Quirinius ordered the census of Yehud this year. They believe that Adonai planted the idea in his mind to make sure the rightful Messiah's mother would travel here in time to bear the Chosen One."

The tea kettle whistled. He poured two cups and placed one in front of me. "You've met these Notsrim. Do you think their son is the Messiah?"

I shrugged. "If Adonai has chosen Yeshua to restore the kingdom of Yisroel I would think He would have found better accommodations for the family than a barn."

Commander Shaul dropped a slice of lemon into his tea. "Tradition says that the Messiah will come from humble origins."

"But then there's the child himself. When my son was born my wife said he looked like a lizard for a month. But this Yeshua–his skin was smooth and his eyes were wide open. And he had hair already. Yet the father said he had been born only two days ago."

"When Yitzchak's[1] son Esav was born, he emerged from Ribka's[2] womb with a full head of red hair and a beard."

---

[1] Isaac.
[2] Rebecca.

27

"Those were different times. Adonai visited your tent in person and men lived to be nine hundred years old."

He shrugged and sipped his tea.

"You of all people can't possibly believe that Yeshua is the real deal."

"Not for one moment," he replied with a smirk. "It's far more likely that King Antipas is the Messiah than this carpenter's son."

Placing my finger against my lips, I said, "Careful, Commander. The walls have ears. And remember that we spent the best years of our lives in the service of this king's father. It's because of old King Herod that we're here today."

Stretching his arms out, Commander Shaul replied, "Yes, and what a blessing! To think that I gave up the life of a priest for all this."

At that moment, a lizard emerged from a hole in the wall and scampered across the floor. One thing you could say for my commander: his timing was impeccable.

"Anyway," he sighed wearily, "Go out there and see what you can find. Talk to your friend, the seller of stolen goods."

"Right," I replied, slowly rising to my feet. "If anyone is trying to unload chests of scented ointments, Reuven will be the first to sniff them out."

CHAPTER 3

Bethlehem's marketplace can't compare to the grand bazaars and souks of Yericho and Amman. But if you're traveling to the Temple, our proximity to Yerushalayim makes Bethlehem an ideal stop to purchase lambs, turtledoves and grain for your ritual sacrifices at prices far below what you'll pay in the Holy City. And if you have any shekels left over our merchants offer plenty of goods to bring home. On any given day you'll find spices and tea from the East, Egyptian cotton, Nabataean[1] camel-hair rugs, love potions and herbal medicines from Ethiopia and an endless assortment of wooden goblets, gold and silver trinkets, earthenware, candles, lamp oil, dyes and colored tiles. Oh, and if you're looking for fresh goat's milk and fine wool, visit my wife's popular market stall, but get there early, as she often runs out of inventory before noon.

We also offer an impressive assortment of professional problem-solvers. Need to know if a plague of locusts will destroy your barley crop next year? Give Amrita the Astrologer half a shekel and she'll divine your future in a cup of strained tea leaves. Did one of your tent-mates pass away last night? Count on Itzchak ben Akiba, the town mortician, to make sure your old father or uncle is properly buried. Want to recover the silver Shabbat candlesticks that were stolen from your house while you were visiting your in-laws in Chefa?[2] Talk to Reuven ben Peleg.

Reuven was the unofficial leader of Bethlehem's criminal underworld. You wouldn't find him in the central marketplace. His official base of operations, a hashish and wine parlor, was located in a back alley behind a block of warehouses and sheds that served as fronts for brothels, gambling dens and forbidden eateries where sinful Yehudim could secretly indulge their cravings for swineflesh, crabs and oysters.

---

[1]Nabataea was a general name for the lands east of the Jordan River inhabited by Arabs and other non-Jewish tribes.
[2]Haifa.

I knocked on the door of the squat stone building and, a moment later, it opened, revealing a right hand missing an index and middle finger and a narrow face with beady gray eyes and a small pitted nose. Thin lips spread to reveal a grin of large teeth, one of which was made of gold. "Ah, a visit from the Watch. Always a pleasure."

Reuven ushered me into a small dimly lit room. In the center was a large hookah. It was unlit and unoccupied.

"No business, Reuven?" I asked.

He shook his head. "Not a soul and it's mid-day already. Six pounds of fine Perean product and my only customers are mice and horseflies."

I sat down on a stool. "That's too bad."

"It's that cursed Hussein and his opium den!" he spat, sitting on a bench next to me. "Ever since he set up shop my customers have abandoned me for him. Why hasn't the Watch arrested this menace?"

I smiled. "The same reason we haven't arrested you. Opium and hashish aren't illegal."

He grimaced. "You don't understand. Hashish is a gentleman's vice. Sit at my hookah and you escape from the troubles of the world for an hour or so. But opium! It's the tonic of demons! Have you ever seen what it does to a man? It enslaves him in its grip. He doesn't eat or drink. He neglects his wife, his children, his parents. He just lies there, on a filthy mat like a corpse, awaiting death."

I shrugged. "There are no Laws that say a man can't quietly destroy himself with dream herbs."

He waved his crippled hand. "Acchh, spoken like a watchman. I should have known better than to seek sympathy from you. You and your commander will dance on my doorstep the day I am forced to close up shop."

"Not with this knee I won't," I replied. "Besides, I need you to stay in business. You're my eyes and ears on all the illegal activities happening within a hundred-mile radius of Bethlehem."

"That I may be, but I can't live on praise alone." He held out his left hand. I dropped a half-shekel onto his calloused palm. The payoff was merely a formality. Depending on whom you believed, Reuven was either the third- or fourth-richest man in town. He owned numerous properties in Bethlehem and beyond and it was said that he had buried numerous bags of silver and precious gems in the surrounding hills.

"So, what do you want to know?"

"What have you heard about chests of treasure stolen from a family of Notsrim?"

He grinned. "Ah. I knew it was only a matter of time before you'd come around asking about that. A king's tribute of gold and aromatic ointments. Seldom do I see more than a pouch of these fragrant substances in a year. But a whole chest full of each! For the benefit of a carpenter's son, no less!"

"You wouldn't happen to know where any of these valuables might be?"

He stroked his chin. "Senior Constable, you and I have known each other for a long time. You're well aware of my reputation as a purchaser and re-seller of goods whose rightful ownership is often—unclear. So, naturally, once I heard about this theft I put feelers out amongst my many connections with an offer to pay top price for these items. To my great disappointment, no one has yet approached me."

"You're not the only fence in Yehud."

"True, but none of my—competitors—would know what to do with a chest full of myrrh. I, on the other hand, am well connected with many wealthy aristocrats, including the wives of Roman patricians who would be more than willing to reward me handsomely for any rare ointments and scents I might procure, regardless of their origin."

"If you don't have the chests where do you think they are?"

He shrugged. "There are two likely scenarios. One, the thieves are far away from here. It would be easier to get rid of such luxuries in a big city like Yerushalayim or Caesarea Maritima."[1]

"And the other?"

"The chests are still here in town, hidden away somewhere, because the thieves didn't realize what they were stealing or who they were stealing them from. Even the most hardened miscreants wouldn't want to be known as the men who stole from the Messiah. Unless, of course, they were pagans."

"If one of them did approach you would you help us restore the treasures to their rightful owner?"

He smirked. "You mean give up the opportunity to earn hundreds of shekels just to win the gratitude of the Watch?"

With a straight face, I replied, "Yes."

He shook his head. "No."

Before I could speak he pointed to the sky. "But I would do it for El-Shaddai.[2] Just in case He has chosen this child to become the true king of the Yehudim."

I nodded in appreciation. "I never thought of you as a religious man, Reuven."

Rubbing his hands together, he replied, "Even a thief understands the value of a speculative investment."

---

[1] A Roman coastal town on the Mediterranean Sea.
[2] One of the oldest Hebrew names for God.

CHAPTER 4

When I left Reuven's hashish den I had no intention of returning to the Watch house. I was still tired and needed to recover the sleep I had lost last night.

As I opened the door of my house my spirits were immediately lifted by the aroma of simmering lentils.

Ahhh, home.

Few watchmen could afford to own their own houses. Constables Amos and Elihu lived with their parents. Commander Shaul still lived in the house given to him by his father-in-law, even though his wife had died many years ago. I lived in the modest stone house my father had built with his bare hands before I was born.

There were two rooms; one large open area with two small windows on the rear wall and a smaller bedroom. Behind the house were a well, a small pasture and a cattle pen where we kept five goats, four ewes, four lambs and a ram.

The main room was sparsely furnished. Next to a small oven, four chairs surrounded a round table. Against one wall were two chests and a shelf upon which stood two Shabbat candles and a Kiddish cup.[1] In another wall was a hearth where the flames of a fire now licked a cauldron of lentil stew.

I sat down at the table, grateful to be off my feet. A few minutes later the back door opened and the most beautiful woman in the world entered carrying a bucket of water. "Shalom,[2] my husband."

Naomi was nearly my height. Her long, dark hair framed a narrow face with slanted hazel eyes and thick lips. Her exotic olive skin was only now beginning to show the wrinkles of age, and even after more than twenty years of marriage she still maintained the svelte figure of her youth. But she was no delicate creature. Every morning she woke up early to coax milk from the goats and shear wool from the sheep, which she rolled in a barrow to her stall in the

---

[1] A ritual wine cup.
[2] *Shalom* has various meanings, including hello, goodbye and peace.

marketplace. For protection against thieves and ruffians she concealed a kitchen knife in the folds of her cloak. Her father had trained her in knife-fighting, a valuable skill she had, thank Adonai, never had to put to practical use. Naomi's business was very successful. She rarely returned home with unsold inventory and often earned the equivalent of half of my monthly pay in a single day.

"Shalom, my wife."

She placed the bucket on the table and removed her head covering. "You are home early today. Supper will not be ready for several hours."

"How was business?"

"Excellent. The census pilgrims cleaned me out by noon and I didn't waste a minute haggling." She poured water into the cauldron. "How about you? Did you find the thieves who stole the Messiah's treasures?"

My jaw dropped. "How did you hear of this?"

"I know how to put two and two together. You were out for a long time last night. And then this morning everyone in the market was talking about chests of diamonds and herbs stolen from a family of Notsrim."

"Did any of these rumor-mongers suggest who might have stolen these treasures?"

"Some say the Arabs. Some say the Romans. A few say the father made the whole thing up."

"Your information is certainly no worse than what I've seen and heard already. The Sanhedrin is leaning hard on Shaul to solve this thing, so, naturally, he's on my case."

"What will you do next?"

"I've spoken to Reuven. He will keep his eyes and ears open."

"Ahh, yes. I've never understood how that man has evaded the stoning pit."

"We live in ambiguous times, my wife. Reuven gives a generous share of his ill-gotten profits to the synagogue every year. And you'll never find a calf fatter than the one he brings to the sacrificial altar on Rosh Hashanah.[1] In exchange for his generosity the Sanhedrin tends to look the other way."

She frowned. "Maybe that's why everyone is crying out for the Messiah. To restore the virtuous ways of our forefathers."

I snorted. "You mean men like Aharon,[2] who permitted the children of Yisroel to worship a golden idol and then was rewarded for his sins by being appointed chief priest? Or Bethlehem's favorite son, King Dovid, who arranged the death of Uriah the Hittite so he could steal his wife, Batsheva?"[3]

"Shhhh!" she hissed. "Someone will hear you!'

I dipped a cup into the bucket and drank some water. As always, it tasted like sand and rotten eggs. "We are a sinful people, Naomi. We have always been. That is why Adonai allowed the king of Bavel[4] to destroy the first Temple and exile us from the Holy Land. It's why He allowed Idomite pretenders to become our kings and turn Yehud into a vassal state of Rome. Do you really think He is ready to forgive our transgressions by bringing the Messiah into the world?"

She gazed at me with disapproval. "How could I ever have agreed to marry a man with such a dour view of his people?"

"Because back then I was a handsome and strong warrior and the only man in Bethlehem who would agree to marry a foreign girl with no dowry."

She raised her hands in prayer. "Every day I thank Adonai that our son never inherited your cynical ways."

"It's been two years since he left us to live with the Isiyim in Kumran. His outlook on life may have changed."

---

[1] The holiday marking the start of the Jewish New Year.
[2] Aaron.
[3] Bathsheba.
[4] Babylon and/or Babylonians.

"I'll never know, will I? Those hermits don't allow women in their settlements."

I grabbed her hand and pulled her onto my lap. "With good reason. You would force them to bathe and clean their caves."

She picked a thread of wool off her sleeve. "You must visit him, Gidon."

"The Isiyim don't like outsiders. Especially men who once fought for King Herod. The Isiyim were his harshest critics and he tried to destroy their community in Yerushalayim. That's why so many fled to Kumran."

"He might be sick. Or dead."

"Not our Binyamin. Were the Angel of Death to cross his path our son would wrestle him to the ground and make off with his scythe."

Naomi paused. "There's another reason you must see him. To warn him that some are saying the Isiyim stole the Messiah's treasures."

"Why? What could they possibly want with them? They've all taken a vow of poverty. They don't eat or use anything they don't grow or make themselves. And I doubt they'd ever want to adorn their caves with exotic fragrances."

"Regev the figseller told me that his cousin saw two men in white linen cloaks sitting across the street from the inn last night."

"Isiyim aren't the only people who wear linen. Many beggars do, too."

"Perhaps. But shouldn't you be exploring every possibility?"

I laughed. "Has Commander Shaul hired you to be my supervisor?"

"No, but maybe he should. Your duty doesn't end when your shift is over."

I raised my hand in a mock-fist. "Your father warned me that you could argue better than two rabbis debating how many stars must appear in the night sky before Shabbat can begin."

She placed her hand on my cheek. "You would have preferred a simple, stupid girl who couldn't tell an aleph from a bet? An educated wife keeps you sharp."

"Yes, my love," I said. "Although always remember that I married you for your beauty. Your intelligence was a bonus. Praise Adonai that after twenty-one years you still possess both in ample quantity."

She rose from my lap and grabbed my hand. Glancing toward the bedroom, she said, "These are not the only qualities I possess that have not diminished with time."

Rising to my feet, I pulled her close and said, "As King Shelomoh[1] used to say when people appeared before him to settle disputes, 'I'll be the judge of that.'"

---

[1]Solomon.

CHAPTER 5

Two days passed and I was no closer to figuring out who had stolen the treasures. I interviewed dozens of people, from census pilgrims who had stayed at the inn the night of the theft to the usual gang of beggars who slept outside its gate. No one had seen anyone coming or going that night.

At least the Notsrim were no longer living in the barn. Sagiv had moved them to a room at the inn paid for by a group that called itself "The Friends of the Messiah." I didn't check in on them because I was too embarrassed to admit that my investigation was at a standstill.

As I was leaving the Watch house, Uriel cornered me and grabbed my arm. "Senior Constable, have you recovered the Messiah's gifts yet?"

Commander Shaul had taught me a good all-purpose phrase to utter in situations like this. "Inquiries are proceeding."

I expected him to start haranguing me. Instead he smiled and said, "Well, I'm sure you're doing your best. But come with me. I want to show you something."

He guided me over a series of small rises to the largely uninhabited southeast side of town. Out here the sandy soil was barren of trees and brush and the wind that bore down from nearby hills created swirling plumes of dust that stung the eyes and clung to the skin like ticks. Yet in the middle of this desolate place a group of people was gathered on a plot of land. I turned to Uriel. "What is this?"

He clapped his hands. "We're building a home for the Messiah!"

Two men were digging a well. Five more, including Yosef, were placing stones to form the foundation of a wall. In the shade of a lean-to, several women were weaving thatch for a roof. Off to one side, sheltered under a canopy, the girl Miryam sat with the child Yeshua cradled in her arms.

I turned to Uriel. "Is this land legally purchased?"

He nodded. "The Friends of the Messiah bought it and transferred ownership to Yosef."

"Has he been issued a residence and construction permit?"

He shook his head. "Such requirements are waived for those who can prove that they are descendants of King Dovid."

Gazing at Yosef, I said, "You're telling me that an illiterate Notsrim knows his entire lineage dating back more than five hundred years?"

The saltseller smiled. "We're helping him fill in the details."

"Is our magistrate, Reb Lemuel, aware of this?"

"Not yet, but he has no grounds to reject the application."

I walked over to Yosef, who was mixing mortar. "So, you have decided to stay here."

He nodded. "Our son should be raised in the village of his ancestors."

A wagon arrived at the compound. Three men began unloading sacks of sand and limestone and buckets of water. "You have a lot of help."

"Yes!" he beamed. "Many people are donating their time and materials."

"And once this house is finished how will you earn a living?"

"I will re-open my carpentry business here. Uriel ben Teman said he will buy me new tools."

I watched one of the well-diggers remove a large stone from the shaft and throw it into a pile. "Bethlehem already has a carpenter."

"That is true, but I have been told he cannot keep up with the demand for tables, chairs and bed frames so there will be plenty of business for me. When Yeshua's treasures are restored I will sell some of it to raise money to build a proper wood shop."

I felt a little uncomfortable. "I wouldn't get your hopes too high. There's been no sign of the chests since you reported them missing."

He smiled and placed a hand on my shoulder. "I have faith that Elohim will help you restore them to His Chosen One."

Scratching my head, I replied, "Faith is a good thing. But it's important to keep in mind that Bethlehem has had its fair share of messianic claimants over the past few years. In fact, right now there are two men claiming to be the king of the Yehudim—"

"They are pretenders! Yeshua is the true Messiah!" I turned around to see the girl, Miryam, standing behind me. She looked even younger than she had when I first laid eyes on her that night in the barn. In Yehud most girls were married by their eighteenth birthday, but she didn't look a day over fourteen. She was still a child, so I spoke to her like one.

"I understand why you would feel this way. Most young mothers believe that their first-born sons are special—"

"I am a virgin!"

It took me a moment to regain my speech. "Excuse me?"

"I have never lain with any man, including my husband!"

I looked at Yosef. "Is this true?"

He looked down at his feet to avoid my gaze. "Yes. Miryam was thirteen when we married. She had not bled, and it is forbidden to lie with a maiden who has not been in niddah.[1] Nine moons ago, she finally became a woman. On the night her bleeding ended she was purifying herself in the mikveh, preparing herself for me when…when…"

Stepping forward, Miryam exclaimed, in a voice filled with pride, "An angel visited me and said that my womb would receive the seed of Heaven and that I would give birth to a son who would become the savior of the world."

I should have stopped right there. But my watchman's curiosity got the better of me. "Did anyone else witness this angel's visit?"

"No."

"Is it possible that this—visit—was a dream?"

She shook her head vigorously. "No! For right after the visit I felt the presence of the Holy One. Not long afterward, my belly began to swell with child."

Gazing back and both between her and Yosef, I asked, "And did the two of you ever—um—fulfill your marital duty?"

---

[1] Menstruation.

"Of course not!" she snapped. "It would be a sin to defile the womb carrying the Messiah with the seed of any man, even that of my husband."

I pulled Yosef aside. "Um, did anyone, er, confirm your wife's–virginity– after she became pregnant?"

He looked at me as if I were an idiot. "We have never lain together, so there was no need to."

My discomfort level was rising. It didn't help that several of the roof-thatchers were gathering around us. I chose my words carefully. "I mean, did a physician or a midwife look to see–"

Yosef waved his hand, dismissively. "Miryam was visited by an angel! Yeshua was conceived and begat by a virgin, as foretold by the Prophets! Can any other man who claims to be the Messiah say the same?"

I didn't recall any of Bethlehem's long line of would-be messiahs saying that they were born of virgins. Several of them didn't know who their fathers were, but I doubted that their mothers were ever visited by unearthly visitors. At least not angels, anyway.

I made a mental note to talk to a rabbi about this virgin-birth claim. I'm not sure how it would help the investigation. Maybe I just needed to feel assured that there was more to this story than the testimony of two parents. Still, against my better judgment, I plodded on.

"Who delivered the baby?"

"I did!" answered one of the roof-thatchers. Aviv the midwife had guided hundreds of newborns into the world, including my own son.

I gently clasped her arm. "Mother Aviv, may I have a word in private?"

"Of course, Senior Constable," she replied, flashing me a toothless smile. "How is your little boy doing these days?"

She was nearly 65 years old and a bit forgetful. But now wasn't the time to remind her that my "little boy" was 20 years old. "He's fine, thank you."

"Good, good," she said. "I remember how handsome your baby was when he was born. He had almost as much hair as Yeshua the Messiah."

"That's what I would like to talk to you about, Mother Aviv."

She laughed. "Well, your son was trouble right from the beginning. Your wife was in labor for almost two days–"

"I mean I want to discuss the birth of Yeshua."

"Oh, yes. The Messiah emerged from his mother's womb as if Adonai himself was guiding his entrance into the world. I've never seen such a perfectly formed newborn. No wrinkles, no swelling on his eyes, no mottling or blood on his skin. He didn't even cry."

I plunged forward with my next question. "When you were delivering the baby, did you uhmm, notice whether the mother was–you know."

She blinked innocently. "What?"

I looked down at my feet. "A virgin?"

"She claims she was, and still is."

Steeling my nerve, I asked, "I mean was there any–physical evidence of her virginity?"

"Oh! You mean the kiroom habtoolim, or virgin's veil. Well, I couldn't say, because the baby was crowning when I arrived."

I cocked my head in miscomprehension. Like all men, I knew next to nothing about the mysteries of childbirth. In fact, I knew even less than most, for when my son was born I was a hundred miles away, fighting Nabataeans.

Sensing my ignorance, she replied, "Yeshua was beginning to emerge from her womb. Had the virgin's veil been there it would have been broken by that time. But I have no reason to doubt her word."

Before I could ask another question, I heard an angry voice ask, "What does the divine nature of the Messiah's conception have to do with the theft of his treasures?" I turned to see Uriel standing behind me, his arms crossed in disapproval.

"Nothing really," I was forced to admit. Apparently, all of Yeshua's followers believed that this virgin birth was genuine. I, however, had serious doubts. Too many men had used magic tricks and lies to convince the gullible that they were the Chosen One, cheating them of their money and possessions before riding off into the desert, never to be seen again.

With a little bit of common sense, it was easy to debunk the claims of such charlatans. Require them to prove their direct lineage from King Dovid. Test their knowledge of the Torah and the Prophets. Demand that they work a miracle, such as restoring sight to a blind man or curing a leper.

But how did you test an infant? How aware was little Yeshua that many people, including his parents, believed that he would someday grow up to become the king of the Yehudim based on questionable claims of missing treasures and angelic visits? In the warmth of his mother's womb had Adonai told him of his destiny in hushed whispers? Would he ever be able to meet the exalted expectations thrust upon him by his followers? More ominously, what would happen if he didn't?

Since such questions were the province of rabbis, rather than lowly watchmen, I left Yeshua and his followers to their work and returned to the Watch house after completing my morning patrol.

Commander Shaul waited until I had poured myself a cup of tea before accosting me. "Senior Constable Gidon, what is the status of your investigation into the theft of the chests from the Notsrim?"

I responded exactly as I had for the past two days. "Inquiries and fact-gathering continue, but there has been no further progress in identifying the culprits."

He nodded. "Seeing that this is the case, it is time for you to end your investigation."

I blinked. "What?"

"You have a new assignment: to capture the Kanai[1] who have been desecrating the synagogue."

I groaned. "What did they do this time?"

"Last night they smeared camel dung on the front steps."

I sighed. If living under Roman rule wasn't causing us enough trouble, we now had to deal with yet another group of religious fanatics who believed they could hasten the age of the Messiah by attacking those they accused of collaborating with our oppressors.

Like most agitators, the Kanai committed their relatively harmless acts of vandalism under cover of darkness. They never attacked people, only buildings where they believed acts of capitulation had taken place. Bethlehem's synagogue was a frequent target since it was run by the Sedukim and occasionally hosted meetings attended by Sanhedrin members and Roman bureaucrats. Reb Lemuel's home had been vandalized several times. One time they covered his gate in pig's blood. Another time they nailed two wolf skulls to his door, a reference to Romulus and Remus, the twin founders of Rome who had been raised by a she-wolf. The Kanai were more irritating than threatening and I had no desire to waste my time on them.

"Why must I be involved in chasing vandals? This is work for junior constables."

Constable Shaul shrugged. "Today's is Constable Elihu's day off."

"What about Amos?"

"Junior Constable Amos is repairing the cracks in the holding cell walls."

"Commander, you know as well as I do that the theft of these gifts is a much larger crime than acts of hooliganism committed by fools."

Looking away from me, he replied, as if reciting a prepared speech, "Senior Constable, how many times must I remind you that it is the responsibility of the Sanhedrin to prioritize our assignments?"

---

[1] Later known as the Zealots.

"You've never taken me off an investigation, because you know that eventually I always get my man. Even if takes a year or more."

The commander's left eye twitched slightly. After years of serving together, I knew how to read his expressions. "Someone told you to stop my investigation."

He didn't respond.

"Who was it? Reb Lemuel?"

He remained silent, which in our unspoken language meant *yes*.

"Why does our magistrate not want me to solve this crime?"

Commander Shaul pursed his lips and replied, "Since no progress has been made he and the town merchants now want people to forget that the theft ever occurred. It creates the impression that Bethlehem isn't safe. The last thing they want to do is chase away the pilgrimage trade."

"Since when did the Watch become beholden to spice-sellers and moneylenders? We're servants of the Laws!"

"That may be true, but the Sanhedrin pays our wages, so they have the right to tell us which Laws we must enforce. If you don't agree with their policies, you're free to seek employment elsewhere."

We held our gaze for a long moment. I could easily have removed my sash and truncheon and walked out the door, never to return. I didn't need this job. Between the money my father had left me, the wages I had saved over the years through modest living and the income Naomi earned in the marketplace I could have retired and spent the rest of my days studying Torah, tending our flock or playing Petteia[1] with the old men in the market. Shaul, on the other hand, needed the income from his job to support his status as a community leader and all the obligations this entailed. Hosting lavish feasts for visiting Sanhedrin and priests. Tithing a quarter of his salary to the synagogue. Buying lamp oil and firewood to illuminate his dark and empty house. He had much

---

[1] An ancient Greek board game somewhat similar to chess.

more to lose by disobeying orders than I did. Which, oddly enough, made me more willing to give in when he pulled rank on me.

"All right. Adonai might inflict me with boils for not delivering justice to His Chosen One, but I'll put the theft aside and focus on capturing dangerous manure spreaders. Happy?"

He didn't need to answer. The unspoken gratitude in his eyes told me everything I needed to know.

CHAPTER 6

Three more days passed uneventfully. The treasure thieves and the Kanai still remained at large. But following up on a complaint from a blind old widow, I was able to cajole Zev the butcher into admitting that he had sold her mutton infested with flies and mouse droppings. Zev's contrite confession earned him a rather lenient judgment from Reb Lemuel: the "triple-10" penalty. Ten lashes of the whip, a ten-shekel fine, and a ten-day deadline to make an atonement sacrifice at the Temple. Zev was fortunate; he could have been sentenced to ten years in prison.

I had just arrived at the Watch house when Commander Shaul called me over to his desk. "Senior Constable, what are you working on?"

"Let me see. Oh, yes, I'm about to go have a little talk with Avi the tanner. A few days ago he chased away a man who was trying to steal some of the camel dung he uses for fertilizer. Hopefully, he can give me a description that will lead me to our Kanai vandals."

"That can wait. I need you for escort duty."

I glanced at the door of the jail cell. "I didn't know we had prisoners."

"We don't. You and Constable Elihu are to escort the Notsrim to Yerushalayim for their son's circumcision and birth offering."

I raised my eyebrows. "Whose idea was this?"

"We're under direct orders from the Sanhedrin. They want to make sure that the family arrives and returns safely."

I scratched my chin. "First they stop me from finding out who stole Yeshua's gifts. Now they want me to be his private livery service."

He shrugged. "It's not our place to question their motives."

"But why me? I can barely walk."

"We need a level head in charge. Constable Elihu is a hothead, and as a Sedukim he is philosophically opposed to messiahs in general."

"Then why not send Junior Constable Amos?"

"Because he's not a trained fighter."

I grinned. "You're expecting trouble?"

He tapped his truncheon. "You know as well as I do the dangers of traveling the Pilgrim's Highway."

I nodded. The Pilgrim's Highway was a meandering road connecting Bethlehem to Yerushalayim. Thousands of Yehudim traveled the highway every year, their wagons and carts laden with goats, lambs, doves, wheat and other offerings destined for the sacrificial altar of the Temple. Those who traveled without weapons or bodyguards were easy pickings for the gangs of bandits who lurked in the surrounding hills.

"How will we be traveling?"

"In a covered mule cart."

"Where is this cart?"

"It's at the inn. Constable Elihu is there now. Get going as soon as possible. You must return before nightfall."

When I arrived at the inn, Constable Elihu was standing by a mule cart parked in front of the gate, waving his spear at two mobs that were shouting at each other. One group I recognized as Yeshua's followers. Pressed against the gate, clutching clubs and planks of wood, they chanted, "Praise the Messiah Yeshua!" The other, much larger group, shouted, "Galilim heretics go home!"

I squeezed through the crowd and joined Constable Elihu. "What's going on here?"

Pointing the tip of his spear at the anti-Notsrim contingent, he replied, "These righteous men are trying to prevent the false messiah from leaving Bethlehem."

I brought out my truncheon. "Where's the mule driver?"

"He ran off."

I felt a tap on my shoulder. Uriel ben Teman waved an angry finger at me. "Senior Constable, what are you going to do about these hooligans? Three times they've tried to crash the gate and harm the Messiah and his parents. If we hadn't been here to stop them who knows what plague the Almighty would have rained down upon us all?"

I looked around. Both factions were swelling with new members. Violence hadn't broken out yet but it was only a matter of time. I turned to Uriel. "Go get Commander Shaul. Now!"

The saltseller scampered off. We continued to guard the gate and wagon. Both mobs could easily have overcome us but my younger comrade's wild-eyed glare kept them from acting on their impulses.

A few minutes later Junior Constable Amos joined us. "I heard about the fracas and got here as soon as I could."

Sighing in relief, I said, "I appreciate you coming in on your day off."

Grinning, he replied, "I can fill wine amphorae anytime. How often do I get a chance to protect the Chosen One?"

With the three of us wielding our truncheons menacingly, crowd control became a little easier. Which was fortunate because it took another ten minutes for Commander Shaul to arrive. And when he did it was like the Prophet Moshe parting the Yam Suph.[1] The mobs instantly separated and became as docile as lambs. He had that effect on people.

Looking at both groups, he called out, "What's the problem here?"

An angry shepherd waved his crook and shouted. "Your men are protecting the imposter! To circumcise him is a sin against Elohim!"

"No, these men are keeping you apostates from harming the Messiah!" Uriel retorted. This started another round of chanting and jostling.

Commander Shaul drew me aside. "You had one simple duty. Transport the Notsrim to Yerushalayim."

I shrugged. "You may find this hard to believe, but the mob was already here when I arrived."

He replied, with a smirk, "Three watchmen can't break up a gathering of farmers and merchants?"

---

[1] The Sea of Reeds, later misnamed the Red Sea.

Grinning, I answered, "Alas, we clearly don't measure up to the task, which is in dire need of your wisdom and leadership. And your weapon."

Drawing a bronze-plated trunchcon from his pocket, he gazed at the crowd and shook his head. "This won't be easy."

"Agreed," I replied, dodging a well-aimed fig.

"Any ideas?"

I nodded. "I was thinking of a Heshbon feint."

He rubbed his chin, thoughtfully. "Only you could be so devious."

When I returned to the inn twenty minutes later, it seemed like everyone in Bethlehem was there, either siding with one mob or the other or standing on the sidelines to see if a holy war was about to break out. A few enterprising street vendors were selling food. A gambler was taking bets on which side would win. Commander Shaul and Constable Elihu continued to separate the factions while Junior Constable Amos kept his massive frame parked in front of the inn to discourage gatecrashers.

"So?" asked Commander Shaul as he pushed an angry young man back into the crowd.

"All set," I replied.

Several minutes later, a large covered carrus drawn by two oxen pulled in front of the inn. Two Roman guards emerged from the cart. Constable Amos stood aside to let them pass through the gate. They entered the inn. Several minutes later they emerged with two hooded figures fully clothed in robes. One was carrying a small bundle. The guards surrounded them and helped them get into the carrus. The driver whipped the horses and urged the carrus forward. The guards walked alongside, brandishing their spears menacingly. One foolish man tried to climb into it and a guard threw him to the ground. After that the mob quickly dispersed.

Commander Shaul returned to the Watch house while the two constables and I followed the carrus until it had reached the outskirts of town and disappeared behind a hill beyond the first bend of the Pilgrim's Highway.

"Gee, they must have been pretty important for the Romans to get involved," said Junior Constable Amos.

"If you have shekels you can always find a few off-duty guards when you need them," I replied. "They camp out in the taverns, looking for muscle work."

"I wonder how they feel about transporting the Messiah?"

"He's not the Messiah!" snapped Constable Elihu, thrusting his spear into the ground. "There is no such thing. Messiahs are the invention of heretics who wish to overthrow the priestly classes."

"Only a Sedukim would say that!" countered Junior Constable Amos.

"And only Isiyim and you Apocalypts would believe such nonsense!"

"Gentlemen!" I shouted. "Save your debates for the synagogue. Constable Elihu, we have escort duty to perform."

They both looked at me with puzzled expressions. "But the Romans just left town."

"That is true," I replied. "They are escorting a family of Arabs home to Azzah."[1]

"Then…where are the Notsrim?" asked Junior Constable Amos.

Behind us we could hear a mournful bray. We turned to watch a mule-drawn hay wagon approach.

I grinned. "Surely you two have heard of the Heshbon feint?"

They stared at me with blank expressions.

"No? It's a shame you young people know nothing of our military history. Fourteen years ago, Commander Shaul and I were fighting the Nabataeans in the Heshbon plain. One morning, we found our bivouac greatly outnumbered by our enemies. To make it worse, our leader, General Noor, was laid low by an arrow in the thigh. We needed to get him to safety but we knew his train would be attacked if we tried to evacuate him. So, I came up with the idea of dressing Commander Shaul in General Noor's armor and helmet and sending

---

[1] Gaza.

him off on our fastest camel. The Nabataeans fell for this deception and pursued him. Fortunately, their camels were much slower and Commander Shaul was never caught. Meanwhile, we covered the real general with an old burial shroud, strapped him to a mule and brought him back to our field headquarters. It was the perfect diversion."

"Gosh," whistled Junior Constable Amos. "The general must have rewarded you handsomely."

"Well, no, not really. He died a day later," I replied as the wagon stopped. "But the strategy lived on."

Approaching the side of the wagon, I called, "Is everyone here?"

Two hands parted a large clump of hay, revealing the sweaty face of Yosef. "Yes, Senior Constable."

"And the child is well?"

"Yes."

From another part of the pile I heard the muffled voice of the mother. "Why we must hide like fugitives?"

"I know this is uncomfortable, but you must remain concealed. Eyes will be watching this wagon all the way to the Holy City."

"Adonai's love for Yeshua will protect us from harm!"

"Let us hope so, because I'm not convinced two guards are enough," I replied. Turning to Junior Constable Amos, I said, "Go back to the inn and stand by the gate for an hour or so."

He grinned. "To create the illusion that the Messiah never left town, just in case some people didn't fall for the Heshbon feint?"

"Smart lad."

"It's like that gambling game where you hide a grape under one of three walnut shells."

"That's right. And we want to make sure everyone guesses wrong."

He nodded and headed off.

Two men were sitting in the buckboard of the wagon. One turned to me and smiled. A flash of sunlight reflected off a gold tooth. "A brilliant plan,

Senior Constable. In another life such trickery would have made you a highly respected smuggler."

"That's quite a compliment coming from you, Reuven," I said as he slid to the ground. "Are you sure you don't wish to accompany us?"

"No, thank you. I can't stand the smell of mules and hay makes my eyes water."

Pointing to the other man, he said, "Togeh, however, is not only a seasoned mule driver but is also quite adept with a dagger. In case you should run into trouble. Safe journey, Senior Constable. When you return please come with your commander to settle our account. I don't think that he's aware of how Heshbon feints cost these days."

As he headed off, Constable Elihu shook his head. "That man should be stoned to death."

Placing a hand on his shoulder, I said, "Before you condemn him, Constable, know that he lost his two fingers preventing a gang of Assyrians from violating a Yehudi woman and her daughter."

He didn't seem convinced. "How do you know that he hasn't sent word to bandits letting them know we're coming?"

"Because Reuven is a man who thinks about the future. And he knows that his future will be very short if he ever betrays the Watch. Or me."

CHAPTER 7

The Pilgrim's Highway not only serves as a thoroughfare for Yehudim traveling to the Holy City, but it is also a major trade route that connects merchants from all over the world to the vast markets of Yerushalayim. It's one of many such roads that cross through Bethlehem, making our little village an important commercial hub. From here you can travel along eastern routes that lead to the valley of the Nahar al-Urdun[1] and the kingdoms of Nabataea and Persea; western paths that terminate in Ashdod and Caesarea Maritima; and south along the Hebron road, which connects our town to the port cities along the southern coast where vessels from Egypt, Ethiopia and the Hindoo lands deliver tea, exotic spices and fabrics.

Yet despite its grand name, the Pilgrim's Highway is little more than a beaten-down dirt path snaking through hills of scrub and cypress trees. Stiff winds constantly whip up swirls of sand and soil, making it difficult to see more than a few dozen feet in any direction. Constable Elihu, Togeh the driver and I wore keffiyehs over our faces but even these couldn't keep the dust out of our nostrils.

Fortunately, springtime is not a particularly busy travel time. In our first half hour the only person we passed was an old beggar. I dropped a half-shekel into his bowl and hoped that the journey would remain uneventful. Still, you could never be too complacent. Constable Elihu was holding his spear and I knew he had at least two daggers concealed in his cloak. I was armed with my truncheon, a dagger and my old battle sword. I had thought about bringing my old wooden battle shield but after years of using it as a well cover termites had eaten through most of it, so home it stayed.

Togeh and I sat on the buckboard while Constable Elihu walked. Occasionally, I would check on our human cargo. I was convinced that the heat and the hay would make the baby wail like a hyena but he was blessedly quiet.

---

[1]The Jordan River.

We were riding through a small chasm when I ordered Togeh to stop.

"What's wrong?" Constable Elihu asked.

"There's an ambush up ahead, just beyond the hill on the left."

"How do you know?"

I pointed at small wisps of dust swirling in the air from beyond a curve in the road. "Shuffling feet. Nervous. Anticipating our arrival."

Drawing my sword, I turned to my fellow watchman and asked, "Feel like taking on some bandits?"

Constable Elihu grasped his spear with two hands and nodded.

Leaning over the hay pile, I shouted, "Yosef, did you hear what I said?"

"Yes," his muffled voice answered from under the straw.

"Should they defeat us, surrender immediately and give them whatever they want. Maybe if they see you have nothing worth stealing they'll let you go." Inwardly, I thought, *Not likely.*

Waving my sword, I shouted, "We know you're out there! Honestly, the way you drag up dirt a blind man could see where you're hiding!"

Nothing happened.

Slipping the truncheon into my left hand, I yelled, "Well, we're not going to stumble into your trap, so you might as well show your faces. Or run away. I don't care which, but decide. We need to make it to Yerushalayim by midday."

A moment later, five swarthy men dressed in ragged cloaks emerged from around the bend. Three were armed with clubs, one wielded a trident and the largest man carried a spear.

"Let us travel in peace," I said. "We're simple farmers and have no money or valuables."

The man with the spear stepped forward. "Really? I've never seen farmers armed with weapons before."

I shrugged. "The Romans are paying top prices for hay these days."

"How stupid do you think I am?" the leader bellowed. "You are watchmen from Bethlehem and you are escorting a family of Galilim to the Temple."

Who tipped them off? I wondered, avoiding Constable Elihu's glance. "You are mistaken."

"If this is so, you will not object if I thrust my spear into your wagon to make sure?"

"Quite the opposite. I will object very much."

He laughed. "So much so that you are willing to lose your life over it?" Waving the other men forward, he said, "Give us the family and we will let you return home."

I shook my head. "What kind of guards would we be if we agreed to such loathsome terms?"

He grinned. "Guards who will live to tell the story of this day to their grandchildren."

I dropped off the wagon and raised my sword and truncheon. "Tales of cowardice aren't worth telling."

"Good. Killing you will be far more enjoyable."

They charged. The leader thrust his spear at me. I dodged and slammed it out of his hand with my truncheon. Two men cautiously approached Constable Elihu, their clubs raised. He held them off by waving his spear and dagger. The fourth man lashed out at me with his club. I parried it with my sword and as he was recovering I plunged the blade through his shoulder. He fell to the ground.

The leader lunged at me again. I swung my truncheon, trying to knock the spear away but he held on fast. I was more experienced in battle, but he was at least ten years younger than me and apparently learned quickly from his mistakes.

From several feet away, I heard a shout of pain. Constable Elihu's spear was sticking out of the belly of one attacker. As he tried to wrench it free, his other foe knocked him to the ground.

I should have been paying more attention to my own skirmish, because the leader suddenly clipped the side of my neck with the tip of his spear, drawing blood. I kicked out with my right foot and landed a solid blow to his groin, doubling him over in pain.

Constable Elihu's opponent was standing over him, his club raised to deliver a fatal blow. In desperation, I flung my dagger at him with all my might. The handle hit him in the nose. He dropped the club and Elihu jumped up and plunged his own dagger into the man's chest.

As the leader rose unsteadily I slammed my truncheon into his forehead, knocking him out. "Where's the last one?"

Constable Elihu shook his head.

I heard a loud moan. "Togeh!" I recovered my sword and ran to the other side of the wagon. The driver lay on the ground, clutching his arm.

"Senior Constable!" Elihu yelled.

I whirled around to see the fifth assailant standing on the edge of the wagon. He raised his trident into the air.

"No!" I screamed.

I watched the three points begin their horrifying descent toward the middle of the hay pile. There was no way he could miss his targets. And I was too far away to stop him.

And then the weapon clattered harmlessly onto the buckboard. The assassin's hands were clutching at an arrow that protruded from his throat. Seconds later another pierced his chest and knocked him to the ground.

Without thinking, I leapt into the cart and spread myself as wide as I could on the hay pile. "Elihu! There's an archer! Protect the Notsrim!"

Constable Elihu joined me in the cart.

"Is everyone all right?" I asked the hay.

Miryam's head appeared. "We're fine. Adonai's love for Yeshua is protecting us."

"Tell Him to keep up the good work," I replied. We were sitting ducks. I had my sword and truncheon, but I wasn't sure how effective they would be in deflecting arrows.

I looked up to see the archer descending from a hill, creating a swirl of sand and dust in his wake. He was shouting something I couldn't understand.

"Constable, he might have a bow but now it's two against one."

Constable Elihu nodded. "It's a good day to die."

"Trust me, Constable, it's never a good day to die, but I know what you mean. Let's do this."

We jumped out of the wagon. Constable Elihu retrieved his spear and I waved my sword. The archer was less than twenty yards away from us and closing fast.

Constable Elihu drew back his arm to launch his spear. "Wait!" I shouted. "If he wanted us dead he could have killed us by now."

When the archer was ten yards away, he stopped, lowered his bow, and shouted "Shalom, Shalom! I am your friend, not your foe!"

He slowly advanced and then stopped a few yards away from us. He was dressed in a white linen cloak and his head and face were covered by a keffiyeh.

"A filthy Isiyim!" Constable Elihu spat, his spear still raised.

The archer nodded and looked at me. "I may be a filthy Isiyim, but I come from a good family. Wouldn't you agree, Father?"

The only part of his face I could see were his hazel eyes. But I recognized them instantly. "Binyamin?"

He unwound the keffiyeh and I found myself staring at my son.

"Aren't you going to say, 'It's good to see you?'" Binyamin grinned. "If you can't do that, could you at least ask your Sedukim companion not to kill me?"

"Stand down, Constable," I ordered. Disappointed, Constable Elihu lowered his spear and sheathed his dagger. There was so much to discuss, but first things first. I ordered the watchman to bind the hands and feet of any bandits who weren't dead, while I tended to Togeh. He had been hit hard on the arm but nothing seemed to be broken. Constable Elihu returned and said that all of our attackers were dead. I didn't bother to ask him if any had been alive when he examined them. Some things were best not knowing.

I then addressed the hay pile. "You can come out now."

Yosef and Miryam emerged. "I told you that that Adonai's love for our son would protect us!" she said, clutching the unruffled infant to her breast.

"The perfect child," I murmured.

Binyamin moved in to take a closer look. "So, this is the little one who's been creating such a stir."

The mother beamed. "Yes! And you are?"

"Binyamin ben Gidon," he replied.

"*My* son," I added.

Yosef nodded. "I am Yosef, this is my wife, Miryam, and this is—"

"Yeshua," Binyamin replied. "News travels fast."

I had a thousand questions but the only one that formed on my lips was, "How do you Isiyim know about him? I thought you people never left your caves."

Tapping his chest, Binyamin said, "If that were so, would I be here right now? In fact, we have informants all over Yehud." Glancing at Constable Elihu, he said, "After all, when you're hated by both Yehudim and Romans, it's always good to know what your enemies are up to."

"You deserve our enmity!" Constable Elihu snapped. "Your heresy and flagrant disregard for the Laws are the cause of our oppression by the idol-worshippers!"

"Really?" Binyamin laughed. "The last time I checked, it was your beloved priests who were paying tributes of gold and silver to both the Romans and their Idomite vassals."

Constable Elihu stepped forward. I pushed him back. "Constable. Please take care of Togeh." Grumbling, he stalked off.

Turning to my son, I said, "Now, what in the name of Avraham,[1] Yitzchak and Yaakov are you doing here?"

---

[1] Abraham.

"We knew that there was a plot to attack the Notsrim. But we didn't know where. My mission is to protect the child at any cost."

Pulling him out of earshot, I murmured, "What possible interest do you Isiyim have in him?"

He shook his head. "I do not know. All I was told is that the baby must arrive in Yerushalayim and be circumcised."

"And they only sent you?"

He shrugged. "No one else was needed."

"Have you been following us the whole time?"

"No, I just arrived here."

"You were trailing the first wagon, weren't you?"

"No, I knew that one was a decoy."

"How did you know?"

He grinned. "Because you weren't guarding it."

"And you didn't feel it necessary to tell me until we were attacked by brigands?"

"It wasn't you I was assigned to protect."

I shook my head, choosing not to dwell on the fact that he considered the life of the baby more important than that of his father. But what could I expect? Two years had passed since I had last seen him, on the day he left my home and headed east to join the mysterious Isiyim. Considered merely strange by most Yehudim and heretics by the Sedukim, their philosophy rejected the trappings of wealth, family and privilege. They believed that the priests in Yerushalayim were corrupt puppets of Rome and that Adonai no longer viewed the Temple as the spiritual center of the Yehudi faith. While a small population lived in poverty in Yerushalayim, most Isiyim had moved to Kumran, a wilderness of desert and jagged hills pockmarked with caves that served as their homes. It was said that they anointed their own priests and conducted sacrifices in strict accordance with the Laws. Only men were allowed to join their community. Over time, this would have guaranteed their eventual extinction. But it wasn't an issue for they, like the Apocalypts, believed that the age of the

Messiah was imminent and that the restoration of the Kingdom of Yisroel would somehow guarantee their survival.

"Do you believe Yeshua is the Messiah?"

He shrugged. "I don't know, but he and his followers are under Elohim's protection."

"And your proof of this?"

"That I happened to find this wagon seconds before the infant's assailant was posed to strike."

"Coincidence. Or luck."

"How do you account for the fact that, in spite of being outnumbered, none of you were seriously injured?"

Reaching for my neck, I replied, "Really? Then what do you call—"

I stopped. There was no blood. No gash. No pain. But I had felt the spear tip slicing through my skin. "What the—"

Binyamin cocked his head. "You were saying?"

My faith in Adonai is strong, especially when I emerge from a victorious takedown of a thief with only cuts and bruises. But even minor wounds take days, if not weeks, to heal.

Rubbing my neck again, I wondered if a miracle had occurred. Perhaps, but I didn't have time to dwell on it now. I called Constable Elihu over and said, "We must search the bodies to see if we can find out who ordered them to attack us."

The watchman shook his head in horror. "No one but a cacher may examine the dead!"

I sighed. It wasn't easy being a watchman in a community bound by strict rules regarding the handling of just about anything that drew a breath. Technically, no one was allowed to touch the dead other than cachers. They collected corpses and brought them to a mortician for purification and burial. According to the priests, anyone else who touched a body or was stained with its blood was considered impure. Only a ritual cleansing in a mikveh could remove the corruption.

But you couldn't be a soldier without spilling blood. When a fellow warrior fell in battle on a lonely plain in the desert hundreds of miles from the nearest Yehud village, you pushed aside your aversions, removed your comrade's weapons and any keepsakes to return to his family and buried him as quickly and respectfully as possible. Then you wiped your foe's tainted blood from your weapon and moved on.

That's why retired soldiers made ideal watchmen. Our military experience taught us that when a cornered thief was lunging at your heart with a knife you couldn't worry about impurities when you crushed his skull with your truncheon. And you couldn't wait for a cacher to search the thief's body because the recovered loot needed to be returned to its rightful owners quickly and the tattoos on his back might tell you which of the many gangs of brigands he had once belonged to. It was a job that sometimes required you to bend the Laws to uphold them. The Sanhedrin understood this, which was why the Watch had its own mikveh. In our line of work, you often needed physical and spiritual cleansing several times a day.

Constable Elihu had never been a soldier. He had been a watchman for only seven months. And although he was a formidable opponent in a fight he had never killed a man—until today. Had this skirmish occurred in Bethlehem, I could have pawned him off on a fellow Sedukim to walk him back from his theological crisis, but right now I didn't have the time. We were still an hour away from Yerushalayim and who knows what other miscreants were waiting in ambush in the hills beyond?

Binyamin began to search through the pockets of the assailant he had killed. "Don't worry. I'm a cacher."

"Under whose authority?" Constable Elihu sneered.

"Our own priests," Binyamin answered. "All Isiyim are cachers. We have to be since none of your city cachers are going to venture out to our enclave to take care of a body."

Constable Elihu shook his head in disgust. "Sacrilege! Only the Temple priests can appoint cachers!"

"Is that so?" asked my son, moving on to the next corpse. "And where in the Torah is this written? I have read every word and I don't recall any mention of cachers at all."

"Just because it is not mentioned specifically doesn't mean the authority is not inherently proscribed—"

"Oh really? I thought you Sedukim believed in the literal translation and administration of the Laws. No interpretations allowed whatsoever."

"You ignorant—"

Once again I had to separate them. "Gentlemen, in another time and place this would be a fascinating debate. But not now. We have a family to deliver."

Both men glared at each other and then separated. Binyamin and I searched the remaining bodies but found nothing that might have told us who they were. We then dug a shallow grave and buried them, covering the dirt with large stones. Yes, these men had tried to kill us, but they, too, were the children of Adonai and no corpse deserved to become carrion for vultures and hyenas. To my surprise, even Constable Elihu helped. If a Sedukim and an Isiyim could put aside their differences long enough to provide a decent burial for their common foes, maybe the time of the Messiah was imminent.

CHAPTER 8

We knew we weren't far from Yerushalayim when peddlers began appearing on the side of the road selling turtledoves, goats, lambs, and grain for those who needed offerings. As we approached the walls that surrounded the Holy City, they were joined by money changers, beggars and whores.

We reached the Damascus Gate and stood at the end of a long line of visitors waiting to get past the Roman checkpoint. I turned around and said, "I think it's safe now."

Yosef and Miryam emerged from the hay. Yeshua was awake. He gazed at the surroundings with a studied expression.

An old woman emerged out of nowhere and thrust a bony finger at the Notsrim. "Destroyer of the Yehudim! A curse upon you!"

Stepping between her and the wagon, I grabbed her arm and said, "Move along, crone!"

She slapped my hand away. "Heed my words, for I am the Prophet Avital! Twenty years ago El-Shaddai warned me of this day, when the false messiah would come to Yerushalayim for his circumcision and birth offering!"

Binyamin and I looked at each other. *How does she know this? Unless she's in cahoots with our would-be assailants—*

"You've got the wrong family," I replied.

Glaring at Miryam, she said, "You believe your child is the Chosen One, but our savior he will not be! He will die a painful death, hanging from a tree, and all of Yehud shall suffer for it!"

Two men in priestly robes suddenly stepped forward and pushed the old woman aside. A third approached us and laughed, "Sorry about that. She's a crazy old hag. Says the same thing every time a family with a newborn son comes here for the birth rituals. You're the third one today. Please don't let this spoil your pilgrimage, and welcome to Yerushalayim. I assume you're heading for the Temple?"

"Yes," I replied.

"Well, then, once you're through the gate, follow the signs of *Shin*. Looks like this." He separated the fingers of his right hand to signify the Hebrew letter that represented divine power. "And if you're not bringing your own sacrifice I recommend you only deal with the approved vendors on the Temple plaza. Sure, you'll pay a little less if you buy a lamb from one of the street vendors but the priests are very picky about what they allow on the altar."

Thanking him, we crossed through the Damascus Gate and entered the city that had served as the center of the Yehudi faith since the time of King Shelomoh. Yet, even with its storied history, most first-time pilgrims, having seen the huge walls that had been rebuilt to restore grandeur to this ancient place, were disappointed once they entered. If you raised your eyes high enough you could see King Herod's old palace perched upon a hilltop, but the first thing most people noticed was the dirty, wild-eyed faces of beggars and children who swarmed visitors like angry bees. They slapped the sides of the wagon as we passed.

Binyamin headed off to the Isiyim quarter to purify himself in their mikveh. Constable Elihu and I would wait until we returned to Bethlehem so we continued on to the plaza outside of the Temple. Yosef bought a fat turtledove and I joined him and hundreds of other pilgrims in the sacrifice line while Constable Elihu and Togeh stayed with the mother and the infant in the wagon.

When it was his turn, Miryam handed the baby to Yosef. With the possible Messiah in one hand and the turtledove in the other, he entered the Temple alone.

Binyamin rejoined us as Yosef emerged with the baby twenty minutes later, his face frozen in an expression of horror.

"Did you look like that after I was circumcised?" asked my son.

"No, because I was off fighting Nabataeans," I replied. "My father accompanied your mother to the Temple for yours."

Yosef began to sway and Miryam immediately ran over to him and wrenched Yeshua from his grip. Patting Binyamin on the shoulder, I said, "Well, at least that's one ritual you Isiyim won't have to see, being celibate and all."

He smiled. "Not so. In the past year, two gentiles converted to our faith and joined our community. Have you ever witnessed the circumcision of an adult man?"

I shuddered at the thought. "No, and I hope I never will."

The infant was fast asleep. I watched in wonder. "Binyamin, your mother said that after yours you didn't stop crying for three days. This one slumbers like a lion who has just feasted on a gazelle. Nothing seems to bother him."

Binyamin rubbed his beard. "A Yehudi who doesn't complain? That truly is a miracle."

The trip back to Bethlehem was uneventful. On the outskirts of town, I stepped out of the wagon and ordered Comrade Elihu to make sure the Notsrim returned to the inn safely. When the wagon was out of earshot I turned to Binyamin. "It would gladden your mother's heart for you to pay her a visit."

He shook his head. "I cannot."

I sighed. "The desert has turned my boy into a man with a heart of stone."

"You don't understand. When you become an Isiyim you give up your former life. Family. Friends. Possessions."

"Why?"

"So we can be free of the trappings of wealth and power that would distract us from living our lives in accordance with the Laws."

"Isn't honoring your parents one of the Laws?"

He shrugged. "We believe the best way to honor them is to devote our lives solely to the worship of the Almighty."

I looked at him for a long minute. "And where does Yeshua fit into all this?"

"Our rabbis ordered me to protect him."

"Do they believe he is the Messiah?"

"I don't know."

"Yet you're willing to kill others to save his life."

"Like you, I am a soldier. I follow orders, not question them. And now I must go."

"Is there any message you'd like me to convey to your mother?"

He wound his keffiyeh around his face until only his eyes showed. "No. Goodbye." He turned and ran toward a distant hill. I watched until he disappeared behind a crest and then limped into town with a heavy heart.

After a trip to the Watch mikveh, I returned to the inn to see how the baby was doing. Sagiv told me that the Notsrim were visiting their construction site. I meandered over there and was surprised to see that the house was nearly finished. It was a modest yet sturdy stone dwelling with a small goat pen and a well in the back.

Erez the flower seller greeted me at the door. "Senior Constable! Come and see the gifts from the Friends of the Messiah!"

After kissing a finger and touching the wooden mezuzah mounted on the doorpost, I followed him inside. The interior had been divided into a living and eating area and two smaller bedrooms. The main room had a stone hearth and was already furnished with a full-sized bed on a wooden platform and a table with four chairs. But I noticed they still had the old wooden cradle.

"I've never seen a house built so quickly," I said to Yosef, who was sitting on the floor with his wife, who, as usual, was holding the infant.

Yosef nodded. "Yeshua's followers want us to start living here as soon as possible."

Gazing at the baby, I said, "You should have Zacchari ben Adam, the town's physician, tend to your son's circumcision."

"There is no need. He is healed already!" exclaimed Miryam.

I bent down to speak into Yosef's ear. "Your wife is very young and doesn't understand the delicate nature and proper care of the male organ after a circumcision—"

Apparently, she heard me. "I have two younger brothers! When I was eight my mother taught me how to treat their circumcised penises with turmeric and honey to promote healing and prevent infection."

I blushed. To hear a young girl say such things! I was glad Constable Elihu wasn't here, for he might have been tempted to arrest her for sinful speech. But before anyone could stop her, she removed Yeshua's swaddling cloth. "Behold! See for yourself!"

I looked. So did Yosef and Erez.

"She's right. It is fully healed," murmured Yosef, as if he could barely believe it himself.

I rubbed my chin. "Normally it takes a week for the incision to heal properly."

"For normal infants," replied Erez. "But not for Elohim's Chosen One."

Her face beaming with pride, Miryam dressed the baby and placed him in the cradle. I bowed to her and said, "I apologize for doubting you."

"You are forgiven," she replied.

"I think we shall be fine now," said Yosef, gently urging me to the door. Somehow, I got the impression that he had had enough excitement for one day. So had I.

By the time I returned to the Watch house it was nearly sunset. After making a report to Commander Shaul—leaving out any mention of Binyamin's role—I returned home. Naomi was adding salt and saffron to a pot. The greasy aroma of fish filled my nostrils. I was so hungry my stomach began to gurgle loudly.

I sat down at the table and massaged my aching knee. "What a day. How fortunate I am to come home to my lovely wife making my favorite stew."

She didn't turn to face me. "So? Tell me about your escort mission."

Removing my boots, I replied, "It went fine."

"No surprises?"

"Nothing we couldn't handle."

"No unexpected visitors?"

I paused. She still would not face me. "Like whom?"

"Like our son, perhaps?"

I sighed. You couldn't keep a secret in this town. "How did you find out?"

"Togeh told my friend Rivkah about your encounter with the bandits and how a mysterious young Isiyim suddenly appeared out of nowhere to help you."

She placed a bowl and spoon in front of me. Even in the dim light I could see the tears in her eyes. "Would it have been so hard for him to pay his mother a visit?"

"Naomi, we both had to kill men today."

She shrugged. "Ending the lives of murderers is a mitzvah[1] as far as I'm concerned."

"I invited him here. He would not come."

"What was his excuse? Our house is not clean enough for a cave-dweller? We're not observant enough for him?"

"It's complicated," I replied, spooling the thick, fragrant stew into my mouth. Apparently, she had also gotten her hands on cumin and pepper, which were hard to come by these days. "The Isiyim have their rules, just like all the other sects."

She slammed her hand on the table. "Rules! I'm so sick of rules!"

"Naomi, our whole covenant with Adonai is based on following His rules."

"Do not treat me like an ignorant savage!" she snapped. "I am as well-versed in the Torah as you!"

---

[1] A righteous deed.

I could only nod in agreement. The Yehudim of Oxyrhynchus had an egalitarian attitude toward educating women. Growing up there, Naomi had spent nearly every Shabbat studying our ancient Scriptures in the synagogue alongside her father and cousins and could read and write Ivrit far better than I could.

"Does pledging his loyalty to a community of fanatics absolve him of his responsibility to honor his father and mother?" she asked.

"He said that the best way to honor us is to devote himself to prayer." Realizing that this wouldn't mollify her, I added, "I think he was afraid of seeing you."

"Afraid of his own mother?"

"Yes. You two were very close. If he saw you he might be tempted to break his vows. I think that's the real reason the Isiyim live in the desert. To avoid the urge to return to their families."

She sat down and wiped her eyes. "It's my fault. I introduced him to the writings the Sedukim refused to teach him. How obsessed he was with Yeshayahu's[1] condemnation of those who oppress the poor and powerless! Do you remember the day he left us? He said that those filthy hermits were the spiritual descendants of the Prophets and thanked me for enlightening him. Better I should have taught him the right way to butcher a sacrificial goat or which years you can and can't grow crops."

I said nothing. Twenty-one years of marriage had taught me that when my wife was consumed with righteous indignation it was better to remain silent.

She poured herself a cup of wine and consumed it in a single gulp. "If my own son truly believes that protecting a baby is more important than visiting his own mother, all I can say is if that son of a carpenter doesn't turn out to be the Messiah I'm going to be angrier than Iyov[2] on the ash heap."

---

[1] The prophet Isaiah.
[2] Job.

CHAPTER 9

"Wake up! Wake up!"

These words, and several sharp jabs to the chest, stirred me from a deep slumber. "What? What?"

"Get up, husband. Shaul is here."

I blinked. It was barely dawn. Groaning, I put on my morning tunic. "Where is he?"

"Outside."

The commander stood a few feet away from the door. He knew how grouchy I could be this early in the morning. "Commander," I yawned. "To what do I owe the pleasure of this unexpected visit?"

"Get dressed and come with me, Senior Constable," he replied, curtly.

Naomi appeared in the doorway. "Come in and have some tea, Shaul. I just bought some black hibiscus from the Hindoo lands."

He bowed, stiffly. "Thank you, but we don't have time."

"You know I'm useless without my morning tea," I grumbled as I changed into my cloak and donned my skullcap and sash.

He said nothing as we walked to the northwest part of town. This was always a sign he was following an order with which he didn't agree. We stopped in front of the Bet Shafa. This three-story apartment building was one of the most luxurious dwellings in all of Yehud. It was set off from the road and the rooms in back offered beautiful views of distant hills steeped with wild grape vines. Every unit was fully furnished. Gourmet meals and wine were included in the rent and were prepared in a ground floor kitchen that was larger than my entire house. Its owner lived in Yerushalayim and a heavyset man named Chanoch served as its caretaker and concierge. He met us at the main door and led us up a narrow stairway to the third floor.

"Let us through!" Commander Shaul shouted as we pushed our way down a hallway crowded with people to a door guarded by Junior Constable Amos.

He stepped aside as the commander knocked on the door. "Bethlehem Town Watch. Please allow us entry!"

The door opened wide enough to let us through. Once inside, Commander Shaul pushed it closed.

We were in a large, brightly lit room. In the center stood a large wooden table surrounded by chairs. In the corner there was a raised bed frame with a thick down mattress. A divan was upholstered in linen. Ornate tapestries draped two large windows and large woven rugs covered most of the floor. Twelve oil lamps gave the room a golden hue.

Next to the bed a handsome young couple dressed in colorful cloaks sat on two upholstered chairs. Between them was a large bassinet of ornately carved cedar in which lay a sleeping infant.

"Senior Constable, this is Nogah ben Zilpah, his wife and their newborn son, Yochanan," Commander Shaul said.

"Congratulations," I said. "When was he born?"

"Yesterday, an hour before dawn," replied the proud father.

Still unsure of why Commander Shaul had brought me here, I asked, "And how long have you been in town?"

"For three days. Like so many others, we're here for the census, since I am a descendant of King Dovid. My wife, Devorah, was not due for another month, but apparently Elyon willed that my son be born in the birthplace of his ancestors."

Great. Another census family with a newborn son. I was beginning to wonder whether these mothers-to-be ingested pepper to induce labor.

"Have you traveled from far away?"

"Yes, our family has lived in Dor for several generations. We are goatherds."

I nodded, gazing at the surrounding luxury. Goatherding must have been a profitable profession in Dor, a coastal town on the Mare Nostrum. Most of our local goatherds dressed in sackcloth and lived in tents.

Turning to Commander Shaul, I said, "Commander, thank you for introducing me to this delightful family, but I am wondering why my presence is required?"

He waved his hand toward a corner of the room. I turned and suddenly noticed–

Three wooden chests.

I looked at the commander. He nodded. I walked to one of the chests and lifted the lid. A fragrant sweet aroma wafted from pouches filled with small stone-shaped pustules. The second contained reddish-brown pebbles that gave off a sharp, spicy aroma. The third was filled to the brim with gold coins of various sizes and shapes.

Turning to Commander Shaul, I asked, "How did these get here?"

Licking his lips, he said, "Several hours ago I was informed that three princes from foreign lands visited this apartment last night bearing chests of treasure to celebrate the birth of this child, whom they proclaimed to be the Messiah."

I could feel anger souring my stomach. "Really? And who was this mysterious informant?"

"Me."

I turned to see a tall man dressed in a blue and white cloak and a black skullcap standing by the door.

Commander Shaul cleared his throat and bowed. "Reb Lemuel."

I bowed as well. In addition to being the town magistrate and a member of the Sanhedrin, Reb Lemuel ben Kfir came from a long line of wealthy Yehudim and was an advisor to the Temple priests on administrative matters. His craggy face, salt-and-pepper-hued beard and delicate build made him look like an old man, even though he was at least five years younger than me. His family had lived next door to Naomi and her father when they moved to Bethlehem from Egypt. She always remembered him as a weak, humorless boy prone to breaking out in tears at the slightest insult or injury.

He turned to Commander Shaul. "Commander, it is my understanding that you put your senior constable in charge of the investigation of an alleged theft of wooden chests from a family of destitute Notsrim."

Commander Shaul nodded. "Yes, Reb Lemuel."

"Then in order to settle this matter once and for all I give your senior constable permission to question me directly."

Commander Shaul cast an anxious glance at me. Generally, only superior officers spoke with community leaders. Reb Lemuel was breaking protocol. I had to word my questions very carefully, making sure that I did not show any signs of disrespect for his authority.

"Thank you, Reb Lemuel," I said. "Were you here when these princes arrived?"

"No. I was at home."

"Forgive my confusion, Reb Lemuel, but how did you learn of this fortuitous visit?"

"Nogah came to me himself after the princes left."

Trying hard to suppress a smirk, I asked, "Reb Lemuel, was there anyone else here other than the family when these royal visitors arrived? Did anyone else see them come or go?"

Reb Lemuel glanced at Commander Shaul before looking me straight in the eye. "According to Nogah ben Zilpah, no one else saw them. But his word can be trusted. He is well respected in Dor and, like me, is a Sedukim."

You didn't need to be a mindreader to understand what he was really saying: *How dare you even think that this man is lying?*

As I opened my mouth, Commander Shaul's subtle head-shaking silenced me. I nodded. What was the point? This whole conversation had been orchestrated long before I arrived.

Turning to the commander, Reb Lemuel said, "The presence of these gifts and Nogah's testimony of their origin proves that the Notsrim's claims of theft are falsehoods. I suggest that you end this irrelevant investigation and assign your men to more productive activities."

Commander Shaul nodded. "Yes, Reb Lemuel."

"Good. Starting tomorrow I will appoint one of my own private guards to replace your junior constable. Since Yochanan is clearly the anointed Messiah, his family will require more robust protection than the Watch can provide."

Again I stopped myself from ending my career with a sarcastic retort. The awkward silence was broken by a howl from the bassinet. The mother picked up the baby and cradled him in her arms. For a premature infant, he was very large, with chubby arms and a squarish head. His big brown eyes blinked in the bright light. I made a funny face, and he smiled back at me.

Commander Shaul cleared his throat. "Senior Constable, we have our orders. Let us give this family some privacy."

Nodding respectfully, I headed for the door. Glancing backward, I noticed that the baby's eyes were following me.

As we the left the apartment the mob pressed against us.

"Is it true there are treasures in there?"

"They stole them from the baby Yeshua!"

"That's a lie! This one is the real Messiah!"

Commander Shaul grabbed Junior Constable Amos by the shoulder. "Reb Lemuel will have his own guard here tomorrow. Constable Elihu will relieve you this afternoon. Will you be all right until then?"

The big watchman waved his truncheon. "I once stopped a pack of wolves from breaking into my father's stable. I think I can fend off these people for a little while longer."

"Even so, you'd better put the fear of Adonai into them," I whispered in the commander's ear. He nodded and turned to the mob. "This apartment is under the protection of the Sanhedrin. Anyone who attempts to invade it or harm anyone who is guarding it will receive swift and merciless justice!"

That quieted everyone down. They respectfully withdrew to create space around our grateful colleague.

When we had returned to the Watch house, I said, "For a small village we seem to attract more than our share of messiah-seeking foreign luminaries bearing precious gifts."

He shrugged. "You heard what Reb Lemuel said."

"Yes, and I found it quite interesting that he referred to young Yochanan as the Messiah. I thought the Sedukim are against the whole Chosen One idea."

"Even traditionalists can see the need to change their point of view when reliable evidence is presented."

"Hmmm," I replied. "You know what I also find interesting?"

He sighed. "No, but I'm sure you'll tell me."

"Despite our learned magistrate's claims, no one actually saw these princes deliver the chests to the Dorans."

"True, but no one witnessed anyone delivering them to the Notsrim, either."

"Yes, but Yosef reported the visit and the theft more than a week before these chests suddenly appeared in Nogah's apartment. Chests that contained the same treasures as those stolen from Yeshua."

"Are you suggesting that these are the same chests?"

"Yes."

"Why would someone want to steal them from one family and give them to another?"

Sometimes I felt sorry for my commander. He was honest and righteous and, unlike me, didn't have a single cynical bone in his body.

"Someone really wants Yochanan to be the Messiah. But I think these Dorans are imposters."

He looked surprised. "Why do you say that?"

"Did you notice that there was no mezuzah on the doorpost?"

"So what? It's an apartment, not a home."

"Every apartment in Bethlehem has hooks on the doorposts for renters to hang their mezuzim. Even our poorest census pilgrims hang them on their tent flaps. Yosef and his family, as poor as they are, nailed a simple wooden mezuzah to the doorpost of Sagiv's barn. It's now on their house. But there was only a hook on Nogah's door."

"Maybe theirs was stolen."

"Okay, but did you notice that there were no Shabbat candlesticks or Kiddish cups anywhere in the room?"

"It's not Shabbat. Maybe they're storing them somewhere."

"Do you know any Yehudim who don't display these ritual objects in their homes as a sign of respect to the Almighty?"

"So, perhaps Nogah isn't particularly observant."

"Have you ever met a non-observant Sedukim?"

"They're from Dor. Maybe they do things differently on the coast. Besides, there's no tradition that says that the Messiah's parents must be ultra-religious."

"Fine. But since we're now talking about the boy, did you notice how large he was?"

"No."

"Did you see him smile at me?"

"Only after you made a childish face at him."

I had to remind myself that his short marriage had never been blessed with children. "Newborn babies are tiny and look like lizards. And they're nearly blind at birth. They don't start seeing anything far away for several weeks, and don't start smiling until they're a month old or more. Yochanan looks at least several weeks old. And he clearly saw me, even though I was standing halfway across the room." Of course, the same things could be said about the infant Yeshua but I wasn't about to stir *that* pot.

The commander was silent for a long while. "You may be right. But these are not matters for us to investigate."

"I thought our job was to solve crimes."

"Our job is to keep the peace and, when possible, apprehend those who have broken the Laws. None have been broken here."

"The stolen treasure—"

"Remains stolen, if it ever existed at all."

"You saw the chests in the Dorans' room!"

"Yes, I did. With sworn confirmation from Nogah of their delivery, a claim that is supported by Reb Lemuel. Now, if there were definitive proof that these are the same chests that were stolen from the Notsrim your suspicions might be justified. But other than the statement of a poor carpenter and an old man with Isiyim sympathies, you have none. Do you see the problem here?"

Yes, I knew what the problem was. It wasn't about justice or the truth. It was about politics. My refusal to let the Sanhedrin's views influence my investigations was one of the main reasons I had never advanced beyond the rank of senior constable. Not that I minded. As my father used to say, "The further you are from the tempest, the less likely you are to be struck by lightning."

Commander Shaul fingered his sash, a sign that he was losing patience with me. "Drop it, Senior Constable."

"But–"

"Our long-awaited census starts tomorrow, Baruch ha-Shem.[1] Guarding Roman census takers is our priority for the next few days. After that, we can send the Notsrim on their way and put this whole affair behind us."

"But they now have a home here!" I protested.

"A dwelling that was built without the permission of Reb Lemuel, who, as you know, must approve all residence requests. The Notsrim never made such a request, and, therefore, after the census is officially completed they must return home, along with all the other pilgrims."

He waved a finger at me before I could protest. "This is a legal decision, Senior Constable. I understand your frustration so I'm giving you the rest of the day off to calm yourself."

---

[1] "Praised be His Name." Another way of saying, "Thank God."

I returned home, stewing in anger. It was still early morning but I would never get back to sleep. I sat down at the table. Naomi rose from the bed and joined me.

I tossed my sash on the table. "Why do I put up with this idiocy? Is this why I devoted so many years of my life to defending Yehud against our enemies? So I could spend the rest of my life licking the boots of the rich and powerful?"

She placed a cup of water in front of me.

"I fought to save my people from those who were trying to destroy us. I killed countless men, many of them younger than our son. I fought because I believed that our way of life was worth protecting. In a world full of idol-worshippers we Yehudim were the only ones who believed in a God who commanded us to be servants of truth and justice."

Naomi nodded. Just as I didn't interrupt her occasional tirades, she offered me the same consideration.

"I joined the Watch for the same reason," I continued. "To bring justice to the victims of crime. To reveal the truth hiding behind lies. But now, the powerful have committed a great wrong against the powerless and I can do nothing!"

I wanted to explode. Instead, I struck the cup and sent it spilling to the floor. A stupid gesture. Water was far too precious to be wasted.

Naomi picked up the cup and placed it on the table. "My husband, I don't believe that you will let this injustice go unpunished."

"You have no—"

"Shhh!" she hushed. "Your sense of justice has nothing to do with being a watchman. Even when you were still a skinny soldier you would always come to the protection of the weak and defenseless. Remember that time in the marketplace when you stopped a crowd of men from stoning a leper? Or last year, when a mob wanted to lynch Ahab the fool for stealing lamp oil from the synagogue? You hid him in one of Reuven's sheds until you could prove that his cousin was the real thief. You might think you are subservient to the rich and powerful, but when you truly believe a serious miscarriage of justice has occurred, you find a way to the truth, no matter how much harm it does you. That's why I married you."

I smiled. "I thought it was because I looked good in battle armor."

She laughed. "That, too."

"Even though I'm the son of a tanner, a trade so reviled that even the lepers and cripples won't marry one?"

"I've told you time and time again: It wasn't important to me to marry a man who was either rich or high born."

It was hard to imagine such a statement coming from a woman whose family had once possessed great wealth. Her father, Shimon, came from a long line of wealthy artisans who had lived in Oxyrhynchus since it had been conquered by the Greek general Alexander several hundred years ago. Twelve years after his wife died giving birth to Naomi, they left Egypt and settled in Bethlehem. Here he established a highly successful goldsmithing business that catered to clients throughout Yehud. He built one of the largest homes in town, surrounded by groves of lemon and fig trees.

Naomi grew up to become an exotic olive-skinned beauty with hair as black as night. By all rights, she should have married into one of Yehud's aristocratic families. But when she was seventeen a series of bad business ventures and crippling arthritis drove Shimon into bankruptcy. After selling their home to pay his debts Shimon and Naomi moved into a small two-room hut that had once served as the quarters for his gardener. With no sizeable dowry, her marriage prospects quickly evaporated. Still, with her beauty and intelligence she could have had the pick of Bethlehem's tradesmen. Why she agreed to be wed to a lowly soldier I will never know. She knew that I would be away for months at a time and chances were high that I wouldn't come back at all.

She had spent the early years of our marriage tending to my father and raising our only child in a home that constantly stank of urine and manure, the elixirs of my father's profession.

Sensing my doubt, she grabbed my hands. "And because you are the man I married, I know you will do what's right for the Notsrim."

"But what if doing what's right costs me my job?"

"Adonai will provide for us."

I looked into her eyes and said, "Have I ever told you that you're way too good for me?"

She pinched my cheek. "Not often enough."

CHAPTER 10

Yesterday I was dealing with messiahs and stolen treasure. Today, I was playing bodyguard to a Roman census taker. More accurately, a skinny, dour Assyrian journeyman hired by our occupiers, who had far more important things to do than count Yehudi rabble.

The work was as dull as sheepherding. I would knock on a door or shake a tent flap and then step out of the way so the Assyrian could write the occupants' names on a scroll.

It was an easy day to be a watchman. All crime ceased. Pickpockets kept their hands to themselves. Gambling dens temporarily transformed into prayer rooms. Whores exchanged their gaudy dresses for form-covering burkas. Even the marketplace preachers suspended their daily rantings. For a few days we were nothing more than humble, obedient, pious villagers, not even remotely involved in activities that might be against the Laws, or, even worse, subject to Rome's infamous sin taxes.

We were making our way through a cluster of houses and tents when a door opened to reveal a familiar grizzled face. "You! Why are you not investigating the crime that has been committed against the Messiah?"

"Good morning, Uriel. We're taking time out from that for the census," I replied, making room for the Assyrian.

"Uriel ben Teman of the tribe of Asher," snapped the old man. "I am 67 years old, a retired vendor of fine salt crystals. Four months ago I moved from Ashdod to Bethlehem to spend my remaining days cherishing the memory of my wife Rachel, who was born here. Anything else you'd like to know, idol-worshipper?"

The census taker scribbled notes on a scroll. "No, that's all I need."

As we were leaving, Uriel grabbed my arm. "Well? What are you doing about the stolen treasures?"

Turning to the Assyrian, I said, "Why don't we take a little break?"

He frowned. "We still have eight more dwellings to visit in this area alone."

I gave him a half-shekel. "Go get yourself something to eat. I'll catch up to you in a few minutes."

After the census taker was out of earshot, I turned to Uriel and said, "You may not know this, but the three chests have been found."

"I heard!" the old man spat. "They were stolen from Yeshua and given to imposters!"

Looking around to make sure no one was listening, I said, "My commander has ordered me to end my investigation."

"That doesn't surprise me. He's a tool of Reb Lemuel and the Sedukim!"

I didn't have time to get into an argument. "Unless you have stronger proof of this theft than your own testimony there's nothing more I can do."

He shook his head. "What's the point? The Sedukim will do anything to discredit Yeshua's claim."

"Why?"

"Because when Yeshua comes of age Elohim will use him as the vessel to bring about the biggest transformation in the Yehudi faith since the Almighty gave the Torah to the children of Yisroel at Mount Sinai. The Temple, the priests and their outdated and corrupt rituals will be destroyed. Antipas and his Idomite pretenders will be deposed. The rich and powerful will lose everything and the poor and humble will be exalted."

His words had a familiar ring to them. "You sound just like my son, the Isiyim."

He smiled. "Binyamin speaks very highly of you."

My jaw dropped. "You've met him?"

He looked both ways before replying. "I am the Isiyim's agent here in Bethlehem. I keep them informed about the sins committed by our blasphemous overseers. Binyamin is my main contact."

I had to suppress my anger at the thought of my son holding clandestine meetings with this old man without once stopping by to visit Naomi and me. Now I truly understood how she felt.

Uriel leaned in closer and whispered, "Anyway, even if nothing comes of it I now have irrefutable proof that the Dorans' treasures are the same as those that were stolen from the Notsrim."

"Show me."

The Assyrian was heading back our way, his hands loaded with olives. "Not now. Come back here three hours after sunset. Make sure you're alone." He closed the door. After a few more hours of census-taking we quit for the day.

When I returned to Uriel's house later that evening, his settlement was unusually quiet. This was because most of the tents were gone. Once the census pilgrims had been counted they had packed up to return home, satisfied that their identities as descendants of King Dovid had been officially registered on a scroll that would probably end up locked away and forgotten in some minor clerk's office.

I knock on Uriel's door. There was no response. I knocked again. Nothing.

Then I smelled it. The faint but familiar odor of decay. Fifteen years in the army heightened your awareness of death.

I couldn't enter the house without a witness. Fortunately, Adonai sent me one in the form of Junior Constable Amos. I could hear the telltale scraping of his enormous feet heading this way.

I caught up to him and yelled, "Junior Constable!"

Flashing a good-natured smile, he replied, "Good evening, Senior Constable. Checking up to make sure I'm conducting night patrol instead of napping?"

"Not this time. Come with me!"

Uriel's door was stuck. "Break it open!" I ordered.

He smiled. "With pleasure."

Leveraging all of his considerable weight, he planted a large foot on the door and kicked the door open. The darkness inside only heightened the terrible stench. Lighting a small torch I always carried with me at night, I cautiously entered the room. Spotting an oil lamp on a table, I lit it.

Junior Constable Amos gasped and ran outside. The yellow glow illuminated the body of Uriel. He was sprawled on his back in a puddle of blood.

I bent down to examine him. There were two large vertical gashes in his chest only an inch or two apart. My heart sank as I recognized the kind of weapon that could cause such wounds. I then examined his hands. Small white threads were embedded under the fingernails of his left hand. His right hand was clenched in a fist. I bent open his stiffened fingers to reveal something shiny embedded in his palm. I gently worked it loose and held it to the light. It was a bronze medallion, oval in shape, attached to a broken leather chain. On one side was an etching of a pomegranate; on the other side, a vine.

Why would Uriel so forcefully hold on to such an object, even in death? Had he chosen to die rather than let his murderer take it from him? The bronze was tarnished and cracked. It didn't look particularly valuable. Might it have had sentimental value? Had it belonged to his wife or his children?

Junior Constable Amos returned a few minutes later, wiping drops of vomit from his mouth. I felt sorry for him. The first murder victim was always the hardest.

"Please forgive me," he said in a trembling voice.

"Of course," I replied. "Very few murders are committed around here, but when they occur they usually look like this. It's something you'll have to get used to."

I could tell that he was reconsidering his career choice. Amos was big and strong, well-liked and much easier to supervise than Constable Elihu. I didn't want him to quit, so I needed to move him past this occupational obstacle.

"Junior Constable Amos, if you're going to succeed in the Watch you must learn to separate what you see in front of you from what you feel. Do you understand?"

He nodded, weakly.

"Good. Please examine this man's wounds and tell me what you observe."

Summoning all of his courage, he bent down to observe the corpse. Several times I could see him gagging. But then, almost imperceptibly, the fear and revulsion in his eyes were replaced with concentration and curiosity.

"How was he killed?" I asked.

"S-stabbed," he stuttered.

"How many times?"

"I-I don't know."

"Look closer. Examine the wound if necessary."

He didn't touch the body but lowered his face until it was within inches of the wounds. "Twice." Looking even closer, he shook his head. "Wait. The incisions are symmetrical."

"And what does that tell you?"

He thought for a minute, and then his eyes lit up with recognition. "He was stabbed once with a knife that had two blades side-by-side."

I nodded. "A forked dagger. Each blade was probably no longer than four inches. The incisions are separated by about two inches, meaning that the knife itself was probably–"

"Nine inches long," interjected the constable.

"Smart lad. Who typically uses double-bladed daggers?"

He rubbed his beard. "Almost no one. They're not practical in a knife fight since the short blades put you at a disadvantage versus a foe with a longer blade. The few I've seen are mostly ceremonial, designed to look like a serpent's tongue. I've heard that Egyptian assassins carry them for show as well as…"

His voice trailed off.

"Go on," I said. "As well as?"

With great discomfort, he gazed at me and murmured, "Isiyim."

"That's right." I patted him on the shoulder. "I'm sure my son has one."

"You don't think…"

"That Binyamin killed him? As his father, I hope he wasn't involved. As a watchman, however, I must be open to the possibility that he–or one of his fellow Isiyim—are responsible. The question is: Why? Uriel was their informant. What reason would they have to kill one of their own?"

He shook his head.

Placing the pendant in my pocket, I said, "Constable, please bring Commander Shaul here. It's going to be a long night."

After he left I began searching for evidence. There wasn't much to look for. Like most homes in Bethlehem, Uriel's house consisted of a single room. Threadbare rugs covered most of the wood floor. A stove was still warm with the embers of a recent fire. On a table near the rear window stood an old Kiddish cup and two enamel Shabbat candlesticks. There were several large chests. One held two sets of plates, bowls and cooking utensils. Another was packed with purple pouches adorned with overlapping symbols of fish monogrammed in yellow thread. I looked inside one. It was filled with gray and blue crystals of salt. In the center of the room was a table with two plates, a wine amphora and two half-empty bronze goblets.

In the corner stood a platform bed with a large down mattress and blanket. It looked and smelled like it had been recently occupied.

I looked under the bed. A small box held another purple pouch filled with gold and silver coins. There were also large clumps of dust, a dead mouse, and– wait, what was this? I reached as far as I could and pulled out a folded piece of fabric. It spread open to reveal a long silk scarf. It was red and adorned with delicate patterns of seashells stenciled in black.

I heard footsteps approaching. I quickly hid the scarf in my pocket as the door opened and Commander Shaul and Junior Constable Amos entered.

The commander bent down to examine the body. After a moment he stood up and turned to me. "Have you found anything that would point to a motivation for this crime, Senior Constable?"

I shook my head. "Not really. I don't think they were here to rob him. None of his possessions were disturbed or taken, including his money."

He pursed his lips. "I agree with yours and Junior Constable Amos's conclusion about the cause of death. The saltseller was killed by Isiyim."

"Excuse me, Commander, but that was not my conclusion. Yes, a forked blade was most likely the murder weapon, but we don't know if it was wielded by Isiyim."

"When is the last time you saw an Egyptian here in Bethlehem? At the request of King Antipas the Romans forbid them from traveling to Yehud."

I decided not to remind him that I was married to an Egyptian immigrant.

"Besides it is no secret that the saltseller was an Isiyim sympathizer."

I didn't ask the commander how he knew this. Like me, he had many eyes and ears in town. "Then why would they kill him?"

"You should know better than anyone. You met with him earlier today. Perhaps he no longer shared the Isiyim's contention that the Notsrim infant is the Messiah?"

I needed to be circumspect about what I disclosed to him. Shaul was my superior officer and my friend but Uriel had been right in claiming that he was beholden to Reb Lemuel and the Sedukim who comprised the majority of the Sanhedrin. Until now this had never really bothered me. But the events of the past few days had convinced me that there was some kind of messianic power struggle going on in theological circles far above my station and that the most influential factions were throwing the contest in favor of the Dorans. As I possessed neither wealth nor a noble bloodline I tended to instinctively side with the underdog.

"Uriel still believed that the scholars' treasures were stolen from Yeshua."

"Maybe he did something to insult his Isiyim paymasters."

Or perhaps whoever murdered him wanted to make it look like he insulted his paymasters, I didn't say.

"Anyway," Commander Shaul continued, "Did you find anything else that may help us identify his assailant?"

It was time to be selectively honest. I held out the pendant. "Uriel was holding this when he died."

He gazed at it. "I've never seen such a bauble. Do you know what these symbols mean?"

"No."

"Probably some kind of Isiyim talisman." He handed it back to me.

"If it was, it didn't help him in the end."

We examined the table. "Two wine cups. He may have had a visitor here before he was attacked."

Commander Shaul removed the lid from the amphora and sniffed. "This smells terrible."

"May I have a look, Commander?" asked Junior Constable Amos. "As the son of a vintner I am very good at identifying wines."

Commander Shaul nodded. The young watchman stuck a finger into the wine and licked it. After a moment, he said, "This isn't Yehud wine. It isn't sweet, like ours, and there are raisins and herbs mixed in. It tastes like Greek wine—quite likely from the island of Crete, judging by its sour taste and faint scent of sea salt."

I was impressed. "You're a man of many hidden talents, Junior Constable."

He blushed. "Thank you, Senior Constable."

"Does your father sell this wine?" asked Commander Shaul.

Junior Constable Amos vigorously shook his head. "He wouldn't dream of selling wine that isn't kashrut[1] here in Bethlehem. But he and an Arab partner own another wine shop in Caesarea Maritima. They sell wines from Assyria and the Greek and Roman provinces, including Crete." After a moment he added, "Along with our fine Yehud vintages, of course."

"Of course," the commander nodded, gravely. "That may explain why the saltseller was murdered."

---

[1]Kosher.

I cocked my head. "Please enlighten me, Commander."

"He was meeting with one of his Isiyim contacts and, intentionally or accidentally, served him forbidden wine. The Isiyim was so insulted that he killed the saltseller in a fit of rage."

"Uriel may have had another visitor who left before he was murdered."

"I find that very difficult to believe in the face of all the other evidence."

It was at that moment that I decided not to tell him about the scarf. He was already convinced that the Isiyim were responsible for Uriel's death, and nothing more I could say right now would change his mind. I would pursue my own investigation, with the scarf as its foundation. The less he knew about the methods I might need to employ to discover its origin the better.

Commander Shaul turned to me. "In any case, we need to properly dispose of the body. Since you were his friend I'll leave it to you to arrange for Itzchak ben Akiba to remove it. Later, I'll send a priest to purify this cursed place."

"What about his possessions? And his money?"

"Does he have any living relatives?"

"It was rumored that he had two married daughters."

"Do you know their names? Or where they live?"

"No."

"Well, I'm certainly not sending anyone to look for them. If we can't find a will or other legal documents here we'll get Pakra the junkman to sell the saltseller's belongings. And we'll use the proceeds to pay for his burial and the purification of his home and give the remainder to the synagogue in his memory."

"The Isiyim won't be happy about that."

He frowned. "Since they probably murdered him I doubt they'll venture out from their caves to file a claim."

I didn't approve of the commander's sudden rush to judgment on the cause of Uriel's death or his refusal to actively locate the old man's heirs. For the first time in my life I felt that I couldn't trust my longtime friend. His sudden willingness to abandon the quest for the truth was unbecoming of a man of his bearing and reputation.

If he wasn't willing to seek justice for Uriel's death I would do it myself, using every resource at my disposal. That included taking half of Uriel's stash of gold and silver coins for expenses. If Uriel's daughters weren't found I would give whatever I had left to Yeshua, since I'm sure the saltseller would have wanted it that way.

When I returned to Uriel's home early the next morning it was strange to see the dwelling completely empty. Even the bloodstains had been cleansed from the floor. The room smelled of lavender, a sign that a Levite had purified the premises. But would anyone ever live here again? Doubtful. No one would want to step foot in a place where a murder had been committed. In time, it would become a sanctuary for rats and lizards.

Other kinds of distasteful creatures were on my mind when I made my next stop. Four men were sitting around the hookah in Reuven's hashish den, smoking the Persian dream herb through long copper tubes. Two wore only loincloths. I quickly looked away and approached the proprietor, who was sitting behind his counter placing coins into a wooden box.

He greeted me with a languid wave of his crippled hand. "Ahh, Senior Constable. There's room for one more. From what I hear you're a man who could use some relaxation."

"No thank you," I replied. "But it looks like you've got a full house today."

"Yes. Business has been booming since Hussein closed his opium den and left town."

"Why did he do that?" I was almost too afraid to ask.

"It's very difficult to run a business with two broken arms. A most unfortunate...accident."

Waving a swirl of acrid smoke away from my face, I decided that the less I knew the better. "I'll never understand why men waste their time and money on such foolishness."

"Allow me to address your perplexity." Pointing a finger at the hookah, he continued, "You see, their days are burdened with endless toil, pain and misery and their nights are filled with the nagging of their wives. Here, for a half-shekel they can find a few hours of blessed relief."

"You're just lucky Adonai doesn't mention hashish in the Torah."

He grinned. "True. I suppose during the forty days the Almighty taught the Prophet Moshe the Laws governing the slaughter of animals and the treatment of skin conditions He somehow didn't feel it necessary to address herbal remedies. Besides, the Prophets Yirmiyahuw and Yechekel[1] were devotees."

"I don't remember the rabbis teaching this in my religious studies."

"That's because the Sedukim excised those parts from their versions of the Prophets' writings. I have copies of the originals if you wish to see for yourself."

Shaking my head, I said, "Some other time. I'm not here for a theology lesson."

"Then it must be for yet another favor that requires my—special—knowledge."

"That's right. I'm sure you're aware that Uriel ben Teman was murdered last night."

He frowned. "Yes, the saltseller was one of my regular wine patrons. The rumormongers say the Watch believes that the Isiyim killed him."

Looking around to make sure no one was listening, I murmured. "I can't speak for my fellow watchmen, but Commander Shaul and I don't always agree on things. For example, he thinks you're a dangerous parasite who should be stoned to death without the benefit of a trial. I, on the other hand, consider you to be an unsavory yet necessary source of information on Bethlehem's criminal

---

[1] The prophets Jeremiah and Ezekiel.

activities. So far, I've been able to convince him to give you the benefit of the doubt."

Spreading his arms in a dramatic manner, Reuven said, "And for this advocacy I am constantly in your debt, as you never hesitate to remind me."

"That's right. And part of that debt includes identifying this."

I removed the scarf from my pocket and placed it on the counter so his customers couldn't see it. Not that they would have noticed anyway. In a low voice I asked, "Do you recognize it?"

He leered at me. "Of course I do. The question is: Do you?"

"It's a whore's scarf. They're always red. And if the whore works in a brothel it's usually embroidered with its symbols."

He smiled. "Senior Constable, I never would have thought of you as an expert on the customs of practitioners of transactional affection."

"Don't get smart with me!" I snapped. "I found this in Uriel's house."

He rubbed his chin. "Planted, perhaps, by someone who may have wanted to besmirch his name? Or to make it appear as if a whore murdered him?"

"Doubtful. I found it under his bed and only after a thorough search. A conspirator would have placed it near his corpse. And as you can see, there's no blood on it."

"Maybe she wasn't wearing it when she killed him. Or perhaps she left it there on a different night."

"You know as well as I do that a whore would never leave her scarf with a customer. It would be like a soldier leaving a battlefield without his shield. And notice how it's not dirty or covered in dust? That means it wasn't under his bed all that long. I think this whore was there last night. She may have witnessed Uriel's murder. She was either working with the killer or was there by chance when he arrived."

"If the latter is true how did she survive? From what I have heard, no other bodies were found anywhere near the saltseller's home, nor was there a trail of blood that may have suggested another victim of an attack. This tends to support the theory that she was somehow involved."

I nodded. "Perhaps. I intend to find out. But first I need to figure out where this scarf came from. As a watchman I'm familiar with the scarf designs of the two brothels here in Bethlehem—"

"Three," Reuven interrupted.

"Really?" I asked. "I know only of Izebel's[1] Palace and Delilah's Delights."

"Batsheva's Oasis," he replied. "One of my new—partnerships. The influx of census pilgrims in recent weeks has created an increasing demand for pleasures of the flesh."

Before I could speak, he waved a hand. "Don't worry, Senior Constable. We will close it down once our temporary guests have left town."

Lifting up a corner of the scarf, I said, "No Yehudi brothel would allow scarves with seashell images."

"Correct," he replied. "Thus, we must assume that the saltseller was cavorting with a gentile whore."

"There are no gentile brothels in Bethlehem!" I snapped, with perhaps a little more righteous indignation than was necessary. Noticing his grin, I added, "Are there?"

"Rest assured, Senior Constable, that no such establishment would be permitted here by those of us involved in this ancient profession. That isn't to say that such a venture wouldn't be extremely profitable. Since the time of Hagar, Avraham's Egyptian concubine, we Yehudim have had a healthy appetite for heathen flesh. But to experience this particular form of pleasure you must venture beyond the limits of any Yehud town. There's one near Gedara that features dark-skinned Nubian girls. And I've heard rumors that there's another near Sychar where the girls have skin the color of bronze and eyes that are frozen in a perpetual squint."

"You wouldn't happen to know where this scarf comes from, would you?"

"It so happens that I do. How much do you know about the gods of the Greeks?"

---

[1] Jezebel.

"Heathen idols are not something they teach in the synagogue."

"A pity, since their myths are quite charming. Among the Greeks—and the Romans, too, since they worship the same false gods—the seashell is a symbol of Aphrodite, the goddess of love. The Romans call her Venus."

"Is this goddess an oyster?"

"Hardly. In their religion Aphrodite is the most beautiful woman in the world. She was born in the sea, apparently emerging from a seashell. Now, whether her parents were snails or scallops is beyond my limited knowledge, but I do know that Aphrodite's temples are always adorned with shells. And before you ask me how I know this I will admit that I hire boys to collect shells from the shores of the Sea of Salt. I keep them in stock for Romans who stop here on their way to make an offering to Aphrodite at her temple in Caesarea Maritima. I have heard that extravagant orgies are held in its central chamber where the priestesses do the most delightful things with their—"

Tapping the scarf, I said, "The brothel, Reuven."

He grinned. "This particular establishment offers the charms of young Greek and Roman lovelies to gentiles who consider our Yehudi whores to be unworthy of their coin. And, of course, to sinful Yehudi men who wish to sample the pleasures of forbidden flesh."

"Where is this place?"

With a dramatic flourish he placed his good hand on his forehead. "All this time I have spent paying back the enormous debt I owe you has made me quite forgetful."

I placed one of Uriel's silver coins on the counter. He winked and dropped it into the coin box.

"Ah yes, my memory is coming back. Mind you, I have never been there myself, but I have heard that it's located a short way south of here, not too far from the Hebron road."

"Thank you." As I turned to head for the door he grabbed my arm and whispered, "Let me make sure I understand you correctly, Senior Constable.

You intend to visit a brothel of foreign whores? If word of this gets out what will your commander say? Or your wife?"

In one quick move I grabbed his uncrippled hand and squeezed it tightly. "Nothing. Because they won't find out, will they?"

Spending nearly half of my life clenching a sword, spear and truncheon had given me a very strong grip. As I squeezed harder, Reuven's eyes began to water. "Not from me, Senior Constable."

Just in case he didn't get the message, I whispered, "Good. Because I'm sure you wouldn't want the Sanhedrin to find out that the candles you donated to the synagogue last year were rendered with swine fat."

Beads of sweat rolled down his forehead. "Just that one batch."

"Of which I still have three in my possession. Each of which is stamped with your seal."

I released his hand. Rubbing his fingers, he grimaced and said, "Safe travels, Senior Constable."

CHAPTER 11

After my conversation with Reuven, I headed home. I removed my Watch sash and armor and put on my walking boots. Fortunately, Naomi wasn't there so I didn't have to tell her that I was going in disguise to visit a brothel. I'm sure she wouldn't have approved. For similar reasons I didn't inform Commander Shaul, either. I would have a great deal of explaining to do when I returned, but right now I had a murder to solve. If I had to cavort with whores to move my investigation forward, so be it.

The Hebron road connects Bethlehem to that ancient village where the Patriarch Avraham is buried. From there it meanders in a southwesterly direction until it reaches the port city of Eilat. It is the main trade route for merchants who import wares that arrive by sea from Egypt and Ethiopia.

A half-hour walk led me to a wooden sign painted with red seashells. Behind it a lightly trodden path cut through two small hills. It led to a clearing in which stood a large two-story house. Two young women sat on a bench by the door. They wore thin white togas that barely covered their long legs and ample breasts. Their long blond hair framed round faces caked with white makeup and bright red lips. They looked nothing at all like our Yehudi whores, who, in spite of their vocation, always wore modest clothes and head coverings. I could understand how an old widowed man like Uriel—or any man for that matter—could be enticed by such exotic creatures.

As I approached, the whores laughed and began chattering. I may not be a scholar but I've always had a natural talent for languages. In addition to speaking and reading Aramaic and Ivrit I can converse quite well in Latin and know enough Arabic and Persian to successfully negotiate purchases of goods from traveling merchants. But I couldn't understand a word spoken by either whore. So, I removed the scarf from my pocket and held it out. Their smiles vanished. One quickly got up and entered the building. The other backed away from me.

A moment later, the first whore stood at the door and beckoned me inside. Looking around to make sure no one was following me, I entered the sinful establishment.

This wasn't my first time inside a brothel. Every once in a while the Sanhedrin order the Watch to raid our own hometown fleshpots. It is never a pleasant task. Ours are small, dark and stink of sweat and sex. There are usually three or four tiny rooms with a filthy straw mat on the floor, upon which lies the whore, who is generally dressed for the act in an old sackcloth. The customer is expected to finish his business quickly. If he tarries too long, the whoremaster, usually a large man with a face permanently frozen in a scowl, smacks his club against the door as a warning to either pay more or get out.

Thus, the interior of this gentile brothel came as a complete shock. A large room with high ceilings was brightly lit with oil lamps. The walls were adorned with exotic tapestries. Light streamed through arched windows, which were covered in meshed netting to keep insects out. Nearly every inch of the floor was covered in intricately patterned Persian carpets. In one corner stood a marble statue of a naked woman standing on a large seashell, her right hand extended in a gesture of beckoning. The scent of cloves and honeysuckle filled the air.

Four more whores reclined on several richly upholstered Roman-style lounges. They gabbed excitedly among themselves as they pointed at the scarf still dangling from my hand.

An older woman emerged from a doorway in the back of the room. She was short and plump and wore a red gown patterned with seashells. Her long gray hair was pinned to her head in a bun. She approached me and began speaking in a language I recognized but didn't understand. I responded with the only phrase I knew in that tongue: "I sorry, I no talk Greek."

She tried again, this time in Latin, which I did understand. "Welcome to House of Aphrodite, home of finest Greek and Roman nymphs of love. I is Mistress Helena."

"I am…Gidon of Bethlehem." I replied.

Her smile turned into a scowl. "Yehudi? Not place for you."

I held out the scarf. "I am trying to find the owner of this scarf."

Her eyes widened. "Ahh, you find!" Pointing to one of the whores, she said, "Is to Diana. Fall off when she gets water from well. Wind blow to Bet-le-hem, yes?"

Before I could react, Mistress Helena snatched the scarf and handed it to the whore, speaking rapidly to her in Greek. The girl held the scarf away with two fingers, her face tight with fear.

"How did you know the scarf was in Bethlehem?"

She hesitated. "You from Bet-le-hem. If scarf in Hebron, man from Hebron bring back, yes?"

I admired her tenacity. Still, I wasn't going to let her off the hook. "I found the scarf under the bed of a dead man. If your… girl…was with him, I must speak to her."

Mistress Helena shook her head. "Diana here last night."

"Were any other girls in Bethlehem last night?"

"No. All here all night."

I knew she was lying, and she knew I knew she was lying, and we both knew there was nothing I could do about it. The Watch had no jurisdiction here.

Out of the corner of my eye I saw one of the whores wiggle her finger at me. The expression on her face made it clear she wasn't seeking transactional affection.

Now it was my turn for subterfuge. "Can Yehudi…have pleasure with your whores?"

"Nymphs," Mistress Helena snapped.

"Yes, er, nymphs."

She shrugged. "You have money?"

With a great deal of guilt and trepidation, I held out one of Uriel's gold coins. "Yes."

Her eyes lit up. It only took a moment for her to grab it from my hand. She turned to the whores and started barking in Greek. They looked away, as if to say, *Please don't choose me.*

Mistress Helena pointed to two of the whores. "Choose Athena or Hera. They love Yehudi before. No surprise."

Pointing to the whore who had gestured at me, I said, "I want that…nymph."

Mistress Helena frowned. "Demeter? Skinny. No chest. Only good to love young boys first time."

"I like skinny girls with flat chests."

She shrugged. "No refund." She waved a hand at the whore, who nodded and walked over to me. Grabbing my hand, she silently led me through the rear doorway to a hallway. On the right was a kitchen. To the left was a ladder leading to the second floor. Feeling very uneasy, I followed her upstairs to another hallway with four closed doors. She opened one and beckoned me to follow her inside.

I hesitated. Demeter didn't look a day over 16, but she carried herself with the seductive confidence of a royal concubine. I had never committed adultery nor had I ever coveted another man's wife. Noticing my anxiety, Demeter leaned in until her lips were inches away from my left ear. In broken and heavily accented Aramaic she whispered, "You want to know about scarf come now."

Sighing with relief, I followed her into the room. It was small and furnished only with a bed and end table, but it was attractively decorated with silk tapestries depicting scenes of copulation involving men, women, bulls, lions and other animals I didn't recognize. The scent of lilacs filled the air. For a moment I almost forgot why I was here.

Demeter sat down on the edge of the bed. "Sit."

"I prefer to stand," I replied. "You speak Aramaic?"

"Yes. I born in Sidon."

"I thought you were all Greeks."

She smirked. "Big lie. Mistress Helena is only real Greek. Athena, Diana and Hera are half-Greek. Penelope, Eurydice and I are half-Roman."

"And the other half?"

"Our mothers are Arab, Persian, Assyrian, who knows? Greeks and Romans rape them."

I nodded. "How did you end up here?"

"When I am five I am sold to rich merchant in Perea. I become maid. I learn Greek and Aramaic. When I have first blood, he lay me and sell me to Mistress Helena."

"When was that?"

"Three years ago."

I wasn't surprised. Most whores were the products of rape or adultery or the orphaned daughters of parents who met their end at the hands of bandits and soldiers or were felled by disease. Others were the unwanted daughters of poor families. As soon as they could walk these young girls—and sometimes young boys—were sold to slavers. The lucky ones ended up as house servants. But most found their way into brothels. Like Reuven's hashish house and Bethlehem's gambling dens, prostitution was a sinful activity that was tolerated because it also happened to generate a great deal of taxable revenue, a portion of which found its way into the coffers of the synagogue and the Temple in Yerushalayim. Watchmen learned to accept this and other hypocrisies as professional facts of life.

Did the Greeks and Romans consider prostitution to be sinful as well? If so, why would they have named a brothel after one of their gods? At least we Yehudim acknowledged its sinful nature by naming ours after the wayward women of our Scriptures.

"Okay, so tell me about the scarf."

"Is not Diana's."

"Even I knew that. The girl treated it like a leper's tunic."

She nodded. "Belong to Cassandra."

"Cassandra. Is she here?"

"No. I not know where she is."

"When is the last time you saw her?"

"Yesterday. She go to Bethlehem to love old Yehudi."

"You mean Uriel ben Teman?"

"Yes. He make deal with Mistress Helena to let Cassandra stay with him two nights a month."

"Your Mistress Helena doesn't like Yehudim very much."

She smirked. "Hate Yehudi men. Like Yehudi money."

"How did Cassandra travel from here to Bethlehem? I doubt she walked there alone."

She shook her head. "Driver from old Yehudi take her there and back in cart."

"Did this man take her there yesterday?"

She said nothing.

"Well?" I asked.

"You give money to Mistress Helena. She keep all."

It took me a moment to understand. I placed two of Uriel's silver coins into my palm. She gazed at them and said nothing. I added two more. She grabbed them. "Cassandra go with driver late afternoon. But she not come back with him. Come back alone late. She tell Mistress Helena scarf is gone. Mistress Helena beat her and throw her out."

"Did Cassandra tell her what happened?"

"No. All Mistress Helena care is scarf is gone and Cassandra not paid. She throw her out forever."

Demeter dabbed her eye with a long finger. "Later I hear knock on window. Is Cassandra, on ladder. I invite her come in, but she say no. She tell me she see old Yehudi dead and go away with man who hide her."

"Did she say who the man was?"

"No, but man give note to Cassandra. Tell her give to friend she trust. Friend must give note to nosey Yehudi from Bethlehem who return scarf."

She lifted a corner of the mattress and drew out a small folded piece of parchment. Handing it to me she whispered, "I think this for you."

I unfolded and read the note and then quickly placed it in my pocket. "Thank you."

"I no want Cassandra dead. She is good friend."

I nodded. "If I find her I'll make sure no one harms her."

She smiled. And then her face hardened. "Now you must yell."

"What?"

"Make pretend sound of love."

"Why?"

"So Mistress Helena not be–" She struggled for the word. "Suspicious."

She reclined on the bed and began to moan, loudly.

"Do it!" she hissed.

With hesitation, I said, "Oh."

"Loud!"

"Ohh!" I yelled, finding the whole thing ridiculous. "Oh, ah, ahhh!"

"Yell my name!" she murmured between her loud cries. "Make noise like I am love goddess!"

It took me a moment to remember her name. "Demeter!"

"You love best nymph in Yehud, not call dog!" she snapped. "Louder! Pretend real!"

"Demeter, Demeter, Demeter!" I shouted.

She pulled me down beside her on the bed. "Bounce! Old witch must hear!"

We began to bounce, side-by-side on the bed, while she moaned loudly. It was embarrassing to think that the thumps could be heard in the parlor below. After a few minutes she whispered, "Now stop!"

After the bed stopped wobbling she gazed at me and giggled. "Good."

"Do you think we fooled her?" I whispered.

"Hope so." She placed a hand on my cheek. "If worried we can love for real."

I removed her hand. "You are a beautiful girl but I am a married man."

She shrugged. "Does not stop other men."

"I'm not like other men."

She stared at me for a moment and nodded. "No, you not. You good man. Foolish, but good. Stay little while. When you go, tell old witch I am best nymph in world."

Several minutes later, I gave her two more silver coins and left the room. I returned to the parlor, feigning an expression of satisfaction.

Mistress Helena's face was tight with suspicion. "You done already?"

I shrugged. "I tried to last longer but Demeter's love made me finish fast." Two of the other whores started giggling. Holding out another gold coin, I added, "I give you more to thank you for letting me love best nymph in Yehud."

As I headed home I wondered if paying for a whore but not committing adultery with her was a sinful act. Was it also a sin that I was spending Uriel's money, which rightfully belonged to his children? On the other hand, I was using it to find his killers, so wasn't this justified?

There was only one way to resolve this dilemma. Pesach was only a few weeks away and I had been saving my largest ewe for our Seder.[1] Instead, I would offer her as an atonement sacrifice at the Temple. Such was the price of pursuing the truth.

---

[1] The Seder is a Jewish ritual ceremony and meal conducted on the first and second nights of Passover.

CHAPTER 12

Commander Shaul was waiting for me when I returned to the Watch house. "Where have you been?"

"I was chasing new leads in the murder investigation."

"On the Hebron road?"

Who had been following me? I wondered. "A good investigator explores every path available to him."

"Well? What did you find out?"

"Nothing. It was a dead end," I lied. "But I have another path to pursue."

"Put that aside for now, I have another job for you to do first."

"What is it?"

"You are to go to the Notsrim and convince them to return home."

I was stunned. "Why?"

"You know why. They're not legally permitted to live here. And their presence is becoming disruptive. Many foolish people still insist that this Yeshua is the true Messiah."

"As descendants of King Dovid they have as much right to live here as you do."

"The Sanhedrin thinks otherwise. They believe that their continued presence threatens public order."

I laughed. "Yosef is a middle-aged carpenter. His wife is a teenage girl. The baby is incapable of doing anything other than sleeping, eating, crying and messing himself. They're a danger to no one."

He sighed. "Look, Senior Constable, between you and me I don't care whether they stay or go. But the Sanhedrin is getting nervous. The last thing they want to see is civil unrest caused by factions supporting two competing infant messiahs. If the Notsrim are out of the picture we'll only have to deal with one."

"We can achieve the same result by ordering Nogah and his family to return to Dor."

"Perhaps, but their claim is substantiated by the princes' gifts."

"Which were stolen–"

"With the death of the saltseller, there is no longer an independent witness who can testify that any such gifts were ever in the possession of the Notsrim."

Another thought occurred to me. "If Yosef never saw the chests, how did he know they contained frankincense, myrrh and gold?"

Commander Shaul rubbed his chin. "I don't know."

"All the more reason–"

"There is no more reason. The Sanhedrin decides what we will and will not do. They support the claims of the Dorans and we must respect the wisdom of their decision. The faster we get the Notsrim out of here the more quickly order will be restored."

"And what about Yeshua's followers?"

"They're welcome to follow them back to the Galil."

"And if Yosef refuses to leave?"

"Then the Sanhedrin will forcibly remove them."

"They can't do that!"

"Of course they can. The Sanhedrin has the authority to approve or reject residency in any Yehud village where they have legal authority. That's why our towns are mercifully free of lepers and sodomists."

"Are you saying that Yosef and his family are profane abominations?"

He raised an eyebrow. "Me personally? No. But the Sanhedrin assigns false messiahs to the same category."

"How can they–"

Fingering his sash, he said, "Senior Constable, this discussion is over. You have my orders. Report back to me when you have completed them."

Seething, I stormed out of the building and headed along the road toward Yosef's house. I didn't know what I was going to do when I got there. What if I couldn't convince them to leave, especially since I wasn't convinced myself?

But that was the problem. I didn't have the authority to act according to my personal convictions. There was a chain of command starting at the bottom with watchmen and working up through Commander Shaul to Reb Lemuel to the Sanhedrin and the priests in Yerushalayim, who supposedly received their orders directly from Adonai. Break a link in the chain and the Almighty might open up the earth and swallow us up as he did to the followers of Korah who rebelled against the Prophet Moshe in ancient times. But I wasn't so sure. Ever since His last miracle of guiding the Hashmunayim to victory over the Seleucids four generations ago, He had largely stayed His hand from direct involvement in human affairs.

Maybe He had a purpose in letting the Romans turn Yehud into a vassal state and tax us to near penury. Maybe it was His divine plan that every time we rose up in revolt the Romans brutally put it down, killing and enslaving thousands of innocent women and children along the way.

I wasn't a priest or a rabbi and thus was unqualified to interpret His will. But I might bend the chain of command a little, without breaking its links. Commander Shaul had ordered me to talk to the Notsrim. But he hadn't given me a deadline for completing this task.

I reached into my pocket and felt the piece of parchment.

Closing my eyes, I prayed, silently, *Adonai, if you want me to convince Yosef and his family to leave Bethlehem instead of investigating the murder of Uriel ben Teman, send me a sign, such as a bolt of lightning, an earthquake or a burning bush and I shall obey Thy will.*

I opened my eyes. The sun was still shining. The sky was clear. The earth was solid beneath my feet.

I would not be speaking to the Notsrim today.

The chain of command might stretch to Heaven. But I knew in my heart that the Almighty had other plans for me.

CHAPTER 13

Hundreds of flies swarmed before my eyes and dug into my skin as I sat in a mound of sand, barely sheltered from the mid-morning sun by the shade of a cliff. After leaving home at sunrise the next day it had taken three hours for my aging legs to traverse the barren hills and valleys of the Yam ha-Melah path, which leads from Bethlehem to the desolate wilderness of Kumran and the sweltering Sea of Salt beyond. I was still several miles away from this fetid body of water and yet I could already smell its telltale aroma of brine and decay.

In my many years as a soldier I had battled and bivouacked in deserts ranging from the craggy wastes of the Negev to the desolate plains of Nabataea, but none could hold a candle to the sweltering, spirit-crushing oppression of Kumran. Only those who considered suffering to be a virtue could possibly live here without going mad.

No one came to Kumran without a good reason. I was only here because of the parchment Demeter had passed on me. On it was an Ivrit phrase that translated to "pit of a thousand dead vipers." Only two people would have understood its meaning and the shared memory it evoked.

Twelve years ago, I was on sabbatical from the army after nearly a year away from my family. I only had a month off and I wanted to do something special for my eight-year-old son. I decided to take him for a swim in the Sea of Salt, on whose crusty surface you could float like a flower petal.

My knee hadn't yet been pierced by an enemy's arrow, so walking there was no challenge. We decided to stay there overnight so I could give him a taste of what living in the wilderness was really like. Carrying satchels of camping gear, water and dried food, we left early one summer morning and followed the Yam ha-Melah path into a hilly and desolate terrain inhabited mainly by lizards, scorpions and vultures.

We rested in the shade of a canyon surrounded by hills. Binyamin wanted to search for the caves where strange wild-eyed hermits were said to live like savages, surviving only on insects and moisture collected in spider webs. I let him go and rested against a boulder.

I must have dozed off, for the next thing I remembered was Binyamin tugging at my cloak. His face was flush with excitement, for he had discovered a wondrous pit of sleeping snakes. After my heart rate returned to normal, I let him cautiously lead me to his discovery.

It indeed was a large fissure filled with hundreds of gray and black speckled desert vipers, whose venom was capable of killing a camel. From my vantage point of several yards away I threw a few stones into the pit and saw no signs of movement, leading me to the welcome conclusion that they were all dead. Deciding not to push our luck, we gathered our gear and continued on to Yam ha-Melah. We both agreed not to tell Naomi about our discovery of this "pit of a thousand dead vipers." A mother had enough things to worry about.

I now found myself sitting fifty feet away from the same pit. Over the years shifting sands made it blend into the surrounding landscape. Were the vipers still there? Or had some brave soul removed them? I didn't feel compelled to find out.

After a half hour or so of shooing away insects and scorpions I saw a man approach me from a ravine. He wore a white linen cloak and his face was shrouded in a keffiyeh.

"Do you need assistance, stranger?" he asked.

"Perhaps," I replied, slowly rising to my feet. I held out the parchment. "I am looking for whoever wrote this."

He looked at it and nodded. "Come."

Wrapping a sash of white cloth around my eyes, he grabbed my left arm and began guiding me along a gently sloping trail. The air grew heavier as we proceeded, indicating the approaching proximity of Yam ha-Melah. Eventually we began traveling uphill along a rocky path. He didn't speak to me and I knew better than to try to start a conversation. My bad leg throbbed in pain. My clothes were drenched with sweat and with each step I found it harder to inhale the thick, salty air. But my guide offered me no respite. How ironic would it be, after having survived years of avoiding death in desolate battlefields, were I to die less than a day's walk away from my home?

Finally, he stopped and removed the blindfold. I was standing in a large clearing surrounded by hills pockmarked with cave entrances. There were several small patches of wheat and flax. Inside a fenced-in pen several scrawny goats leisurely chomped on hay.

"Stay here," my guide ordered before heading off to a rise and disappearing into a cave.

I waited. A short man with a long black beard emerged from another cave and sat down at a grindstone. He removed a double-bladed knife from his pocket robe and began to sharpen it. There didn't appear to be any bloodstains on it. After a few minutes he stopped to inspect his work. Apparently satisfied, he returned to his cave. A short time later, an old man limped out of another cave and headed for the goat pen, which he began mucking out. After filling a small wheelbarrow with manure he rolled it away, presumably to a nearby garden.

After this brief burst of activity, nothing happened. The day was half over, I was hungry and parched and my clothes were so drenched with sweat that I was afraid of drowning should I risk taking a short nap.

After what seemed like days, another old man descended from a cave and approached me. "Come."

"Where are we going?"

"You must be cleansed of impurity before your meal."

"Who said anything about eating?"

He waved a hand at me. "Come."

Sighing, I followed him to a small stone building. He pointed to a door. "Have you ever entered a mikveh before?"

Irritated that he thought I was an ignorant heathen, I glared at him. "Yes. And I am circumcised as well. Do you need proof?"

My sarcasm apparently went right over his head. "Disrobe inside and leave your clothes on the step. Stay inside until we return for you."

The mikveh was shallow and made of rough stone. The water was lukewarm and had the stale aroma of sweat and mildew. Clearly it was not made for comfort. I submerged my entire body and rubbed the sand and dirt off with a pumice stone. When I felt I was clean I recited a brief blessing and waited. After a short time another man entered, motioned me to stand up, and looked me over. I must have passed the purity test for he recited a short blessing and handed me a towel, a tunic, a white linen cloak and sandals. When I was fully dressed he passed me on to the man who had brought me there. We returned to the clearing where he spread a threadbare blanket on the ground.

"Where is my son–"

"Shhh. You must eat. Sit."

Sighing, I obeyed. He handed me a waterskin and a handful of figs. The water had a metallic taste but the figs were fresh and sweet. Or perhaps I was so hungry that a bowl of hay would have tasted good right now.

When I had finished I turned to him. "Now can you tell me where my son Binyamin is?"

"He is in the mikveh, cleansing himself of sin."

"I didn't see him when I–"

"You were in the visitors' mikveh. We use our own."

That didn't surprise me. "I didn't see any other buildings in the area."

"This is only one of our enclaves. There are many others. This one is called Bet Ha-Tamid. It means–"

"–House of the Torch. Believe it or not, I spent five years studying the Torah with Rabbi Taavi ben Harun. As did Binyamin."

He nodded. "A learned and righteous man, for an infidel." Later I learned that this was the highest compliment an Isiyim could pay someone outside their sect.

"What sin did my son commit?"

"He brought a whore into our community."

"You mean Cassandra? That whore has information about the death of Uriel ben Teman, who was one of your informants in Bethlehem. Binyamin found her and offered her protection. He wanted me to come here so I could interview her."

He nodded. "We are aware of his intentions. But you cannot speak to the whore."

"Why not?"

He raised an eyebrow. "Did you not hear me? She is a whore. Righteous Yehudim cannot be exposed to the whore's corruption."

"I'm a watchman. I deal in corruption every day. Do you see any boils on my skin? Do I look like I'm turning into a pillar of salt?"

"The whore is kept alone."

"Is she a prisoner?"

"No."

"Then why do you let her stay?"

He shrugged. "There is a great debate among our rabbis over what to do with the whore. Some want to give the whore sanctuary. Some want the whore to be cast out like a leper."

"What is your opinion?"

"My opinion doesn't matter. I am just a lowly flax weaver."

And I am just a lowly tanner's son, I wanted to say, but held my tongue. "Can you tell your rabbis that I can't find out who killed Uriel unless I speak to Cassandra?"

"That would be a violation of the laws of our community."

"I'm not a member of your community."

"Yet, here you are, in our sacred desert which is watched over by Elohim. While you are our guest you must follow our rules."

"I respect your traditions. But know this: back in Bethlehem, the Sanhedrin is blaming the death of your informant Uriel on the Isiyim. I'm the only one who's trying to bring the real murderer to justice. If an Isiyim is guilty of this crime, I'm sure you'd execute him rather than hand him over to the authorities. If this is so, send me on my way. But if the Isiyim are innocent of this crime and you don't want your sacred desert overrun with Idomite and

Roman soldiers, you need to help me. Ask yourself: What would displease Adonai more: Allowing a man and a woman to speak to each other or permitting your enemies to destroy your community through inaction?"

His lip trembled.

"Of course, I'm not expecting you to answer that question. Go ask your rabbis."

For a long time he stared into space. Then he nodded and walked off.

More waiting. The sun slowly began to descend behind the cliffs. When it was no longer visible he returned. "I have spoken with the rabbis. It is forbidden for any man to speak to a woman in our community."

I sighed. Such a long way I had come for nothing. I stood up and prepared myself for the long walk home. The settlement area was now bathed in shadows but beyond it the sands would still be hot and bright.

I turned to him. "They said I can't speak to her in your community."

"Yes."

Smiling, I said, "Then maybe it's time to leave your community."

CHAPTER 14

A distant figure shrouded in shadows appeared along the pathway leading out of the ravine. I watched it approach as I stood next to a wooden post that marked the border of the Isiyim settlement. It was getting dark and my aching limbs were not looking forward to the long journey home.

Emerging from the ravine, the figure transformed into a woman wearing a long red dress. A hijab covered her hair. She wore thin scandals that were unsuitable for traveling through the desert and she struggled to stay on her feet. I would have offered to help her but given how much effort it had taken to convince the Isiyim to bring her here I decided not to push my luck. She was escorted by another Isiyim, who remained twenty feet behind her, walking backward so he would not be corrupted by inadvertently casting a glance in her direction. He stopped at the edge of the ravine and sat down, facing away from us.

I spread a blanket on the sand and motioned for her to sit. I then handed her a waterskin. She nodded gratefully and squeezed a stream of warm water into her mouth. I sat on the sand next to the blanket and gazed at this vessel of sinfulness who might hold the key to Uriel's death.

"So, you're the one Binyamin chose to lure to this desert paradise," she said in Aramaic.

I smiled. "He's my son."

"Ahhh. Well, please don't punish him. He's in enough trouble already," she replied before gulping down more water.

She was a small girl, probably no older than 18, but her body pleasingly filled out her dress, which was stenciled with House of Aphrodite seashells. Her eyes were blue, and strands of red hair poked out from beneath her hijab. Her pale, freckled face was soaked in sweat and dust.

"I assume you are Cassandra?" I asked.

"No, you're confusing me with the many other whores who live with these crazy cave-dwellers."

Noticing my puzzlement, she laughed, bitterly. "Sorry. You spend two days cooped up in a dark room and see if you don't get a bit ornery." Looking around, she said, "Why are we meeting here?"

Waving a hand at her escort, I asked, "He didn't tell you?"

She shook her head. "He didn't say a word to me. He just came to my room and waved for me to follow him."

"According to Isiyim rules, a man cannot speak to a–er–"

"Whore," she offered.

I nodded, gratefully. "–In their community. To get around that, I convinced them to let me speak to you outside the border of their settlement."

She laughed. "In a strange way that makes sense. I'm sure they'd rather suffer a plague of locusts than have a woman like me in their midst."

"You may be the first. Have they mistreated you?"

"Actually, for a gang of celibate men they've been a lot nicer than I expected. They've given me candles and a straw mat to sleep on and leave food and water outside my door twice a day. Otherwise, they leave me alone. It's actually nice not having a man come to my room every hour. If this were a Roman camp I'd have been passed around like a jar of cheap wine."

I smiled. In addition to her beauty she possessed a nimble wit. *Just like my Naomi,* I reminded myself. I could see why Uriel had favored her. "You speak Aramaic very well."

"Thank you. Maybe that's because I'm half Yehudi."

That surprised me. "You don't look Yehudi."

She laughed. "If I were paid a shekel every time a man said that I'd have built such a dowry that even King Antipas might take me for one of his wives."

"How did you end up in a Greek brothel?"

She shrugged. "How do any of us? My father was a red-haired savage from the frozen lands in the north. He was captured by the Romans and sent to work at one of their garrisons in Caesarea Maritima. My mother worked in the kitchens. One night he raped her and I was the result. She was 16 at the time. Her parents cast her out of her house and we lived on the street for many years.

When I was twelve she sold me to a slaver, who eventually turned me over to Mistress Helena. He never told her I was half-Yehudi. Neither did I. Since I could speak Latin she was able to pass me off as a half-Roman, half-barbarian whore. The day I arrived I was deflowered by a fat Etruscan quartermaster and I've been earning my room and board on my back ever since."

I nodded in sympathy. But I was not here to discuss her past, as tragic as it was. "You know why I am here?"

She nodded. "You're trying to find the men who killed the old man."

"Did you know him well?"

"Yes. He was one of my regular customers. And the only Yehudi."

"How long had you known each other?"

"I thought you wanted to find out how he died."

"We'll get to that. But I need to know the full story of your—relationship. You don't have to talk about the—intimate aspects."

She sighed in relief. "Praise Jove and Elohim. I'm trying to forget that part."

"Just tell me the rest. How long had Uriel been visiting your establishment?"

"For several months. Mistress Helena met him when she went to Bethlehem to buy salt."

"I thought he had retired."

"He only said that because he didn't want to pay taxes. He was still secretly selling salt to a small group of private customers. Mistress Helena was one of them."

"How did you meet?"

"One day he came to the house to deliver the salt. I think he just wanted to see what a gentile brothel was like. He saw me and offered to pay Mistress Helena triple the normal rate to have me stay with him overnight at his house. She said she was fine with that because she didn't like 'Yehudi filth fouling her beds.'" She laughed. "She never found out that half of me was fouling her bed several times a day."

Recalling my recent visit to the House of Aphrodite, I wondered how valuable Uriel's gold coin must have been to convince a Yehudi-hater like Mistress Helena to let me dally with Demeter in her own establishment.

"How often did you…would you…"

"Go with him? Twice a month. Always on the first night of the full moon and on the first night when there was no moon in the sky."

I nodded. Uriel had been killed on the first night of the new moon.

"How did you travel from here to Bethlehem?"

"He would send a driver to pick me up."

"Was it always the same driver?"

"No."

"Would the driver wait for you?"

She laughed. "You mean like listen at the door until the old man was done? No. He'd return to take me home in the morning."

"Tell me what happened two nights ago."

She swept a fly off her sleeve. "I was picked up shortly before sunset and dropped off near his house."

"When you arrived did you see anyone suspicious?"

"I'm a red-haired whore. If anything, I'm the one who would have raised suspicions."

I smiled in agreement. This would especially be true in a small town like Bethlehem. "Go on."

"First he served me dinner. A slab of old mutton, tough as leather, and that awful Crete wine he thought I'd like because I was supposed to be a Roman whore. Then we went to bed."

"And how long did that…last?"

"Old men never last long. A few thrusts and he was through."

I turned my head away to hide my embarrassment. Yesterday I had shared a bed with a whore and pretended to be engaged in a carnal act. Yet, for some reason talking about it with Cassandra made me feel like I was committing a far more serious sin.

"What did you do...after?"

"Normally I stay with him until morning. But that night he told me he had to meet with someone and I must leave early. So I went out through the back door to the privy to clean up. He always keeps a basin of water and a washcloth there for me. A few minutes later I heard shouting coming from the house."

She shuddered. "I should've run away. But instead I returned and peeked through a crack in the back door. The saltseller was on the floor. Blood was all over his clothes. Two men were standing over him."

"What did they look like?"

"They were tall thin men dressed in light-colored cloaks."

"Did you see their faces?"

"No. They wore keffiyehs."

"How about weapons?"

"They were holding daggers."

"What did the daggers look like?"

She tapped her chin to focus her memory. "They had two short blades close together. I didn't think much of it until I saw the men here using the same ones."

"Did they say anything?"

She nodded. "Yes. One of them said something I couldn't understand."

"I know several languages. Can you remember what it sounded like?"

She rubbed her temples for a moment and then said, "It sounded like, 'denboronatvero.'"

I didn't recognize the word. "What happened after that?"

"I ran away so they wouldn't find me. I didn't know what to do. It was too early for the driver to come back and if I went to the authorities they might have arrested me. So I ran out of the town and began walking home. On the Hebron road, in the middle of the night! It was lucky I wasn't killed—or worse."

"Why did you leave your scarf there?"

"I didn't mean to. I didn't take it with me when I went to the privy. And I was too scared to go back into the house to get it."

She sighed. "If I had I would've saved myself a lot of trouble. When Mistress Helena found out I didn't have the scarf and hadn't been paid she threw me out of the house."

"I know. Demeter told me. Why didn't you tell Mistress Helena what happened?"

She scoffed. "That old witch would have turned me over to the next Roman guard who stopped by. I was hoping she wouldn't find out until later, so I could lie and say the old man was killed after I had left. You see how that worked out."

"How did you meet up with Binyamin?"

"He found me sitting outside the House of Aphrodite after Mistress Helena banished me. He said he was a friend of the saltseller. He had come to his house to meet with him and then found the body."

"How did he know you had been there?"

"He found my scarf on the bed. He knew about my visits and where it came from."

But I found the scarf hidden under the bed, I thought.

"He knew I'd never kill the old man, so when he found the scarf he thought I'd been kidnapped by the killers. He searched all around Bethlehem and the surrounding hills. When he didn't find anything he decided to look for me at the House of Aphrodite. He offered protection."

I removed the parchment from my pocket. "And he gave you this to give to Demeter."

"Yes. He told me to tell her what happened and to make sure she gave it to any watchman who brought the scarf back."

Not just any watchman, I thought. Only one he knew would be thorough enough to look under beds for evidence and who wouldn't let the risks of visiting a gentile brothel dissuade him from pursuing the truth.

"Do you know who might have wanted to kill Uriel?"

"He told me he had many enemies."

"Were you aware that he was a spy for the Isiyim?"

She grabbed the waterskin. "I didn't even know what an Isiyim was until I was brought here. What a strange place this is. Who would want to live in caves in the desert without women for company?"

I've often wondered the same thing, I thought.

A shadow crossed her face as twilight approached. It would take us at least three hours to get back to Bethlehem and I had no desire to keep one eye out for bandits and the other for vipers and hyenas. "Come on," I said, rising to my feet.

"Where're we going?"

"Back to Bet Ha-Tamid."

"But they told me I couldn't come back."

"We'll see about that."

The Isiyim who had accompanied her here flinched when I tapped him on the shoulder. "We need shelter for the night."

He shook his head. "You agreed to take the whore into your custody."

"Yes, I did. But I didn't expect it would be sunset when you brought her to me. It's too dangerous for us to stay out here."

"We cannot allow heretics and whores to corrupt our community."

"Is the moral fortitude of your community so fragile that it could be shattered by an old man and a young woman who are only seeking a place to sleep?"

He didn't respond.

I tried a new tactic. "Since when do Yehudim turn away strangers in need of shelter? What if Avraham had not opened his tent to the visiting angels? What if Lot had refused to give them sanctuary in his home?"

He thought about this for a moment, and then said, "Wait here."

As we watched him disappear into the ravine, Cassandra asked, "Who are Avraham and Lot? Are they friends of yours?"

Stifling a chuckle, I replied, "They're my—our—ancestors. The Torah tells the story of how one day three visitors came to Avraham's tent. He insisted that they stay with him. It turns out they were angels whom Adonai had sent to test Avraham's worthiness to be the father of our people. Later, two of them visited Avraham's cousin Lot in Sodom. He took them in as well. But when the townspeople heard they were there they demanded that Lot hand them over for them to violate. Lot refused."

She nodded. "A brave man."

"To mollify the mob, Lot offered them his virgin daughters."

She frowned. "But not a nice man."

We waited for a few minutes in silence until the Isiyim returned. He motioned for us to follow. Another Isiyim met us halfway and Cassandra and I parted ways. My escort took me back to the compound. After another session in the mikveh, he pointed at a cave entrance and told me I would spend the night there.

Carefully climbing the hill, I entered the cave and followed a dimly lit passageway to a large chamber that reeked of smoke and sweat. A fire burned in a stone hearth with a chimney flue that bore into the ceiling. Something was bubbling in a pot. Seven mats were spread around the room. Four of them were occupied by thin men with gaunt faces and long beards. Even in the stifling heat they were still fully dressed in their linen cloaks and head coverings. They gazed at me with disinterest, as if I were no more important than the beetles and spiders that scurried along the stone walls.

I sat down on a mat and waited. Several minutes later, Binyamin entered and sat down on next to me. "Father."

Suppressing my emotions, I nodded tersely and said, "So, this is where you live."

"Yes, this is where we live." He stuck a ladle into the pot and filled a clay bowl with something brown. "Eat."

"I'm not—"

"Eat!" It was as an order, not an offer. And from his expression I knew that this wasn't an act of kindness from a son to his father, but a ritual grounded in the ancient tradition of Yehudi hospitality that forbade discussion until the visitor had eaten his fill.

The stew was thin and tasteless. To wash it down, he handed me a cup of salty water. I had had better meals in the army.

I finished the stew quickly and placed the empty bowl on the ground. "Thank you."

He nodded. "Now that the meal is done, you can tell me: Why are you here?"

"Because it wasn't safe for Cassandra and me to return to—"

"No," he interrupted. *"Why are you here?"*

I paused, thinking about everything that had happened since the fateful day he had re-entered my life, bow slung across his shoulder, on the road to Yerushalayim. The prodigal son coming to his father's aid. But it hadn't stopped there. He was a character in this story of dueling messiahs and murder, hovering around the edges like a phantom. And then I knew.

"Because *you* wanted me here," I replied.

He nodded, slowly.

Looking around at the other men, I said, "Can we speak in private?"

He shook his head. "There is no need. We all know each other's secrets and sins."

"But they don't know about mine."

"Anything you say will not travel beyond our enclave. What happens in the outside world is of no concern to us."

"Really? You seemed to spend a lot of time in Bethlehem, meeting with Uriel ben Teman."

Even in the dim light I could see him wince. But none of the other men seemed to care. "That was a role assigned to me by the rabbis. I was the saltseller's appointed—liaison."

"For what did he merit such service?"

"He was our eyes and ears."

"A curious choice, since his lifestyle hardly reflected Isiyim values. Drinking foreign wine, bedding gentile whores."

He flashed a brief smile. "He also had a weakness for oysters."

I waited. "So?"

"It is not your place to define our values."

I stopped myself from starting an argument. This wasn't the time or venue. Besides, I was outnumbered.

Focus on why you're here. Why he needs you.

"You felt guilty that Uriel was murdered when he was supposed to be under your protection. As an Isiyim you wouldn't be able to find his killer alone so you manipulated me into getting involved."

He said nothing. Which meant he wasn't disagreeing with me.

"That's why you hid Cassandra's scarf under the bed. Because you knew that only an experienced and thorough watchman would think of looking there. And it's why you gave your note to her friend. You knew I would follow this investigation wherever it led."

He shrugged. "In Yehudi tradition there are few things nobler than the pursuit of the truth, something your Sanhedrin masters have never understood."

"I didn't come here to get into a debate over Yehudi factions. I came to learn what Cassandra knew of Uriel's death."

Binyamin looked away. "Did she give you the answers you were looking for?"

"Not all. But at least she eliminated several questions."

"Good."

"Your rabbis must not have been happy when you brought her here."

Looking around the room, he replied, "Yes. I was nearly excommunicated. But I have influential friends. So I was merely punished."

"How?"

"I was given eighteen lashes. It was a merciful punishment. I deserved many more. And afterward I had to cleanse my sins in the mikveh using water from a well I had to dig myself. It took half a day for my shovel to strike water and another to shore up the walls. Yet, much good comes out of this. I am purified and now we have a new source of water, a blessing in this parched land."

I stared at him. Could this be the same mischievous boy who used to pull the beards of old men and bear his backside at girls who passed him on the street?

"Did the whore tell you how the saltseller was murdered?" asked Binyamin.

"Yes. She saw the double-bladed knives the murderers were holding. And that the men wore the kind of cloaks you Isiyim wear."

"To make it look like we were responsible."

"How do I know you weren't?"

He shook his head. "The Isiyim did not kill him."

I threw up my hands. "Well, that settles it then. Now I can go back to Commander Shaul and Reb Lemuel and tell them, 'In spite of all the evidence to the contrary, my son assures me that his people didn't murder Uriel.' They'll laugh me straight to the stoning pit."

"Then you must convince them otherwise. That's why I…why we…need you."

"I need more than your word. I need to understand what's going on here. I know it has something to do with all this messiah business."

Binyamin nodded. "Yes."

"Then tell me the connection."

"All I know is that we have been ordered to protect the lives of the Notsrim and Doran infants."

"Wait—you're supposed to protect *both* of them?"

"Yes. And you must protect them, too."

"Why both? And why me?"

He brushed a spider off his cloak. "The rabbis didn't tell me."

You just blindly obey orders, I thought. *I wouldn't last a week here.* "All along I thought you Isiyim had thrown your lot in with Yeshua. I had no idea you were playing both sides."

A growling voice snapped, "We are on no one's side!" The speaker was a tall man with a sooty face and a scar that ran from his right eye to his lower lip. Thick braids of wild gray hair flowed from beneath his skullcap like the legs of a giant crab and his filthy unkempt beard stretched several inches below his neck.

"This is Rabbi Adiel ben Shalhevet," said Binyamin.

Suppressing a smirk, I said, "You're a rabbi?"

Rabbi Adiel pointed to two of the other men. "So are they."

"Rabbis and regular people live together here?"

"This is our way. We share everything so that no one should live without. Knowledge. Food. Labor. Suffering."

"Rabbi Adiel administered my punishment," said Binyamin, with pride. Noticing my anger, he quickly added, "It was an honor to submit to his lash. He is one of the most revered men in our community."

Staring at the rabbi, who would have fit right in with Bethlehem's beggars, I thought, *If you say that Binyamin's punishment hurt you more than him we're going to have a serious problem.*

Rabbi Adiel nodded. "As I was responsible for inflicting pain upon our acolyte as punishment for his sins, I am also responsible for healing his wounds and his spirit."

As long as I lived I would never understand these people. But maybe I could inch a bit closer to figuring out what was really going on. "Rabbi, why must the Isiyim, and apparently me as well, protect both infants?"

He glared at me with frightening intensity. "They must survive."

I refused to look away. "Why?"

He paused for a moment before answering, "Because the Nochmah says it must be so."

"The what?"

"The Nochmah. The one who foretells our destiny." He sounded like he was reciting from a scroll.

"Is he a rabbi?"

He shook his head. "We rabbis interpret the Laws and provide instruction so that we may fulfill the Covenant Elohim established with our people. The Nochmah interprets the words of the Prophets to tell us what is to come."

I thought about this for a while before asking, "May I speak to this Nochmah?"

Tension immediately filled the air. The other men looked at each other as if I had asked for a meal of pork and snails.

"Only the most senior rabbis are allowed to meet with the Nochmah."

"You want me to prove that the Isiyim didn't kill Uriel. You want me to protect Yeshua and Yochanan without telling me why. You're asking a lot without giving me a good reason in return. Just because you want me to do it isn't enough. If I'm going to risk my job—and maybe even my life—going up against the men who run my town I need to know *why.*"

Rabbi Adiel gathered the two other rabbis around him in a huddle. They began to speak to each other in Ivrit. Years of Torah study had taught me how to read and chant the language, but I rarely heard it spoken in conversation. I gazed at Binyamin. He understood what they were saying. It's a fine thing when a son knows more than his father.

Finally, Rabbi Adiel turned to me and said, "I will confer with our leaders."

After he left I realized how far I was from Bethlehem, where the priests and rabbis dressed in fine robes, lived in lavish homes and always seemed to grimace in contempt when they were forced to speak to the common people.

Turning to Binyamin, I said, "I seem to have created quite a stir around here."

"You are a very troublesome man," Binyamin replied.

I grinned. "A quality you have inherited. And praise Adonai for that, for where would either of us be now had we not chosen to knock down the walls that others built around us?"

"You are a tool of the Sanhedrin," he countered. "You guard the corrals the Sedukim build to keep the sheep from straying."

"How little you know me!" I snapped. "I'm a servant of the Law. Do you think that I spent fifteen years in King Herod's army just to return home and become a tanner like my father and his father before him? I did it so I could escape the bonds of my caste and so I could study Torah, a privilege denied to my father. I learned the Laws so that I could earn the right to enforce them, even if that means I spend most of my time arresting petty pickpockets, drunks and swindlers. It makes no difference to me whether the miscreant is a poor man or a priest. When a crime is committed, justice is meted out in equal measure. Of course, the difference between Isiyim justice and Bethlehem justice is that in our village an offender is usually put on trial before he is punished. And, occasionally, he is found guiltless."

Placing a hand on his shoulder, I added, "Deep down in that Isiyim soul of yours, I think you realize how alike we are."

He shook my hand off. "We're not alike at all!"

"Oh, it's true we may not eat the same food or practice the same rituals or even follow the Laws the same way. That's just about living day to day. No, what we share is an unwillingness to blindly accept things the way they are. We're like Adam and Chavah sampling the forbidden fruit. Yaakov wrestling the angel. Avraham negotiating with Adonai for the lives of the men of Sodom. We obey His Laws, but sometimes we question His actions. When appropriate."

Looking around the room, I said, "Well. At least you used to."

"I still do. Only I do it in a different way."

"And the lashes on your back are marks of dissent?"

He glared at me. "You're just like all the others. You think we Isiyim are some kind of cult whose members blindly follow the orders of our leaders. But we're not that way at all. We're not like the Sedukim, who give their loyalties to the capitulating sycophants posing as priests in the blasphemous fraud of a Temple built by the Idomites. Elohim allowed the Bavel to destroy Yerushalayim because the Yehudim had broken His Covenant with their acts of sinfulness and idolatry. He never meant for it to be rebuilt, especially by a man as evil as Herod. We Isiyim have our own priests and here we're committed to following the Laws the way Elohim intended us to. That's why I joined them."

I waited a long time before replying, "I've always wanted to ask you that question. Your mother and I often wondered whether you joined the Isiyim because of something we said or did to offend you."

His expression softened. "No. You both brought me up well."

"I wasn't there a lot of the time."

"True, but I could always feel your presence and moral authority in our home even when you were gone. If anything, the way you both raised and educated me inspired me to emulate the righteous ways of our ancestors. When I learned about the Isiyim, I realized that they could offer me the life of austerity and piety I craved."

"You could have saved your mother and me a great deal of anguish had you told us this. Instead, one day you just said you were going off to join them and left before we could discuss it."

He shrugged. "For that I am sorry. Perhaps I was worried you might try to talk me out of it."

"You were old enough to make your own decisions. Now, if you told me you were going to start worshipping Baal or Aphrodite or some monkey god that would be a different story."

He laughed. "Mother would have threatened to take me to Yerushalayim to have the priests drive the demons out of me."

"And she would have done it, even if she had to knock you out with a candlestick first."

He smiled and placed a piece of wood on the fire. It brought back a memory from long ago. On one frigid winter morning when Binyamin was eleven, he refused to gather firewood from the surrounding hills, one of his weekly chores. Instead of punishing him, Naomi and I let the hearth and oven fires run out. We neither cooked nor ate for two days. The house grew so cold that icicles started forming on the ceiling. Binyamin spent most of his time huddled in the darkness under a thin blanket. Finally, on the third day, he left the house and returned a short time later, his arms laden with wood. He never disobeyed us again.

I thought about the lashes on his back that, thankfully, I could not see. "You were always an argumentative child. How do you hold your tongue in such an orthodox place?"

"It is true that we strive to follow the ways of the Prophets. But that doesn't mean we don't debate the meaning of the Torah and the Scriptures. Everyone who can read them is encouraged to contribute to the discussion. Even an acolyte like me can refute the opinions of a rabbi."

I waited for a long time before asking, "If you ever felt that your rabbis were acting in a way that conflicted with your own moral beliefs, what would you do?"

Acutely aware that all eyes and ears in the room were focused on him, Binyamin answered, "I would voice my concerns to them in the hope that they would return to the path of righteousness."

"And if your efforts failed?"

"I would leave."

Before I could ask another question, Rabbi Adiel returned. "The Nochmah will see you."

I rose. To Binyamin, I asked, "Will you be here when I return?"

He shook his head. "I will be on night patrol along the lower reaches of the Yam ha-Melah path. I won't be back until mid-day tomorrow."

"May I return here to visit you some other time?"

He raised a finger and replied, "Find the saltseller's killers and protect the two infants from harm. Then we shall see."

CHAPTER 15

Placing a blindfold over my eyes, Rabbi Adiel guided me along a path that meandered through patches of brambles and sharp stones. After what seemed like hours he stopped me and removed the cloth.

We were standing next to the door of a large rectangular structure. Behind it lay a large expanse of rubble.

"What is this?" I asked.

"The remains of a once-sacred place now cursed by Elohim." Pointing to my feet, he ordered, "Remove your sandals. Then you may enter."

"You are not accompanying me?"

He shook his head. "I will be here when you return."

I kissed the mezuzah on the doorpost, pushed the door open and stepped into a small foyer dimly lit by a candle. On the opposite side were another door and a footbath. After dipping my bare feet, I knocked on the door.

From within the next room I heard a faint voice. "Come."

I opened the door and entered a much larger room. There were no windows except for a line of skylights that channeled the glow of the waxing crescent moon into shafts of pale light that illuminated sections of a wooden floor crowded with long benches. On the far side of the room a flame flickered. Waiting until my eyes adjusted to the near-darkness, I carefully stepped through the spaces between the benches until I arrived at the flame's source, a candelabra perched in the center of a wooden table covered with scrolls. Behind the table several shelves overflowed with more scrolls. Next to it was a closed ark, above which a small oil lamp dangled from a chain. To the right of the ark were a ladder and an amphora of lamp oil.

"Welcome, Gidon ben Einan. Approach and sit."

I turned in the direction of the voice, which was husky yet oddly feminine. From the darkness a figure emerged, covered from head to foot in a dark blue burka.

"In case you are wondering, the rubble you see outside this structure is all that remains of a large complex the Isiyim built to serve as a center of study and worship. It was destroyed by an earthquake more than twenty years ago. Legend says that one day a corrupt rabbi incurred the wrath of Elohim by smuggling a statue of the Roman god Neptune into the compound. Angered by this blasphemy, the Holy One made the earth tremble, destroying every room desecrated by the feet of this apostate. Only two buildings survived—this synagogue and a storage shed. The Isiyim declared the entire complex to be impure, and today only its most senior leaders may enter."

When I reached the table the figure motioned for me to sit in a chair and then sat down across from me, gazing at me through the eye slits of a face-shrouding veil. Wrinkled hands emerged from drooping sleeves and pushed aside a bronze yad.[1]

"You're a woman!"

The figure nodded. "Ah. What is said about your astute powers of observation is true."

"Do you work for the Nochmah?"

She paused. "Then again, perhaps I should reconsider my last statement."

I was tired and running out of patience. "Are you going to take me to the Nochmah or not?"

"That depends. Do you deserve such an audience?"

I was to about to open my mouth, but then I realized I had to choose my words wisely. This room had been a synagogue. This woman was probably an assistant of some sort. My answer would determine whether I would be allowed to speak to the Nochmah. Indeed, it was possible that the Nochmah was listening right now from a hidden corner of the room.

"I don't know."

The woman tapped the yad. "Good. Knowledge begins with ignorance. Why do you wish to speak to the Nochmah?"

---

[1]A Jewish ritual pointer used to read the Torah.

"I am looking for answers."

"And why do you need answers?"

I thought for a moment before replying, "Because I need to solve an injustice."

"Good, good. Now tell me: How open are your thoughts to possibilities that are otherwise obscured by narrow-minded thinking?"

My frustration was reaching the boiling point. Hadn't Rabbi Adiel promised me an audience with the Nochmah? If so, why did I have to explain myself to some old woman—

Realization finally penetrated my thick skull. "*You're* the Nochmah?"

She nodded.

"But—but—how can that be?"

"Yes. Astonishing, isn't it? The Nochmah is a woman living in a community of men who have foresworn all contact with the daughters of Chavah. What a scandal it would be if word got out!"

"Are you...a priestess?"

"Me? No. Only the male descendants of Aharon can be priests. But these days, who can truly claim their ancestry with any degree of confidence? The children of Yisroel lost their obsessive talent for recording their lineages many years before the first Temple was destroyed. That's why the Isiyim elect their own priests and rabbis. They believe that these roles are earned through merit, rather than bloodline. Even you, the son of a tanner, could become a religious leader in this community."

Or perhaps the son of a watchman, I thought, thinking of Binyamin. "If you're not a priestess what do you do here?"

"I am a guardian of the past, and a herald of the future."

"You're a soothsayer?"

She chuckled. "Lucky for you no Isiyim heard you compare me to a common fortune teller. I don't dabble with tea leaves and horoscopes. I reconcile the ancient words of the Prophets with the events of today to understand what is to come."

"To the Isiyim?"

"To all the scattered children of Yisroel, wherever they dwell. My agents in Yehud, Egypt, Assyria, Perea, Nabataea, Persia, Ethiopia and Rome bring news that I scry to infer Elohim's intentions."

"Was Uriel ben Teman one of your agents?"

"Oh, yes. Uriel was my eyes and ears in Ashdod and, later, in Bethlehem. His death is a terrible loss."

"It didn't bother you that he dallied with whores?"

"One must use the resources that are available, however questionable their moral character may be. Just as you rely on thieves and other miscreants for information to aid in your investigations. Your son understood this as well when he became our liaison with Uriel. And when he brought Cassandra here. He is like his father in many ways."

"I wouldn't know. Until last week, I hadn't seen him in two years."

"For what it's worth, Binyamin is highly regarded among the Isiyim. Or so I am told. I've never met the young man."

"Why not?"

She shrugged. "He does not have enough seniority. Yet."

"Then why did they allow me to meet with you?"

"Because, in the eyes of the Isiyim, you're an outsider and a heathen, so your visit doesn't violate their spiritual hierarchy."

I paused for a moment before asking, "How you can you help me?"

"You are looking for answers."

I leaned forward. "Ah. You know who murdered Uriel."

She shook her head. "No. But I know why he was killed."

"Is it because he was the only person to see the chests of treasure that had been given to the infant Yeshua ben Yosef, other than the boy's parents?"

She nodded. "Yes."

I paused before asking, "Is Yeshua the Messiah?"

She waited a long time before answering. "He is a Messiah."

I took a deep breath. Could it really be true that this baby would someday become king of the Yehudim? But how could he–

"Wait. What do you mean 'a Messiah'?"

"He is one of two."

It took a moment for her remark to sink in. "What?"

"The Apocalypts believe that there can be only one leader of our people at a time. Even some of the Sedukim are beginning to embrace this belief. But the history of the Yehudim proves this is wrong. The Patriarch Yaakov's twelve sons became the leaders of the twelve tribes of Yisroel. After the exodus from Egypt, the Prophet Moshe and his brother Aharon shared the spiritual leadership of the children of Yisroel during their forty years of wandering in the desert. And before the Bavel destroyed Yerushalayim, the Holy Land was divided into two kingdoms, Yisroel to the north and Yehud in the south. So why should there only be one Messiah? The Isiyim believe that several Messiahs can exist at the same time, each one playing his own role in advancing the progress of our people. And right now they believe that two newborn infants will eventually free the Yehudim from the spiritual abyss into which the Romans and their vassal kings and false priests have herded them."

"If Yeshua is one Messiah, who is the other?"

Her eyes twinkled. "I think you know the answer to that question."

I thought for a moment before answering. "Yochanan ben Nogah."

She nodded. "Yes." Grabbing several scrolls, she continued, "A careful study of the writings of the Prophets foretells the appearance of two Messiahs in Yehud at the same time. In one example–"

Rising to my feet, I said, "Thank you, but I'm here to find a murderer. I don't have time for a religious lesson–"

"Sit!" she commanded. Against the will of my mind, my body obeyed.

"You believe your mission is to solve a crime. But there is much more to it than that. Your fate is linked to the fates of these two infants, and you must understand the context. Because what you do–or don't do–in the next few weeks will determine the future of these two children and all Yehudim. Are you ready to listen?"

I felt the hairs on my neck stand on end. "Yes."

Opening a scroll, she said, "In his testament, the Prophet Yeshayahu foretells the coming of a Messiah who will fight to restore righteousness among our people. This Messiah is Yochanan ben Nogah."[1]

Before I could respond, she grabbed another scroll and said, "And the Prophet Michah foretells the appearance of a different Messiah whose lineage goes back to ancient times, who will nourish his flock in the strength of Elohim and bring peace to the world. This Messiah is Yeshua ben Yosef."[2]

"How can there be two kings of the Yehudim?"

"That is another misconception. None of the prophecies say that the Messiah will restore the kingdom of Yisroel."

I waited a long time before asking, "Then what *will* they do?"

"Yeshua will grow up to become the most famous rabbi in Yehud. He will be known for working wonders such as restoring eyesight to the blind and bringing the dead back to life."

I nodded. "We Yehudi have always been impressed by miracle-workers."

"He will gain many followers among the people. But he will run afoul of the priests and the Romans by condemning the corruption of the wealthy and powerful, while championing the poor and the meek."

"The authorities won't like *that* message."

She nodded. "He will make many enemies who will try to silence him. They will succeed, but his teachings will live on and spread far and wide among the Yehudim, even after his death."

I rubbed my chin and thought about the son of Yosef sleeping in his cradle. And that brought up another question. "Yeshua's mother claims she is a virgin."

---

[1] Isaiah 9:1-7.
[2] Micah 5:1-5.

She sighed. "Ah, yes. The virgin birth. So much time has been spent in disputation of this subject. All because of one word."

"What do you mean?"

She grabbed another scroll. "The Prophet Yeshayahu again. In another prophecy he says that a woman will bear a boy named 'Elohim is with us.'[1] He uses the word 'almah' to describe the mother. Do you know what this word means?"

I had to think back to my Ivrit lessons from long ago before answering. "Young woman?"

"Correct. It can also mean 'a woman of childbearing age' or 'an unmarried woman.' But many claim it also means 'virgin.' Some have interpreted this to mean that the Messiah will be born of a woman untouched by man."

"The mother said she was visited by an angel who told her she would receive seed from Heaven."

She nodded. "That is one way Yeshua could have been conceived."

I was a bit relieved. "So, her claim may be true?"

She pushed the scroll aside. "This is a matter of great debate among the Isiyim. Of course, with Elohim, anything is possible, so some do believe that Yeshua may be an angel in human form. Or even the son of the Almighty Himself."

Did I detect skepticism in her voice? "But there are doubters?"

"Yes."

"What do they say?"

"Well, for one thing, other than the testimony of Yosef and Miryam there is no physical proof of this virgin birth. But the theological argument against it is that the Holy One has always appointed adult men to lead our people and carry out His wishes. If He wanted a divine being to be the Messiah why would He require a woman to bear and nurture it? Surely such a being could descend fully formed straight from Heaven."

---

[1] Isaiah 7:14.

She waved a hand. "Anyway, the nature of Yeshua's conception and birth is irrelevant, since he is a Messiah nonetheless."

"What about Yochanan?"

"Oh, he was conceived the traditional way."

"I mean, what is his fate?"

"He will one day be proclaimed a Messiah and lead a rebellion against the Romans. But he will not succeed. His death will result in the destruction of many of our ancient institutions."

I said nothing for a few minutes, pondering the destinies of these two babies. "If neither of these Messiahs restores the kingdom of Yisroel, why do the Isiyim wish to protect them?"

She pointed the yad at me. "An excellent question. To answer it, you must think like the Isiyim. They believe that the purpose of a Messiah is to hasten Elohim's establishment of a new Covenant with the Yehudim. One where we will earn the favor of the Almighty through piety, prayer and good works rather than by establishing kingdoms, requiring pilgrimages and Temple sacrifices and forcibly converting our enemies. In different ways, and at different times, these two infants will facilitate this transformation. Exactly when and how has not been revealed to me...yet."

She pointed the tip of the yad at me. "But what I do know is that Elohim has chosen you to ensure their safety."

I laughed. "You must be joking."

"Yes, you. A Prophet predicted your role as well."

"Which one?"

"Hannah of Sigoph."

My ears perked up. "A woman Prophet?"

"Why not? Re'ut[1] was one of our most venerated Judges. Devorah[2] was one of our most respected warriors. And Hadassah[3] saved us all from destruction at the hands of Haman."

Looking across the table, I thought, *And the Isiyim trust a woman to foretell the future.*

She grabbed another scroll. "Hannah lived a generation before Yeshayahu. She predicted that during a time of false kings Elohim would choose two brothers to restore His Covenant, and would appoint a warrior to protect them, in her words, 'from the wolf, the eagle and the asp.' The word she uses for 'protector'–'moshiya'–also means 'deliverer.'"

She put the scroll down. "The brothers she refers to are our two infant Messiahs. And I believe you are the Moshiya of her prophecy. You have been chosen to protect them from harm."

Suppressing a smirk, I replied, "I studied all of the Scriptures. How come I've never heard of Hannah?"

"Blame the Sedukim for that. Until they came into power Hannah was nearly as famous as the other Prophets. But the Sedukim refuse to accept the possibility that a woman can be a Prophet. Over the years they've destroyed all but three scrolls of her writings. We have two of them."

I smiled. "The words of a woman Prophet and the woman who interprets them dwelling in a community of celibate men. Who would have thought?"

She shrugged. "The Isiyim don't associate with women but they acknowledge that Elohim communes with those of both sexes. Hannah is held in high esteem here. That's why the Isiyim brought you to me. To help you understand that you must ensure the survival of both Yeshua and Yochanan."

"How can I possibly do that? I'm just a lowly watchman."

"A lowly watchman who somehow was able to convince the Isiyim's most senior rabbis to grant you an audience with me."

---

[1] Ruth.
[2] Deborah.
[3] Esther.

"That's because *they* listen to reason. The Sanhedrin doesn't."

She rose from her chair. "It is time for you to go. You may spend the night in Kumran but in the morning you must return home to fulfill your destiny."

"You wouldn't have an extra Hannah scroll you can lend me?"

She laughed. "I'm afraid not. Even if I did, it wouldn't be a good idea for you to possess it. The Sedukim have little tolerance for heresy."

I nodded in agreement. In Yerushalayim the stoning of heretics was one of the city's most popular public entertainments. As I was rising, I remembered why I had come to Kumran in the first place. "What will happen to Cassandra?"

After a long pause, she said, "I have convinced the Isiyim to allow her to stay for the time being in the storage shed. It is perhaps less comfortable than what she is used to, but, then again, she will not need to lie with men while she is here, so it's an equitable compromise. Now, go, Gidon ben Einan. The Messiahs need you."

Rabbi Adiel was waiting for me when I left the building. Even though I was exhausted I once again cleansed myself in the mikveh. We then returned to the cave, where I spent the rest of the night tossing and turning on a threadbare rug. Binyamin didn't return and I regretted not being able to bid him farewell.

At dawn Rabbi Adiel served me a small plate of lentils and then silently escorted me through the valley to the border of the settlement. He handed me a satchel containing my clothes and turned away from me.

After I had dressed and given him my Isiyim garments, I asked, "Isn't someone going to accompany me to Bethlehem? I am the protector of two Messiahs, you know."

He pointed to the sky. "If the prophecy of Hannah of Sigoph is true the Holy One will walk by your side."

As I began my long trek home I hoped that the Holy One wasn't reading my mind, because as grateful as I was for His company, I would have felt a lot safer with my truncheon and sword by my side.

CHAPTER 16

Apparently, Rabbi Adiel spoke the truth, because I returned home safely. Bandits didn't ambush me. Wolves didn't gore me. And scorpions didn't sting me. Baruch ha-Shem!

Junior Constable Amos met me at the edge of town. "Senior Constable! I'm glad you're back. Everyone was wondering where you were."

"I had some business to attend to."

"Commander Shaul wishes to see you right away."

"I will, after I report to a higher authority." Seeing his puzzled expression, I added, "My wife."

"Please, Senior Constable, he ordered me to escort you to the Watch house right away. If he finds out I didn't…"

The pleading in his eyes was so pitiful I relented. I could make a quick report and then head back home for a well-deserved rest.

Constable Elihu was sitting at the table drinking tea as I entered the Watch house. A tiny smile formed on his face. A moment later, Commander Shaul came in, his face red with anger. "Senior Constable. How nice to see you finally reporting for duty. Would you care to tell me where you've been?"

Glancing at Constable Elihu, I asked, "Can we speak privately, Commander?"

"No, we cannot. Contrary to what you might believe, we are a squad here."

"I was pursuing a new lead in the investigation of the murder of Uriel ben Teman."

His expression didn't change. "Didn't I tell you to put that aside and instead speak to the Notsrim about returning home?"

Tapping my forehead, I replied, "Forgive an old man's failing memory, Commander, for I don't recall being given such an order."

Commander Shaul was only a year older than me. And he wasn't amused. "We needed you here. To bolster our defense against those who tried to murder the Messiah."

I was shocked. "When? How?"

"Archers tried to fire flaming arrows through their window."

My heart skipped a beat. "Was Yeshua injured?"

"I said they were trying to kill the Messiah. Fortunately, Yochanan ben Nogah was not harmed."

Noticing my puzzled expression, he continued, "You see, Senior Constable, contrary to your belief that Reb Lemuel and I are conspiring against your family of Galilim vagabonds, there are actually those who don't wish the Doran infant to fulfill his messianic destiny, either."

Remembering the Nochmah's words, I thought, *Well, you can't blame me for failing to protect the boy. I wasn't here when it happened.*

"I'm sorry, Commander, but my investigation has provided valuable insights into the sequence of events that led to Uriel's death."

"Your time has been wasted. The murderers have been captured."

For a moment I was speechless. "What? Who?"

"Two Isiyim. They were captured outside the city last night."

"By whom?"

"By Constable Elihu."

Turning to the young watchman, I asked. "Really? Tell me what happened."

Flashing a boastful smile, he replied, "Last night I was on patrol and Hiram the stonemason told me he saw smoke rising from the hills somewhere along the western road. Since bandits often camp there I went to investigate. The smoke was coming from Vultures' Ridge. When I climbed up the hill I saw two Isiyim sleeping by a campfire in the embankment behind the Vulture's beak. Their cloaks were stained with blood, as were the double-edged daggers they held in their hands. Fortunately, I was able to disarm them before they awoke. They surrendered without a fight."

I bowed. "Congratulations, Constable. Excellent work." Turning to Commander Shaul, I asked, "Have they confessed?"

"Yes. Reb Lemuel interrogated them after we discovered the saltseller's goods in their possession." He pointed to two purple pouches on his desk.

Recalling my frequent trips to the mikveh during my brief sojourn to Kumran, I thought, *No Isiyim would continue to wear clothes defiled with the blood they spilled.*

"May I see these men?" I asked the Commander.

He shook his head. "No, you may not."

"Why not?"

"Because they are to be handed over to the Sanhedrin in Yerushalayim, where they will be tried and executed."

"As the lead investigator in this case I should have a chance to interview them."

"As I said, Reb Lemuel already heard their confession."

"Then at least let me speak with him so I can write up the report."

He suddenly looked uncomfortable. "That will not be necessary."

"Again, why not?"

He took a deep breath before answering, "Because you are no longer a member of the Bethlehem Town Watch."

I looked around the room. Junior Constable Amos wouldn't look at me. Constable Elihu did and made no effort to suppress the smug expression on his face.

"You're not serious."

"You disobeyed my orders, didn't show up for your shift and didn't tell me or anyone else where you were going or what you were doing. Reb Lemuel wanted to arrest you for sedition and dereliction of duty. I convinced him to have mercy and simply remove you from the Watch instead."

Shaking my head in anger, I snapped, "So apparently, my ten years of service and the hundreds of crimes I solved mean nothing to him?"

He looked away and replied, "I had no choice in the matter."

Yes you did! I wanted to scream. *Your duty is to uphold the Laws and deliver justice. And that means standing up for your fellow watchmen when an injustice has been committed against them.*

But the pain in his eyes convinced me to argue no more with him in front of my former colleagues.

"Hand me your sash of office and your truncheon," he commanded in a voice trembling with emotion.

"I left them at home."

"Then I will stop by your house later to collect them."

I shrugged. "Fine."

He handed me a pouch. "These are the wages that are owed to you." I could tell that there were many more shekels inside than there should have been.

"Now that you are a civilian you are to refrain from any future investigations into the death of Uriel ben Teman. Reb Lemuel considers the matter to be closed. Any attempts to contravene this order will be treated as a criminal offense."

As he spoke, he turned so only I could see the expression on his face. It said, *I know this is wrong, but there's nothing I can do.*

Since there was little more to say, I glanced at Amos and Elihu and said, "Shalom. See you around." It wasn't the best parting speech, but I hadn't had any time to prepare one.

As I stepped out of the Watch house into the bright light of morning, I thought, *Now what?*

I hadn't been without a job since I was five years old, when I began my career working for my father's tanning business. When I turned 21 I joined the army and served for fifteen years before returning home and joining the newly formed Watch. For ten years, six days a week, week in and week out, I had toiled to bring home the meager wages that, along with Naomi's dairy and wool business, kept my family fed, clothed and sheltered.

I wasn't worried about money. I had a few hundred shekels stashed away in a chest buried in the pasture behind my home. And we could probably live comfortably on Naomi's income alone. But I couldn't retire. What would I do all day? Sit on the steps of the synagogue like the toothless old men who were too ill and weak to work? Become a beggar? Move to another town where people never heard of Gidon ben Einan, the only man ever fired by the Watch?

Word of my termination must have gotten around, for I noticed my fellow townspeople staring at me with expressions ranging from sympathy to embarrassment. For years they had witnessed me breaking up fights, wrestling thieves to the ground, thwarting would-be rapists and arresting thieves and drunks. But now, without a sash around my neck or a truncheon in my pocket, I felt naked.

At least I knew I would find sympathy and understanding in the sanctity of my home. Little did I know how wrong I would be.

Naomi was sitting at the table with several friends when I returned home. When she saw me, her face filled with rage. The other women glared at me and quickly left.

She didn't get up to greet me. Instead, she asked, in a cold voice, "Where were you?"

I sat down next to her. "It's a long story. May I have something to drink first?"

"No!" she snapped. "I was worried sick about you! Shaul stopped by at least five times, saying that you had disappeared without telling anyone where you were going. Do you know how worried and ashamed I've been?"

"I apologize. Much has happened over the past two days. Events that required me to range far and wide with my investigation."

"And that includes visiting gentile brothels?"

I was thunderstruck. *How had she found out?*

"There was only one. I went there to find a woman who witnessed the murder of Uriel ben Teman."

"And you needed an entire day and night to accomplish this? Was it enjoyable?"

"Not really. Especially since I had to travel all the way to Kumran to speak with her."

She blinked. "Kumran?"

"Yes," I said. "She was given sanctuary by the Isiyim. After Binyamin brought her there."

Her anger softened. She knew that I would never lie to her. "What was our son doing with a whore?"

"Saving her life."

I told her the entire story of my journey to the House of Aphrodite and the Isiyim, although I left out the part about sharing a bed with Demeter. She seemed particularly interested in my session with the Nochmah. I was hoping she might have a little bit of sympathy for the ordeal I had gone through, but all she said was, "Once again, you are reunited with Binyamin, while I am left only with memories."

I didn't respond. Because she was right.

"And what did Shaul have to say about all this?"

"I didn't have a chance to tell him. He fired me from the Watch."

I told her about my encounter with the commander at the station. She shook her head. "You've always been a rule-breaker."

Now it was my turn to be angry. "Really? Yesterday our son accused me of being a tool of the Sanhedrin. Well, here's what I think: I'm neither a puppet or a rebel. If there's one thing I learned in the army it's that while discipline is important, on the field of battle the rules often change and you must know when to change with them. That's why I am—was—a good watchman. I understood the difference between blindly enforcing the Laws and bending them every now and then to achieve the greater good."

She was silent for a long time. "When you were away at war I worried that you would find an exotic foreign girl and abandon me."

Patting her hand, I replied, "Never once did such a thought ever occur to me. Not then, nor now."

She smiled. "You are an infuriating man, Gidon ben Einan."

I shrugged.

"But you are my infuriating man, until death parts us."

I felt a ray of hope. "Then you forgive me?"

"No. Not yet. Go away and let me be alone for a while so I can pray to Adonai to soften my heart."

"But where should I go?"

She pointed a finger at the door. "You have the rest of your life to figure that out. You might as well start now."

CHAPTER 17

My first act as a retired watchman was to place my sash and truncheon on my doorstep for Commander Shaul to pick up. My second act was to check in on one of the Messiahs I was supposed to protect. When I reached Yosef's home a small group of Yeshua's followers greeted me warmly. None of them looked like they'd be able to shoot flaming arrows through a third story window.

The house was now completely finished. Yosef opened the door when I knocked. Several inches of hair had been trimmed from his head and beard and he was wearing a new cloak and sandals. He was holding a knife with a long curved blade and an olivewood handle. "Good morning, Senior Constable!"

Gazing at the knife, I asked, "Are you expecting trouble?"

He laughed. "No, I was slicing some dates. Please come in."

Yeshua's followers weren't letting up at all in their generosity. The shelves of a new cupboard were stacked with bushels of grapes, olives, figs and loaves of fresh bread and several plates and pitchers. Two new end tables housed a pair of Shabbat candlesticks, a Kiddish cup and three oil lamps. In a corner was a new cradle in which the object of their collective adoration was asleep.

"It looks like you're all settled in."

"Yes. Our home is now complete."

"Indeed. Yours has twice as much furniture as mine and I've lived there for nearly fifty years."

"Thank you. I built it all myself. Once people find out that I am a carpenter they are happy to donate cedar, cypress and nails."

Trying not to show my jealousy, I said, "So…how is the baby?"

"Yeshua is growing bigger every day. And what an angel! He already sleeps through the night."

I quietly walked over to the cradle to get another look at the young Messiah-in-waiting. Yosef was right. He seemed to have doubled in size since the last time–

I stopped. Something resembling a coil of black rope was sticking out of the baby's swaddling clothes. When I peered in for a closer look, it twitched.

Without thinking, I grabbed one end and ripped it out of the cradle. A sharp pain suddenly pierced my right wrist. I dropped it and flattened it with my sandal.

"Get Zacchari ben Adam here right now!" I yelled. Yosef nodded and ran out to fetch the town's physician. Turning to Miryam, I ordered, "Remove the child's clothes!"

Without protest, she placed Yeshua on the table and undid his swaddling blanket. I inspected the baby. On his left leg were two tiny perforations, less than half an inch apart.

Two of Yeshua's followers ran in. "What happened?"

"Yeshua's been bitten by a snake!" I said. "How long has he been asleep?"

"Nearly three hours."

I listened to the baby's chest. His breathing and heartbeat appeared to be normal.

"Wake him up!"

She cradled Yeshua in her arms and gently stroked his hair. The baby opened his eyes and gazed sleepily at her.

"Start feeding him!" I snapped.

She sat down and offered her breast to the baby, who latched on with enthusiasm. I sighed with relief. A victim of snakebite venom wouldn't be awake. Or hungry.

I examined the remains of the snake. It was less than a foot long and as thin as a ribbon.

Several minutes later, Yosef returned with Zacchari ben Adam. The physician immediately took the baby from Miryam and inspected him from head to foot, paying close attention to the perforations. "Baruch ha-Shem, the beast's fangs did not penetrate the infant's skin. He will be fine."

He returned the baby to Miryam and then carefully lifted the dead snake by its tail. "Senior Constable, do you know what this is?"

Now wasn't the time to update him on my change in employment status. "A ribbon viper. During my years fighting the Nabataeans more men died of its bite than in battle."

He nodded. "They are among the most dangerous creatures in the world. It is said they are the direct descendants of the Serpent who tempted the first man and woman with the forbidden fruit in Ehden."[1]

Yeshua began to squirm in Miryam's arms and pointed a tiny hand at me. I had forgotten about my wrist. I looked down at two similar but much deeper fang marks an inch below my thumb.

"Zacchari!" I said, showing him my hand. He examined it and asked, with alarm, "Senior Constable, how do you feel?"

"Fine."

"Are you sure? The viper's bite definitely penetrated your wrist and injected its venom. You can tell by the inflammation around the puncture marks."

"Honestly, I'm all right."

He rubbed his chin. "Then the Holy One protects you as well, for you should be dead right now. Normally, the viper's venom kills within minutes."

I gazed at my wrist and then at Yeshua. Was he nodding at me?

Zacchari placed the snake on a table. "I have never seen a ribbon viper in Yehud before."

"Have you been looking for them?"

"You don't understand. They can't live here. They only eat yellow millipedes, which are found only in the deserts to the east. Perhaps this one found its way onto a wagon and was transported here in a caravan."

His expression told me that he didn't believe it. Neither did I.

"Do you know how it got in?" Zacchari asked Yosef.

"No," replied Yosef. "We didn't even know it was here until Senior Constable Gidon killed it."

---

[1] The Garden of Eden.

Zacchari slit the snake open with a small knife. "Do you see the yellow lumps? They're freshly digested millipede bodies. This snake has eaten within the last day. Perhaps these insects were already in the wagon when the viper sneaked aboard."

Or perhaps somebody captured the beast and fed it along the way, I thought.

The physician turned to Yosef and me. "There is nothing more for me to do, but do not hesitate to call on me if either one of you shows any signs of illness."

After he had gone, I took Yosef aside. "This is the second attempt on your son's life. Perhaps it would be wise for you to leave Bethlehem for a little while."

Yosef's lip trembled. "Did you hear what the physician said? Adonai watches over him."

"Well, at least keep a close eye on your visitors," I replied. "Someone brought the viper into your house. He might have even planted it in the cradle. He could be someone you know. An assassin posing as one of Yeshua's followers."

"Will you try to find the person who did this?"

I sighed. "Not officially. I have been fired from the Watch."

He seemed confused. "Then why are you here?"

"I just wanted to see how the little Messiah and his parents were doing."

Yosef nodded. "I am sorry that you are no longer a watchman. I hope that we are not the cause."

I wanted to say, *Of course you're the cause. You and your Doran competitors. This was a peaceful town until you two started shaking things up, turning otherwise sane people into members of opposing factions who shoot flaming arrows, drop snakes into cradles and murder old men to advance your claims. In a holy war like this, how could a truth-seeker like me possibly survive unscathed?*

But instead, I sighed and replied, "If you're going to stay here you'll need someone besides Adonai to watch over your family day and night. Private guards. Do you have money?"

He shook his head. "I've just re-started my carpentry business. I've spent my last shekels on supplies."

Gazing once again at the newly crafted furniture, I asked, "Would you be willing to trade some of your carpentry work to pay for the guards?"

"Of course. I'll do anything to protect my family."

I smiled. "Good. I know a man whose business could use some refurbishing."

CHAPTER 18

Reuven was cleaning the hookah when I arrived. "Ah, former Senior Constable. I was wondering whether I would ever see your face again, now that you are no longer in need of my special services."

"Word travels fast," I said, sitting on a heavily chipped bench.

He sat behind the counter and took out an amphora of wine. "It's quite likely I knew your fate before you did."

"I don't doubt it."

He filled a cup and placed it next to me. I shook my head. "I'm sorry, but without a steady income I can't afford such luxuries."

"For you, it's on the house. To celebrate the fact that we both now sit on the same side of the Laws."

"No we don't. You're a crimelord. I'm just a regular citizen."

"I meant that our magistrate now looks upon the both of us with disfavor."

"Oh, in that case." I took a sip. "This is very good. Much better than your usual plonk."

"A vintage I keep for special occasions," he replied. "Purchased from the father of your former colleague Junior Constable Amos."

I was about to spit it out when he said, "Senior Constable! I only serve wine that is kashrut, even to the Romans. The vineyard is in Shiloh. Very few amphorae make it down this way. Most of it ends up in the hands of the priests."

I relaxed. "You don't have to call me Senior Constable anymore."

"I don't think I would feel comfortable calling you anything else."

I took another sip. "So. This must a great day for you. One less watchman looking over your shoulder. Too bad you have no customers here to share your celebration."

He frowned. "Only a man with a stone for a soul would exult in the misfortune of a friend. Besides, I never thought of you as a watchman."

Noting my reaction, he quickly added, "I mean, I never thought of you as a watchman in the traditional self-righteous, inflexible sense of, say, your former commander."

"Oh."

"No, never once did I consider you to be the kind of small-minded man who incessantly harasses hard-working purveyors of victimless pleasures instead of pursuing thieves, well-poisoners, slavers and rabble-rousers. Law enforcers who fixate on trivial transgressions inevitably fail to solve the serious crimes that truly threaten our collective peace and security. No, you always understood this and it made for a mutually beneficial relationship. I helped you find the wolves and, in exchange, you kept the hunters from beating down my door."

I took another sip. "Well, from now on you'll have to fend for yourself."

"I suppose I will. Sometimes I think that your commander never raided my shop purely as a favor to you. With you gone, I wonder how long it will be before he stops looking the other way."

"That's not my problem anymore. I'm done with crime-fighting."

He laughed. "I know you better than that. Losing your sash and wooden bashing stick won't stop you from finding out who really murdered my friend Uriel. By the way, did you ever identify the owner of the scarf?"

I hesitated for a moment. Was it a crime for me to tell him everything that had happened since he put me on the trail that led to Cassandra? On the other hand, I was no longer a watchman. And Reb Lemuel had shut down the investigation. Besides, according to the Nochmah, I was being supervised by a higher power now. So, after swearing Reuven to secrecy, I recounted my journey to the House of Aphrodite and the Kumran Isiyim.

Afterward he poured me another cup and said, "I am honored to share my wine with the man El-Shaddai has chosen to protect the two children who are fated to free us from the scourge of the Sedukim. If there is anything I can do to help please do not fail to ask."

"Actually, there is. Do you know of any private guards looking for work?"

He raised an eyebrow. "You believe your life is in danger?"

"Not for me. For the infant Yeshua and his family."

"Has another attempt been made on his life?"

I told him about the ribbon viper. He rubbed his chin. "Ah. You need men who can thwart both the skilled bowman perched on the hillside and the assassin lurking in the shadows."

"Yes," I replied. "Four guards. Two during the day, two at night."

"What about the Doran child?"

"Reb Lemuel's private guards are watching over them."

"May I assume that our esteemed magistrate has not offered the Notsrim similar protection?"

I shook my head.

Reuven nodded. "I can provide these guards. But they will be costly."

I placed four of Uriel's silver coins on the counter. "This should cover their wages for the next two days, minus any amount you want to take off the top."

He waved his good hand. "For such a sacred duty I wouldn't dream of taking a commission."

"Good. Yosef will take over payment starting the third day."

"Really? I was under the impression that he was shekel-less."

Looking around the room, I said, "Don't you think that your establishment could use some new furniture? Look at this bench—it's falling apart. And those chairs by the hookah are so old you can see the worms poking through the grain."

"Ahhh!" he exclaimed. "Yesterday I stopped by the Notsrim's charming little house to drop off my sons' baby clothes. The furnishings are superb."

"Yosef built them all. Give him the materials and he'll make just about anything you want."

He rubbed his chin. "Yes, I agree to this arrangement. When should the guards start?"

"Now," I replied. "And I expect that you won't monopolize all of Yosef's labor, so he can actually earn some money on his own from other customers."

He feigned an insulted expression. "Do you believe that I would tempt the wrath of El-Shaddai by cheating the parents of His Chosen One?"

"No, I always knew you were capable of honesty when it counted," I replied. "When the guards arrive for the first shift they will be asked for a password. It is Nochmah."

He nodded. "Knowledge is a good thing, even among guards."

I stood up. "Good. Thank you for the—"

He placed a hand on my arm. "Wait. Now that you have graciously given me an account of your travels and blessed me with the gift of new furniture at a bargain price, I feel I should return the favor."

I shook my head. "I don't need your charity."

"And I'm not offering it. What I do have is information that may be relevant to the now-ended investigation into the murder of Uriel ben Teman. Unless you are no longer interested."

I sat down. "I'm listening."

"I understand that two men have been arrested for the murder."

"Yes. Apparently, they're Isiyim after all. They had bloodstained clothes and double-edged daggers and were carrying several of Uriel's salt pouches."

"So I heard. Were you able to see them?"

"No. Commander Shaul wouldn't let me."

"Well, I saw them. I just happened to be passing by the Watch house when Constable Elihu was bringing them into custody."

I waited for a moment and then asked, "And?"

"While it is true that their cloaks were spattered with blood, their faces were uncovered. They seemed very familiar. Had you seen them, you might have recognized them as well."

My heart sank. Had I met the captured men in my recent sojourn among the Isiyim?

Reuven must have noticed my dejected look, for he quickly added, "Allow me to relieve your anxiety. The two suspects are most definitely not Isiyim."

"How do you know?"

"Because I never forget faces, especially those of two men who were happily enjoying the pleasures of my hookah the last time you were here. They weren't clothed in Isiyim garments then. In fact, all they wore were loincloths."

I vaguely recalled seeing these men the day I came in to show him Cassandra's scarf. "Yes I remember. However, I didn't get a good look at them."

"Then perhaps you didn't notice the tattoos on their backs?"

My jaw dropped. Tattoos! No Yehudi would ever allow his skin to be defiled with ink. "Are you sure?"

He nodded. "Oh, yes. They're Greek journeymen from Assyria."

"Could they have murdered Uriel?"

"I doubt it. These two were fey, delicate creatures who would faint at the sight of a sewing needle. And they certainly wouldn't spend the night camping in the wilderness. They came into my shop with enough shekels to rent the best room in Sagiv's inn."

"But Constable Elihu said he captured them on Vultures' Ridge."

"Really? Have you been there?"

"No."

"Perhaps you should take a look yourself."

Were I a wiser man I would have left that moment and forgotten everything he had just told me. Instead, I asked, "Why are you telling me this?"

"Because I want Uriel's real murderers brought to justice. Your former commander doesn't have the imagination or the courage to question Constable Elihu's story or the so-called confession witnessed only by our venerable magistrate. But now that you are no longer under the yoke of the Sanhedrin, you can pursue the truth on your own terms."

And risk being arrested for doing what got me fired in the first place, I thought.

He leaned back and crossed his arms. "Of course, I harbor no expectations that you will act upon the information I have just given you. What influence could a humble purveyor of sensory pleasures exert over a man of such independent thought as yourself?"

Knowing that he knew exactly what I would do next, I sighed and asked myself, *If I am no man's puppet, why is it so easy for people to pull my strings?*

CHAPTER 19

After leaving Reuven's shop I took a long, leisurely walk around Bethlehem. Apparently, everyone now knew about my ouster from the Watch, judging by the many townspeople who came up to me to express their sympathy or crossed the road to avoid speaking to me. Fortunately, I encountered none of my former colleagues, although outside the synagogue Reb Lemuel walked right past me as if I were invisible.

Since I was supposed to protect both Messiahs I headed to the Bet Shafa. Two of Reb Lemuel's private guards stood by the gate. I assumed that another was posted outside Nogah's door. Gazing upward, I noticed that the windows of their third-floor apartment had been boarded up. None of the other units were given the same protection. Had it occurred to anyone that if you shot a flaming arrow into the apartment below it could start a fire that might consume the entire building? I considered discussing this risk with Chanoch the landlord but the scowls of the guards convinced me that my presence was neither needed nor desired.

I returned home to the scent of baking bread.

"Are you expecting company?" I asked.

She smiled. "Just you."

I sat down at the table. "I thought you were angry at me."

"I was, until Merav stopped by to tell me what you did."

"That gossip? What rumors was she spreading today? That I was bedding Nubian whores? Throwing dice? Feasting on squid?"

She placed a large slice of steaming bread on a plate in front of me. "No. But she did tell me that you killed a cobra that was threatening the life of Yeshua ben Yosef."

Word traveled fast. "That's not entirely true. It was a ribbon viper."

"It's a miracle that it didn't strike you."

I never lied to my wife. But sometimes I chose to be silent rather than tell her a truth that would distress her. Now was one of those times. Biting into the bread, I savored its warmth and sweet taste of barley and honey. It felt like forever since I had had a good meal. "It was still a pretty foolish thing to do."

She reached out and rubbed my neck. "It's never foolish to protect the weak and powerless."

"Anyone would have done the same thing."

"You're being too modest. It reminded me of the time you saved the life of that young Nabataean soldier."

"I don't remember it." Actually, I did but she enjoyed re-telling the story to anyone who would listen.

"You were fighting the Nabataeans in Gerasa."

"Amman," I corrected her.

"Amman, then. You discovered a soldier hiding behind a boulder and were about to drive your spear into his chest when he covered his face and begged for his life. He told you he was only thirteen years old and had been sold to the army by his father. You knew that if you let him go your fellow soldiers might capture and execute him. So, you told him to play dead until your squad had left the battlefield."

I shrugged. "You don't kill those who can't defend themselves."

"I also remember you telling me how you prevented Moab women from being raped by King Herod's foreign mercenaries."

"Sometimes I couldn't stop them."

"But at least you tried."

"I can't protect anyone anymore. No matter what the Prophets say."

Placing her hand on mine, she said, "If that were true, Adonai would not have chosen you as the Moshiya for his Chosen Ones. He has faith in you. As do I."

CHAPTER 20

Shortly after sunset, I headed out of town along the unnamed road that meandered westward across Yehud through desolate expanses of desert until it ended at the shores of the Mare Nostrum.

After fifteen minutes I reached a hill notable for an outcropping of boulders that resembled the eyes and beak of a bird of prey: Vultures' Ridge.

I climbed through groves of nettles until I reached the crest and then slid down an embankment to a plateau of sand, brush and wildflowers. Under the light of the moon I began to look for the camp of Uriel's alleged murderers.

An hour's search revealed nothing. No impressions in the sand where they would have sat or slept. No charred wood or ashes from a fire. No evidence of any consumed food. And the only footprints, besides those of foxes and rabbits, were my own.

By the time I returned to town it was nighttime. Other than beggars, the only people out this late were tanners' assistants, who were paid to collect buckets of urine and defecation from Bethlehem's wealthier families. When I was working for my father I did the same thing. To this day I could still remember the horrible stench that no amount of scrubbing could ever remove from my skin and clothes.

I hid in a doorway next to a shed and waited. Soon I heard the familiar sound of boots noisily pounding the ground. The unmistakable gait of Constable Elihu. He loved working the night shift. That's when most criminals conducted their activities and the young Sedukim was never happier than when he had the opportunity to bounce his truncheon off the head of a would-be thief.

As he passed, I stepped out of the doorway. "Good evening, Constable."

He quickly glanced at me and replied, "Good evening–citizen."

"Aren't you going to ask me what I'm doing here this late at night?"

His lip trembled. I was no longer his superior officer, but he was having trouble shedding his natural deference to authority and age.

"I trust that you have a legitimate purpose for being out," he replied through clenched teeth.

"Well, yes, I do," I said. "I was hunting ribbon vipers. Apparently, they've migrated here from Nabataea."

His expression didn't change. "Did you find any?"

"No, but perhaps I was looking in the wrong place. I went to the clearing behind Vultures' Ridge, you see."

His eyes widened. "Why there?"

"It's known as a breeding ground for many kinds of serpents. You may not know this, but it's not called Vultures' Ridge because of the boulders on its peak. It's named for the vultures and buzzards that flock there to feast on the corpses of beasts felled by snakebite." I was making this part up but he seemed to accept it without question. "Unfortunately–or, perhaps, fortunately–I encountered no serpents at all."

He nodded. "That is good."

"In fact, other than bushes and nettles, I didn't see evidence of any living thing there. No remains of a fire. No drops of blood. No human waste. No footprints."

His eyes began to blink rapidly. And was that sweat forming on his forehead?

"I find this rather curious, because you said you found the two Isiyim camping there by following their trail of smoke. How do you reconcile this discrepancy?"

Pursing his lips, he snapped, "You're not a watchman anymore. I don't need to explain anything to you!"

"Really? Then maybe *I* should explain it to *you*."

I grabbed him by the neck and shoved him against a wall. Before he could react I knocked the truncheon from his belt and removed a dagger from his pocket and threw it to the ground.

"Assaulting a watchman is a crime punishable by death!" he gasped.

"So is falsely accusing the innocent," I replied. "You see, I have it on good authority that the two men sitting in the cell in the Watch house didn't kill Uriel. Nor are they even Isiyim. They're Greeks who were paid by someone to masquerade as the assailants. If you need proof, remove their clothes and view the tattoos on their backs."

I loosened my grip on his neck to give him enough air to rasp, "Why should I believe you?"

"On the face of it, you shouldn't. But how do you explain the lack of evidence supporting your account of capturing them on Vultures' Ridge? You see, what I think really happened is that someone brought these pretenders into town to be delivered to the Watch. Perhaps their captors didn't want to be given credit for their capture. Maybe they were afraid that the real Isiyim would go after them. Whatever the reason, they wanted a watchman to make the arrest. And who better than Constable Elihu ben Hoshea?"

I relaxed my hold. Tears were running down his face. He wouldn't even look at me. I was no longer worried that he would try to break free or attack me. His guilt had immobilized him.

"The only problem was that it wouldn't look good if you told Commander Shaul that other people captured them. He would ask all sorts of questions: Who were the captors? How did they know where the Isiyim were hiding? No, you needed a cover story, so you made up the tale of finding them in the hills. After all, everyone knew that the Isiyim killed the saltseller. Who was going to doubt the word of Yehud's most incorruptible watchman?"

Stepping back, I said, "You once told me that bearing false witness is a sin second only to worshipping idols. Constable Elihu, in the name of Adonai, do you still swear that your story about capturing the two assailants on Vultures' Ridge is true?"

He shook his head and whispered. "No."

"Am I also correct that these men were delivered to you?"

He nodded. "Yes."

"Who placed them in your custody?"

After a moment, he looked down at the ground. "Reb Lemuel."

I patted him on the arm. "Good man."

No longer burdened by his secret, he took a deep breath and asked, "What are you going to do now?"

"Me? I'm going to accompany you to the Watch house, where you will tell Commander Shaul the truth."

For a moment, I could sense his internal struggle and readied myself to subdue him. But, praise Adonai, he nodded, glumly. "Yes."

The lantern was still on in the Watch house when we arrived. Commander Shaul was sitting at his desk drinking tea. He stood up immediately when he saw me. "What are you—"

Pushing Constable Elihu forward, I growled, "Tell him."

The young watchman stared at his feet. For a moment I feared that he would renege on his promise. Fortunately, his moral inflexibility won out. "Commander, I must confess a terrible sin."

Commander Shaul raised an eyebrow. "Oh? And what might that be? And should former-Senior Constable Gidon be here?"

"Yes," the constable nodded. "He convinced me to tell you that I lied about the capture of the Isiyim."

The commander motioned for the young watchman to sit down. "Go on."

Constable Elihu told the story, adding details he hadn't mentioned to me. On the night of the "capture" Reb Lemuel approached him on the street and said he had arrested the murderers himself and locked them in his storage shed. He offered to hand the two men over to Constable Elihu to give him credit for the arrest. The impressionable watchman agreed and together the two Sedukim fabricated the story of the capture on Vultures' Ridge.

Commander Shaul listened intently. By the look of distress on his face I could tell he knew nothing of this deception.

"Commander, when Constable Elihu brought the two men in did you search them?"

He nodded. "I searched their pockets and found the salt pouches."

"Did you examine their bodies to make sure they were Yehudim?"

He blushed. "No."

"Did you go to Vultures' Ridge to gather evidence to confirm the constable's story?"

"No. I had no reason to doubt Constable Elihu's testimony or Reb Lemuel's account of their confession. Besides, the Isiyim's clothes were covered in blood and they were carrying the same double-edged daggers that killed the saltseller."

"The same *kind* of daggers. But not necessarily the actual weapons."

Commander Shaul pursed his lips. "I concede that possibility."

"Did you interview the two suspects after Reb Lemuel interrogated them?"

"No. Reb Lemuel ordered me not to speak to them, since we're just holding them here until they're brought to Yerushalayim tomorrow."

I mentioned Reuven's claim that the two prisoners were Greeks who had lingered in his hashish den for two days.

Commander Shaul scoffed. "Why should I trust the word of a criminal?"

"Because I stopped by the shop when the Greeks were there as well."

"If the prisoners are the same men will you recognize them?"

"If I see them in their loincloths I might."

He blushed. "That's not enough of a reason to question them."

"Why not?" I asked. "Right now almost everyone in Bethlehem believes that either Yeshua or Yochanan is the Messiah. Any crime that's even remotely related to this conflict must be thoroughly investigated!"

"Does that include running off to brothels?" Commander Shaul retorted, without much conviction. "Some of us are accountable to the authorities!"

"No, you're accountable to the Laws and the administration of justice," I replied. "Once you start taking sides, or become a tool wielded by conspirators, you're no longer a servant of either the Laws or justice. Constable Elihu now understands this."

The young watchman nodded.

Glaring at the commander, I asked, "Did you know that someone tried to kill Yeshua ben Yosef by slipping a ribbon viper into his cradle?"

He looked away. "I heard about the snake. But there is no proof to support your claim that its presence was the result of a deliberate act."

"Well, there's certainly no proof if you don't investigate it. If I were in charge I would question every single man, woman and child who entered Yosef's house during the last few days."

His lip trembled. "Well, I'm not you."

"And apparently you're no longer you, either!" I snapped. "What happened to you, Commander? When you started the Watch you were as stubborn as I was. Committed to uncovering the truth, wherever it led. Never willing to accept a story at face value. But you became complacent. To tell you the truth, until this whole messiah thing started so was I. But Uriel's murder opened my eyes. Plotters are using the Watch for their own insidious purposes. Adonai is watching you, old friend. He is watching and judging you on what you will or won't do next."

His fingers instinctively twirled his sash. But this time, I wasn't backing down. Finally, he stood up and growled, "Gidon, you are a boil on my backside." Grabbing a ring of keys, he slid open a panel on the iron door of the cell and shouted, "Wake up!"

Constable Elihu and I joined him and gazed through a slot the panel covered. The two prisoners were slowly awakening from sleep. The stench of perspiration, rotting food and defecation was overwhelming.

Commander Shaul held up a lantern so I could see them more clearly. They were wearing keffiyehs and white cloaks spattered with dark stains of what looked like blood.

"Are these the same men you saw at the hashish den?"

I looked at them closely. "I'm not totally sure."

To the prisoners, he barked, "Stand up and remove your outer garments!"

Without protest the two men nonchalantly removed their cloaks and keffiyehs and stood facing us wearing only loincloths. They were short, clean-shaven men with pale, smooth skin. One was as thin as a bean plant; the other was pear-shaped.

"Turn around!"

As the lantern light fell upon their backs Constable Elihu gasped. Even in the dim light we could see the image of a beast with the head and torso of a man and the body of a goat engraved in dark ink on their backs. On their right shoulders each had a smaller tattoo of a grapevine.

Commander Shaul slid the door panel shut. Constable Elihu and I followed him back to his desk, where he sat down and shook his head.

Impatiently, I said, "Well? Are you still convinced these men are Isiyim?"

"I don't know what to believe anymore."

"Good. As my old rabbi used to say, 'When a wall of lies crumbles, you must sift through the rubble to find the truth.'"

He raised his hands. "What can I do? These men might not be Isiyim but that doesn't mean they didn't kill the saltseller. Reb Lemuel has already filed charges with the Sanhedrin. I don't have the authority to challenge them."

"Let me talk to the prisoners."

He shook his head. "You're no longer a member of the Watch."

"All the more reason for me to do so. The Sanhedrin can no longer order me around, so I'm free to pursue the truth as a private citizen."

Seeing his hesitation, I urged, "You and Constable Elihu can listen. Nothing that they say can be used in court, but at least you may find out who they really are. We owe this to Uriel."

The commander turned to Constable Elihu. "What do you think?"

The young watchman nodded. "Yes. He should speak to them."

With a deep sigh, Commander Shaul ushered us back to the cell. Sliding the panel open, he once again illuminated the prisoners with the light of the lantern. They were sitting on the floor in their loincloths. I often marveled at the ease with which the Greeks and Romans displayed their bodies. During the summer in Yerushalayim many of their women bared their breasts in public and on their athletic fields near their garrisons the men wore no clothes at all.

"Are you two all right?" I asked. "Is there anything we can do for you?"

"We hungry," said the stout man in a thick accent that reminded me of Mistress Helena.

"Okay. Commander, can we please get these men some food? Thank you. Now, I have some questions to ask you."

"What?"

"First of all, are you Isiyim?"

The thinner man asked, in a similar foreign accent, "You want us say yes?"

Constable Elihu returned with a basket of figs and bread and a wineskin. I held them up to the opening. "I want you to tell the truth. If you lie, you won't get any of this."

I could almost taste the drool on their lips. How long had it been since they had last been fed?

"Then we not Isiyim."

I pushed the food and wine through the slot. They immediately began stuffing their mouths and passing the wineskin between them. I let them gorge themselves for a few minutes before asking, "What are your real names?"

The thin man said, "I Petros, he Vasilis."

"What is your profession?"

They blinked, not understanding.

"What do you do for a living?"

"Ahh," Petros nodded, dribbling wine down his chin. "We Greek actors from Tyre."

Tyre was an Assyrian town on the coast of the Mare Nostrum. It was an important port for ships and soldiers arriving from Rome and Greece. Few Yehudim lived there.

"How did you two end up such a long way from home?"

"King Antipas invite us perform at big party for Romans in Metsada."[1]

I nodded. The Idomite ruler spent much of his time at the palace his father King Herod had built on the peak of this rugged plateau overlooking the southern edge of the Sea of Salt. "When was this?"

"Six day ago," said Vasilis. "You have more figs?"

"Soon. So, if you were hired by the king how did you end up here?"

"Ahh," Petros laughed, nervously. "Is funny story."

"Entertain us, then."

Taking a deep breath, he said, "Well, after party over, we come here for—how you say—vacation?"

"To Bethlehem?" I snorted.

Nodding fervently, he replied, "Oh yes! Greeks know Bethlehem famous for dream herbs and boy whores."

I didn't even need to look at my former colleagues to sense their wincing. "Go on."

"No boy whores but we find dream herb place run by cripple Yehudi with gold tooth."

I nodded. At least part of Reuven's story was confirmed. "How long did you stay there?"

"Hard to remember," Petros said. "How long we there, Vasilis?"

"Two, three days?"

"Maybe."

"So, why were you wearing bloodstained cloaks?"

"That good story, too. We run out of money and cripple Yehudi kick us out. On street strong man take us to house of fancy rich Yehudi who say he arrest us for—what is, Vasilis?"

"Drunk," said Vasilis.

---

[1]Masada.

"Yes, drunk. We no want jail so like good actors we get on knees and beg like babies," said Petros with professional pride. "Fancy rich Yehudi say he free us if we do job."

"And that was?"

"He not say at first. But we say yes. He let us stay in house. Slavegirl give us, bread, wine, almonds. We fall asleep. Later strong man wake us with stick."

"When?"

"Night," replied Vasilis. "Where are more figs and wine?"

"They're coming. What happened next?"

"Slavegirl give us cloaks to wear and funny knives and purple bags to hide in pockets."

"Where did the bloodstains come from?"

"Fancy rich Yehudi strong man spill sheep blood on knives and clothes."

"Did the fancy rich Yehudi tell you why he was doing this?"

"Yes, but I drunk so I not remember. Vasilis?"

"He hire us act like criminals caught by Yehudi watchman," said the stout man. "He say he pay thirty shekels and free us outside Yerushalayim. Thirty shekels! King Antipas only pay ten at Metsada."

"What happened next?"

"Strong man tie hands and put us in shed. Later fancy rich Yehudi come with watchman, who take us here."

I looked at Constable Elihu, who nodded. I grabbed his arm and positioned his face near the slot. "Is this the watchman?"

"Yes!" Petros clapped. "Thin one with crazy eyes."

Constable Elihu's shame filled the room. I guided him away from the slot. "Did you two kill Uriel ben Teman?"

The two men looked at each other with uncertainty. "Who?"

"The man whose murderers you were hired to impersonate."

"No!" shouted both men together. Petros continued. "Fancy rich Yehudi tell us pretend we is killers because watchmen too stupid to catch real killers."

I let the remark pass.

Their accents jogged a recent memory. "Do you know what the word 'denboronatvero' means?"

They nodded. Vasilis replied, "Sounds like Greek 'den boró na to vro.' Mean 'I not find it.'"

I rubbed my chin. According to Cassandra, one of Uriel's killers had said this after they had killed him. What couldn't he find? And if these two Greeks hadn't killed Uriel, why were the real murderers also speaking in Greek?

"Tell me: If the rich Yehudi hired you to pretend to be criminals, why are you telling us the truth now?"

Petros and Vasilis looked at each other. I could see panic spread across their dirty faces. "You not work for fancy rich Yehudi?"

I shook my head. "No." I slid the panel shut.

The Greeks shouted. "Wait! Come back! We not say truth!"

I slid it open again. "You're lying?"

"Yes!" Petros shouted. "We make up story about fancy rich Yehudi!"

"Oh," I replied. "Then the two of you did kill Uriel ben Teman?"

"No!" Vasilis raised his hand. "We not kill! We not do crimes!"

"I suggest that the two of you spend some time getting your story straight," I replied, sliding the panel shut again. Turning to Commander Shaul and Constable Elihu, I said, "Now you see the truth. These two actors couldn't have killed a mouse, let alone a man. Reb Lemuel is behind this masquerade, and Uriel's real killers are still free. What will you do now, Commander?"

As I stared at his ashen face, I genuinely felt sorry for him. If he challenged Reb Lemuel, all he had as evidence of this conspiracy was the testimony of two foreign actors and Constable Elihu. Reb Lemuel would deny the accusations and the Sanhedrin was far more likely to quash the whole thing rather than allow a terrible injustice committed by one of their own to become public knowledge. They might even fire my former colleagues for insubordination. Elihu would always be able to find work. But Shaul was too old to do anything else.

The commander turned to me. "I honestly don't know. What do you think?"

"When will Reb Lemuel take the two Greeks to Yerushalayim?"

"Shortly after sunrise."

"Who from the Watch is escorting them?"

"He is using his own guards."

"Doesn't that strike you as unusual? When is the last time at least one of us didn't serve as an escort?"

It was standard procedure. A watchman—sometimes two—always accompanied the official magistrate's van that brought all prisoners awaiting trial from Bethlehem to the Sanhedrin's prison in Yerushalayim. We were needed to fend off attacks from bandits and, on occasion, attempts by a miscreant's accomplices to free their comrade.

"If the Watch is not escorting them, it can only mean..." My voice trailed off.

Commander Shaul's eyes widened. "They'll never make it to Yerushalayim alive."

I nodded. "Reb Lemuel can't risk the two Greeks exposing his conspiracy, especially in a rabbinical court. Somewhere along the road his guards will kill them and bury them in the hills. A few hours later they'll stumble back into town, their clothes covered with blood, and Reb Lemuel will say a gang of fifty Isiyim overwhelmed them and freed the prisoners. He'll use this as an excuse to whip up anti-Isiyim hysteria and convince the Romans to attack Kumran."

Commander Shaul pondered this for a moment. "Perhaps."

I turned to Constable Elihu. "If the Watch gives custody of these two men to Reb Lemuel their deaths will be on your hands."

The shades of guilt and moral uncertainty that crossed the young man's face were as easy to read as a fable written for children. After a few minutes, he whispered, "We can't let him take them."

171

Commander Shaul stared at us and then began pacing around the room, his hands clasped behind his back. Finally, he stopped in front of Constable Elihu.

"Constable, you have committed a terrible sin."

Elihu's face paled. "I will turn myself into the Sanhedrin for punishment."

"You'll do no such thing," Commander Shaul replied. "You were manipulated by a man who was appointed by the most prominent leaders in Yehud to set the example of lawfulness and integrity. And for all I know other members of the Sanhedrin may be involved. But you are a good watchman, Constable. With a little more experience and maturity you may someday become a great one. So no one outside of this room will ever discuss your participation in this conspiracy, including our two prisoners. But you must go home now. Return here in an hour."

"What are you going to do, Commander?" asked Constable Elihu.

"It's better for you not to know."

The young watchman stood rigidly at attention. "I cannot leave if you intend to harm the prisoners."

"Who said anything about harming them? Now, shoo!"

After a moment of hesitation Constable Elihu left.

Commander Shaul turned to me. "You go, too."

I waved a hand. "You'll need some protection in case they try to harm you when you free them."

A tiny smile appeared on his face. "Who said I was freeing them?"

"I've known you for more than twenty years. During that time I've become fairly good at understanding how your mind works."

He pointed a finger at me. "If the Sanhedrin discovers that you were involved we'll both be arrested and executed."

"Then let's make sure they don't find out."

He returned to the cell and slid open the slot. The Greeks looked up at him.

"Give me your outer garments."

With apprehension, the men fed their cloaks and keffiyehs through the slot. The commander tossed them into the middle of the room. He then unlocked the cell and opened the door. "Go."

Petros and Vasilis stared at him. "What?"

"Get out of here. Leave the city. Quickly. Don't stop running until you're safely back in Tyre. Don't tell anyone who you are, how you were captured, and how you escaped. And never ever return to Yehud."

The two men stood up. "But fancy rich Yehudi—"

"He is lying. He will have you killed on the road to Yerushalayim. If you want to live, you must flee. Now."

The two men looked at each other and then carefully squeezed between us. As soon as they were out of reach they bolted for the door and ran out into the night.

Commander Shaul pointed at the pile of discarded clothes. "Can you get rid of these?"

I nodded.

He turned around and handed me his truncheon. "Now strike me."

"Is this really necessary?"

"Yes. You must knock me out. Otherwise, Reb Lemuel will never believe that the prisoners were able to escape from their cell without my help."

Tapping the truncheon against my palm, I said, "If I do this I could be arrested for attempted murder. I'm in enough trouble already."

He lowered his head. "What kind of trouble? You were never here."

CHAPTER 21

After I shredded the bloody garments and buried them in a field outside of town, I took a leisurely stroll back to the Watch house. When I arrived, a crowd had formed in front of the doorway. Commander Shaul was sitting on the ground as Constable Elihu applied a wet cloth to his head.

I pushed through the crowd. The commander's hair was matted in blood and his clothes were covered in dirt. He looked at me with an expression that seemed to say, *Thank you for helping, but did you have to hit me so hard?*

As I bent down to examine him more closely, a voice said, "Do not touch him."

I looked up to see Reb Lemuel. "He's hurt."

"Only a physician or representative of the Laws may touch him. You are neither," he replied.

And you are a conspirator and a liar, I wanted to reply, but now wasn't the time. At least I had the satisfaction of seeing Constable Elihu doing everything he could to avert his gaze.

I stepped back. Reb Lemuel cleared his throat. "Tell me again, Commander. How did the prisoners escape?"

Commander Shaul rubbed his eyes. "As I told you, Reb Lemuel, as I was opening the cell door to remove the chamber pot one of them jumped me and threw me against the wall. The other one grabbed my truncheon and knocked me out. When I awoke, both of them were gone."

"This was a serious lapse of security on your part, Commander," said Reb Lemuel. "Two murderers now roam the streets."

"I doubt it," I replied. "They're probably miles away from here."

Reb Lemuel glared at me. "If that is true, they've probably gone back to Kumran to seek sanctuary with their Isiyim brethren. We will ask the Romans to send a squad there to end their threat once and for all."

"I doubt they'll go back there, since that's the first place the authorities will look for them," I answered. "I know I'm no longer a watchman, but I would suggest going back to their encampment at Vultures' Ridge to see if there are any additional clues that might help us figure out where they're headed."

I winked at Commander Shaul, who, even in his concussed state, flashed me a small smile. "Yes, that is an excellent idea."

Reb Lemuel shook his head vigorously. "There is no need to return to that impure and sinful place. I've investigated it thoroughly."

"Are you sure, Reb Lemuel?" I asked. "Another set of eyes might be beneficial. For example, we might find evidence of what they were eating. Like bread. Or wine. Or almonds."

Even in the dim light of the Watch house lamp I could see the flush spread across the magistrate's pallid face. He started blinking rapidly and his lips began to tremble. I looked him in the eye and thought, *Yes, I know what you did. What are you going to do about it?*

"No! I forbid any member of the Watch from going there."

"I'm no longer a member of the Watch, so I'll go on my own as a private citizen."

"I forbid that, too!" Reb Lemuel yelled, almost in panic.

"I'm not as learned in the Laws as you, Reb Lemuel, but from my limited understanding your jurisdiction ends at Bethlehem's town limits," I replied calmly, scanning the crowd to guess whose side they were on. A few nodded. I remembered their faces. I might need them later if this got ugly.

"You would be disrupting a crime scene."

"If you investigated it already, I assume you gathered all the visible evidence, so there's nothing more to disturb, is there?"

"Blood was spilled there. The place is impure."

I shrugged. "When I was a watchman, just about every criminal I arrested was tainted with some kind of impurity or another. I've bathed in the Watch mikveh so many times even the centipedes know my name."

A few people laughed. Reb Lemuel glared at me. He might have been wealthier, more educated and more respected than me, but fifteen years of soldiering and two decades of marriage had sharpened my talent for debate to a fine edge. And right now Bethlehem's leading citizen wasn't accompanied by his own guard. The townspeople rarely witnessed anyone standing up to him and they were enjoying the spectacle.

Finally, Reb Lemuel gave in. "Fine. You have my permission to visit the site where the Isiyim murderers were hiding. But you will be accompanied by Constable Elihu."

Commander Shaul raised an arm. "I wish to go as well."

"No," said the magistrate. "You are wounded and must rest."

"I'll let you know if we find anything," I said.

"You will do no such thing. You are not a member of the Watch and thus have no authority. Constable Elihu will report any additional findings to the commander."

I motioned to Constable Elihu. "Okay. Let's go."

"No. It is night time and too dangerous to traverse these roads. You will meet at the western road at sunrise tomorrow. Not one moment before."

It had been a long and eventful day, and as much as I disliked the man I knew he was right. And I could use the rest.

"Will you be all right?" I asked Commander Shaul.

He nodded. "Yes. Constable Elihu will take me home and Junior Constable Amos is on his way to relieve me."

As I turned to go I thought, *After all of this shakes out, the vintner's son might be the only watchman left.*

CHAPTER 22

It had taken me hours to fall asleep that night, so I was exhausted when Naomi's piercing yell awakened me. "Gidon!"

I was getting a bit tired of these late-night and early-morning rousings but I felt differently when a deep breath filled my nostrils with smoke. For a moment, I thought our house was on fire, but the only light in the room came from a candle Naomi was holding as she stood near the front door.

"What's happening?"

"Fire!"

A cloud of smoke engulfed me as I stepped outside. In the distance I saw a yellowish glow illuminating the night sky on the west side of town. Throwing on a cloak, I grabbed a pail and said, "I must go."

"I'm coming, too."

"No. It's not safe. Stay here."

"You know I'm coming so let's not waste time arguing."

I nodded. When my wife had her mind set on something there was nothing I could do to stop her.

Dozens of people joined us as we headed toward the light, most of them carrying pails, buckets and kettles. Bethlehemites might disagree about many things, but in times of crisis we joined forces for the common good.

Along the way we encountered Junior Constable Amos, who was muscling through the crowd. "Where's the fire?" I asked.

"The Bet Shafa!" he shouted. My heart skipped a beat.

When we arrived, fire was raging on all three floors of the apartment building, illuminating a long bucket line of volunteers. The water they were valiantly tossing into the flames was having no effect.

"Does anyone know how it started?" I asked.

A beggar stepped forward. "I saw trails of fire fall from the sky and one of them went into a window on the first floor. Soon after, the whole building was aflame."

Chanoch the landlord was standing near the gate, tears streaming down his face. I grabbed him. "Chanoch! Is there anyone still inside?"

"I'm not sure. Most of the tenants are out here."

"How about Nogah ben Zilpah and his family?"

He shook his head. "I haven't seen them."

I felt a tug on my arm. I turned to see Miryam. She was cradling Yeshua in one arm.

"What?" I snapped.

"The baby is still inside," Miryam said.

"How do you know?"

Glancing at Yeshua, she replied, "We know."

"Is anyone else in the building?"

"No. He is the only one."

I looked up at the boards that covered the windows of Nogah's apartment. Streams of black smoke were spilling through the seams. "The child has surely perished."

"He is alive. You must save him," she said.

"I'll never make it."

"Yes, you will. You will be protected."

I don't know whether it was because of the angelic expression on her face or a momentary lapse of reason, but I grabbed a keffiyeh from a man's head, wound it around my mouth and ran toward the entrance.

"Gidon, don't!" I heard Naomi cry, but I plunged ahead anyway, entering the vestibule. Flames licked the walks of a central stairway. I limped up to the third floor, which was as hot as an oven and so thick with smoke I could barely see.

The door to Nogah's apartment was engulfed in flames. Saying a prayer, I felt searing heat surge through my right hand and arm as I pushed it open.

The walls and furniture were on fire. But the middle of the room was not burning–yet.

Without thinking, I ran across the smoldering rugs to the bassinet. Yochanan calmly looked up at me, his face and clothes black with soot. I scooped him up with my left hand and covered his face with my keffiyeh. Sprinting toward the door, I made it across the threshold seconds before the entire apartment erupted in flames. Clasping the baby to my chest, I held my breath and pressed my charred right hand along the burning walls to guide me down the stairs through a blinding fog of thick black smoke. My hair and clothes were smoldering but I didn't stop until I spilled out of the entrance and stumbled into the street. An old woman in a burka grabbed Yochanan while Chanoch and several men doused me with water and covered me with blankets to put out the flames.

"Gidon!" Naomi screamed as she broke through the crowd and threw her arms around me. "You foolish, reckless man!" Turning to the crowd, she yelled, "Get Zacchari ben Adam!"

Someone held a cup to my scorched lips. Never had Bethlehem's brackish water tasted so sweet.

Nogah ben Zilpah and his wife rushed forward. She was holding Yochanan, who seemed unharmed. "Bless you Senior Constable! Bless you for saving my child!"

"Why—was the boy—alone?" I wheezed, desperately trying to ignore the pain and stench of my burned flesh.

"Nogah and I always take a walk before sunrise. We left Yochanan with our nursemaid. When the fire started she and the guard panicked and ran out without him. If you hadn't rushed in—"

She started crying. Embarrassed, I slowly rose to my feet. Naomi walked me across the road to a bench where a large mob of onlookers surrounded me and gave me more water.

A moment later, the crowd parted. Miryam pushed through and knelt down next to me. Touching my arm, she said, "I told you that you would be protected."

Lunging like a lioness, Naomi growled, "Who gave you permission to touch my husband?"

Through a fit of coughing, I gasped, "Naomi, this is Yeshua's mother."

Naomi blinked and then stepped aside.

Miryam placed Yeshua's hand on my forehead. "And now you are whole."

Hesitantly, I lifted the blanket. Naomi gasped. My right hand and arm were completely healed. No burns, no blisters–even the hair had been restored.

I ran my fingers through my scalp. I distinctly remembered the sensation of flames roasting my skin. But all my hair was still there. And the pain was gone. The only evidence of my descent into the inferno was the burns and soot on my cloak.

I stared into Yeshua's brown eyes. *What are you?*

My attention was diverted by a sudden explosion. The entire apartment building was now a giant conflagration. Burning timbers and ashes swirled through the air, setting adjacent rooftops on fire.

Naomi helped me to my feet and we retreated to a safer distance from the rapidly spreading inferno. The bucket line dispersed. Once a fire like this began to spread nothing would stop it.

Commander Shaul and Constables Elihu and Amos ran up to me. "We must evacuate the town. Will you help us?"

"Of course," I replied.

"Constable Elihu, you take the south side, Junior Constable Amos, you take the–"

Suddenly, someone pointed up. "Look!"

The sky, which until now had been clear, was rapidly filling with thick, gray clouds. Moments later, thunder filled the air. Several onlookers fell to their knees in prayer.

At the front of the crowd, Miryam and Devorah stood next to each other. The infants in their arms were gazing at the gathering storm.

Moments later, the clouds opened, and Bethlehem was drenched in a torrential downpour. The road turned into a river of mud. Cisterns and wells filled in seconds. A fierce wind blew the rain in every direction and sheets of water spilled through the windows of the apartment building, dousing the flames with a violent hiss.

Then, as quickly as it started, the storm ended. The clouds evaporated and within minutes the first glimmers of dawn appeared in the eastern sky.

Crowds of people began gathering around the two families, reaching out to touch the infants.

Aviv the midwife shouted, "Let us give thanks to Yeshua ben Yosef for beseeching Adonai to quell the flames!"

A crowd of people shouted, "Amen!"

A man standing next to Nogah shouted, "No! It is the Messiah Yochanan we must thank for channeling the power of Elyon to raise the storm!"

A different crowd cheered. Others booed.

I could see where this was going. Instead of celebrating this miracle, Bethlehemites were returning to their quarreling ways.

"Yeshua is the true Messiah!" shouted his followers.

"A false Messiah!" countered Yochanan's contingent.

"The three scholars proclaimed him the Chosen One!"

"Really? Then why did they give their treasures to Yochanan?"

"They didn't! The treasures were stolen!"

"Is that so? Did you see it happen?"

"We don't need to see it to know it's true!"

The mobs around each family grew larger. Some were picking up stones, the usual way mob justice was dispensed in Yehud. But such violence had never been directed at infants. Maybe Yeshua or Yochanan could conjure up storms, but could they shield themselves and their parents from a barrage of projectiles? I didn't want to find out.

Commander Shaul and the two constables were trying to separate the two groups, their truncheons held high. I grabbed a broken fence post and joined them.

"You're no longer legally empowered to control crowds," exclaimed the commander as he knocked out a club-yielding thug.

"I wasn't empowered to rescue a baby either, but no one told me that," I replied, tripping an angry man armed with a large rock. "Should I leave?"

"It won't matter in a moment. As soon as they realize how outnumbered we are we'll be powerless to stop this idiocy."

I nodded. That was always the unspoken risk of being a watchman. You only had authority when people believed you had it. When someone else was being chased through the streets and dragged in chains to the Watch house onlookers always nodded in support, since it wasn't happening to them. But a mob often made its own rules.

I looked around for Naomi, desperately hoping that she wasn't caught up in the fracas. If any man laid a hand on her, only Adonai Himself would be able to prevent me from killing him.

Suddenly, without warning, both mobs fell back. I heard the sickening thud of wood hitting skulls. The crowd parted to reveal two large club-wielding guards. They were having an enjoyable time violently restoring the peace.

Supporters of each infant closed ranks around his family. Reb Lemuel stepped into the no-man's land between the two groups. "Is everything under control here, Commander?"

Commander Shaul lowered his truncheon. "We were outnumbered."

"Really?" He gazed at us with a smirk of amusement. "Even with the unauthorized assistance of your disgraced former colleague?"

I started to step forward. Commander Shaul held me back. Later I would thank him, because, left to my own devices, I might have beaten Bethlehem's most prominent citizen to a quivering pulp right then and there.

Sensing my rage, Commander Shaul replied, "Considering that Adonai was watching over Gidon as he ran into the Bet Shafa to save Yochanan ben Nogah, I figured that the Almighty would not object to him trying to prevent the massacre of both infants."

Reb Lemuel nodded. "And what was at the root of this...disturbance?"

Commander Shaul glared at both factions. "Supporters of each child were arguing over which one started the deluge that put out the fire."

"Indeed," said the magistrate. "Don't you feel that this conflict has elevated from a purely theological debate to one that threatens the peace and stability of our village?"

Commander Shaul glanced at me before answering, "Yes."

"Yet, several days ago I gave you an order that would have ended this conflict once and for all. I see that it has not been obeyed. Therefore, I will take matters into my own hands."

He approached the crowd surrounding Yeshua and stepped in front of Yosef.

"Yosef ben Yaakov, as the legal overseer of the Bethlehem Town Watch, I must apologize to you. Commander Shaul was given a direct order to inform you that your family has not been approved for permanent residency in Bethlehem. Had he obeyed this order, you would have had plenty of time to settle your affairs here. But because he failed to do so, it is you who must suffer for his negligence. By sunset three days from now, you and your family must vacate Bethlehem permanently. If you violate this order, you shall be arrested."

This time I wouldn't let my former commander stop me. Stepping in front of Reb Lemuel, I said, "And what about Nogah and his family?"

Reb Lemuel shook his head. "Their permanent residency is approved, as long as they find lodgings–" He gazed at the ruins of the apartment building. "–Somewhere else."

"You can't do that!" I snapped. "Yosef and his family have committed no crime. As magistrate, your job is to dispense justice to all residents of this town, not just those you favor!"

"To whom and how justice is delivered is no longer your concern, former senior constable," he replied, with considerable smugness. "Nor should it be the concern of anyone here."

"You are wrong, Lemuel!" Naomi pushed through the crowd, her eyes ablaze. Waving a finger in the magistrate's face, she continued, "It is the concern of any mother when those trusted with upholding the Laws would put the life of a child at risk!"

Reb Lemuel pursed his lips. "What a woman thinks is of no consequence." He quickly added, "In matters of the Laws."

As respected and feared as Reb Lemuel was, I think even he wished he could have taken back those words. I stepped aside, giving my wife plenty of room. When she finally spoke her voice could have frozen the sun.

"Lemuel ben Kfir, I have known you since the days your mother hired me to watch over you as a toddler. I would need more than two hands to count the number of times I kept you from falling into wells, stepping into hearth fires or getting trampled by mules. This *woman* is the reason you're standing here right now, instead of feeding the worms in the cemetery. So you had better listen to what *this* woman is telling you: Any Yehudi who would put the lives of an innocent family in danger might as well be an Assyrian or a Roman, for, like them, he is no Yehudi at all!"

Several people shouted in agreement. Commander Shaul nodded. "She speaks the truth, Reb Lemuel. Yosef and his family have as much of a right to live here as Nogah and his kin."

"Be careful, Commander," Reb Lemuel responded. "You tread on shaky ground here. Your negligence in allowing the two Isiyim murderers to escape is being scrutinized by the most senior members of the Sanhedrin. Over the years I have been your most stalwart defender, but in light of recent events I am beginning to have grave doubts about your fitness to continue in your current role."

I sucked in my breath, expecting my old friend to lower his eyes and beg to be given another chance. Instead, to my surprise, he rose to his full height and replied, "You know what, Reb Lemuel? I agree with you. I, too, have doubts about my own competency. For example, were I a better watchman, I would have ventured to Vultures' Ridge myself to investigate the area where the two accused murderers of Uriel ben Teman were allegedly camping."

Glancing at me, he said, "I would have interrogated the prisoners myself to gather evidence to build or refute the case against them instead of leaving this task to you. In doing so I would have acted as a true servant of the Laws. Indeed, perhaps I will accompany Gidon to Vultures' Ridge this morning as originally planned."

Not accustomed to having his authority questioned, Reb Lemuel was speechless for a moment. But then his usual arrogance returned. "You shall do no such thing. Your job is to find the men who set the Bet Shafa on fire."

He waved a hand at Yeshua's followers. "You should question them first, since they had the most to gain had Yochanan ben Nogah perished in the flames."

As he turned to go, I grabbed his arm.

"Excuse me, Reb Lemuel."

Shocked that I had the effrontery to touch him, it took him a moment to regroup. "Unhand me, tanner's son!"

Ignoring the insult, I replied, in a very loud voice, "I will, after you tell us how you know that the fire was deliberately set."

I was several inches shorter than him. This gave me a good view of his flaring nostrils. "What?"

"What proof do you have that someone set the building on fire? Were there witnesses?"

I looked around. To my great satisfaction, Naomi and my former colleagues were paying close attention.

I pressed further. "How do you know it wasn't an accident? A fallen candle. Sparks from a fireplace. A spill of cooking oil. So many ways a fire can start other than arson."

"I don't need to answer your questions!" he snapped.

Now it was Naomi's turn to press the attack. "My husband risked his life running into the inferno to save Yochanan. For that alone you owe him an explanation!"

Reb Lemuel looked around in desperation for support. Even his guards looked like they wanted to hear his answer. "We already know that Isiyim bowmen tried to fire flaming arrows into the Messiah's apartment!"

"You have proof that they were Isiyim?" I asked. "Were they the same ones who murdered Uriel ben Teman?"

Looking like a cornered fox, he replied, "I don't know! It's the responsibility of the Watch to find the answers. Maybe if its members spent more time investigating the cause of the fire instead of questioning my authority they might actually accomplish something!"

"What about Vultures' Ridge?" I asked.

"Go there yourself if you wish!" he yelled. "Since the murderers have probably reached Assyria by now, I doubt they'll ever be captured. I refuse to waste any more of the Watch's time on this foolishness."

He snapped his fingers and his two guards moved in front of him to clear a path through the crowd. After he was out of earshot, I turned to my former colleagues. "I've never seen him so agitated."

"He has many things on his mind," answered Commander Shaul. He then leaned in and whispered, "Are you going to visit Vultures' Ridge?"

"Again? No, I think once is enough."

His jaw dropped. "You were there already!"

"Yes. The day you fired me. The place was empty. No campfire, no blood, nothing." I glanced at Constable Elihu. "That's how I knew the story of the Greeks' capture was a fabrication."

"Then why did you want to go back there this morning?"

"To call his bluff. He didn't want me going there. So maybe he arranged for the fire to be set. As a diversion."

"You have no evidence to support this accusation!" snapped Constable Elihu.

"You're right. And he has no proof that the Isiyim started it either, but he was ready to convict them nonetheless. We already know that he lied about Uriel's murderers. Is there any reason to believe anything he says anymore?"

Commander Shaul said, "I would keep such thoughts to yourself."

"It's just conjecture among friends," I replied. "You're the Watch. It's up to you to decide what to do next. I'm just a private citizen, remember?"

He pulled me out of earshot and whispered, "You know I can't openly disobey the Sanhedrin."

"Who says—"

"Listen!" he snapped. "But—unofficially—I'm asking you continue your investigation. Talk to your sources. Look around the remains of the Bet Shafa to see if you can find out how the fire started."

"I know how it started. A witness said he saw trails of fire fall from the sky and enter an apartment."

He sighed. "Flaming arrows again. But if you knew this why did you suggest it might have been an accident?"

I flicked a smudge of ash off my cloak. "Because I wanted to see Reb Lemuel's reaction."

"And what did it tell you?"

"That while he is a liar and a conspirator, he probably didn't start the fire himself or hire someone to do so."

A tiny smile formed on his face. "How will the Watch ever solve crimes without the benefit of your devious ways?"

I shrugged. "That's your problem."

After he and the other watchmen had gone Naomi grabbed my arm. "Let me look at you."

"I told you, I'm fine. At least one of our Messiahs was watching my back. Maybe both."

"You're still coming home to rest. You've done enough for one day."

As we walked through the streets, which were only now beginning to clear of smoke, she said, "If I had known all these years that there would be such excitement every time you left the house I would have accompanied you more often."

"I'm afraid you would have been disappointed. I spent most of my time limping through my patrols, dodging rats and manure."

"Nevertheless, it would still be more entertaining than selling goat's milk."

"But far less profitable. Still, I might ask you to come along the next time I need to speak to Reb Lemuel."

"That man was born a mule and will die an ass."

"If I remember correctly, you were supposed to marry him."

She scoffed. "That was my father's idea. Until I told him I would never wed a man I once had to rescue after he fell into a privy hole. I had to spend hours in the mikveh before my father would let me in the house again. And later Lemuel had the gall to accuse me of pushing him in!" She smiled. "Thinking back on it, I wish I had."

When we arrived home I secured the door with a wood block.

"Why are you doing that?" Naomi asked.

I sat down on the edge of the bed. "Because the people who are trying to harm the two infants may also be going after me. Or you."

She laughed. "Please. You're a hero, not a threat."

"I'm not so sure. My investigations have shaken some very notable trees."

"Yes, but that was when you were a watchman. Those days are over."

I decided not to tell her about my clandestine arrangement with Commander Shaul. Instead, I re-examined my undamaged hand. I could still remember the searing heat from the door and the burning walls. There should have been nothing left but charred skin and bones. If my clothes didn't still reek of smoke I might have believed the whole thing was a dream. Then I remembered the Nochmah's words: *Yeshua will be known for working wonders...*

Naomi sat down next to me. "When will all of this end?"

"Who knows? One thing Reb Lemuel said that I agree with is that this messiah conflict is putting the entire town in danger."

"Do you think that Yosef and his family should be evicted from their home?"

"I wish both families would leave town. The census is almost over and many of the pilgrims are already leaving. Once Yeshua and Yochanan are gone, life can return to normal."

Her eyes twinkled. "Normal as in no more religious conflicts, no murders and no prison breaks? You will go insane with boredom!"

As a man whose future prospects were as desolate as the scrublands that surrounded Bethlehem, I could only shudder in agreement.

CHAPTER 23

To my surprise and relief, I awoke several hours later alive and refreshed. No one had tried to break into my house or burn it down. As Naomi slept I quietly searched every nook and cranny and found no serpents or scorpions, although I had to chase away a vole that had squeezed through a crack in the floor. I carefully opened the back door and found no assassins waiting to stick a dagger in my chest. I filled a bucket of water from the well. It didn't look any muddier than usual, nor did it smell of hemlock or arsenic.

Returning to the house, I began heating the water for tea and then opened the front door. The only thing that assaulted me was the heat of the morning sun. As far as I could tell there were no hired killers lurking in the shadows.

I went back inside and waited for the water to boil and wondered, *Is this what I'm going to be doing for the rest of my life?*

I thought about Reuven. Maybe he could hire me to work in his hashish den or in one of the other businesses he operated under cover of darkness. I could just imagine Constable Elihu arresting me for selling stolen ivory figurines and scarabs. Reb Lemuel would have a field day with that one. He'd be at the front of the stoning line.

I poured myself a cup of tea. Naomi woke up, milked the goats and headed off for the market. A short time later I grabbed my dagger and limped to the ruins of the Bet Shafa and searched for arrows in the debris. I found none. But I did encounter many looters who were scavenging for valuables. Since I was no longer a watchman I couldn't arrest them. I continued to hobble around town, greeting friends, merchants, tradesmen and beggars. They had all seen me running out of the burning apartment building with Yochanan clasped in my arm and treated me with respect and admiration. Several asked to see my miraculously healed arm and hand. I was happy to oblige them. I then headed for the inn and chatted with Sagiv. My prediction had come true. Visitors were now paying him three shekels a night to stay in the barn where Yeshua had been born. I walked to the synagogue and sat on the steps discussing the Torah and the weather with two old men, keeping an eye out for dung-wielding Kanai. Finally, I returned home and mucked out the cattle pen. At least this was one useful thing I could do. Naomi returned and cooked dinner. We ate, talked and went to sleep.

My retirement, day one.

Early the next morning there was a knock at the door. Grabbing my dagger, I carefully opened it. Commander Shaul was standing there, a scroll clenched in his hand.

I stepped outside. "So, they've finally issued a warrant for my arrest?"

He handed the scroll to me. "Read it."

I removed the wax seal and opened it. It was written in ornate Aramaic. After reading it, I grinned. "This has got to be a joke."

The commander shook his head. "I received one as well. King Antipas has invited us to Yerushalayim to receive honors as veterans of his father's army."

"But why today?"

He cocked his head to one side. "Don't you know what day this is?"

I shrugged. "I'm retired, remember? The passage of time means nothing to me anymore."

"It's the twentieth anniversary of the Battle of Teytma."

I scratched my head. "Which one was that?"

"I have no idea. But apparently it was an important one. We're to go immediately to the palace, where King Antipas is staying as a guest of the Romans. He will be bestowing the honors himself."

I was speechless. "Herod's son? Honoring *me*?"

"Not just you. All living veterans of King Herod's army. Or those who show up, anyway. So dust off your battle armor and let's get going."

"I don't have to bring my old shield, do I? The termites have eaten most of it."

"That won't be necessary. I don't think they're expecting us to fight."

"Are you sure? They say that Emperor Augustus uses slaves to stage mock battles in his amphitheater."

"Maybe so, but I can't imagine why anyone would want to watch a gang of old men re-enacting a battle they've spent years trying to forget. Come on, let's go."

I stopped. "Wait. I'm not leaving Naomi alone."

"Junior Constable Amos will guard her at the market and here until we return. I'll meet you at the Pilgrim's Highway in ten minutes."

Surprisingly, Naomi was fully in favor of this little venture. She had always complained that I never received the recognition I deserved for the years I had spent in distant bivouacs far away from home, leaving her to raise our son by herself. She wouldn't even let me go until she had scrubbed the dirt from my "official" battle armor.

It had languished in a chest for nearly eleven years. With good reason, as its cheap leather wouldn't have withstood the assault of anything heavier than a feather. The only attractive thing about it was its emblem, a golden eagle. In the army I was required to wear it but since it offered no real protection I always wore my father's leather armor under it. When I retired from the army, I exiled King Herod's armor to storage. Today I wore both armors because I wasn't convinced that we wouldn't be ambushed on the way to Yerushalayim.

My worries turned out to be groundless. Commander Shaul had rented a mule cart to take us to the capital. No one tried to rob or assault us along the way. I was almost disappointed. It would have been nice to tell the king that two veterans of his father's army had engaged in a skirmish on the way to a ceremony honoring their service.

We were to enter Yerushalayim through the Isiyim Gate. Several dozen Roman guards stood on either side of the slope leading to the entrance. If their purpose was to intimidate us, they were succeeding. With their plated armor, red tunics and curious helmets topped with crests of dyed boar's hair they resembled dangerous roosters. Most wore a protective metal strip on their left leg. I would have given a week's pay to have one of those during my army days. It might have saved my knee.

On a low rise in the distance I noticed something that looked like a giant crossbow mounted on a platform with wheels. "What is that?"

"A Roman siege weapon," replied Commander Shaul. "It can shoot projectiles long distances."

As much as I hated the Romans, I was impressed. With weapons like that, how could anyone ever hope to prevail against them?

We joined a long procession of pilgrims, merchants and tradesmen waiting to pass through the gate. More guards stood at the entrance. I had been through this gate many times and usually there were no more than one or two Romans posted there.

"Why so many roosters?" I asked.

"Extra security for Prefect Coponious, who is attending the ceremony."

"He's come all the way from Caesarea Maritima to watch his vassal honor a bunch of old Yehudim?"

"Not just that. There are reports that the Kanai have been attacking nearby Roman outposts. The Prefect is here to restore order."

A nervous pheasant escaped the grasp of a young boy in the cart in front of us. The driver screamed at him to recover the bird. As we watched the boy chase it Commander Shaul cracked a small smile.

"This whole ceremony is symbolism and nothing more. The Romans are using it to remind us that they and Herod's family have been working together for forty years to keep Yehud from falling into the hands of our enemies."

"But Antipas doesn't rule Yehud."

"True, but some Yehudim, including the Kanai, believe it's only a matter of time before a new generation of Maqabim[1] rises up and throws them out the same way the Hashmunayim got rid of the Seleucids. You remember all those

---

[1] Maccabees.

uprisings after King Herod died? How many Yehudim were slaughtered in retaliation for the acts of a few idiots? The Prefect and King Antipas don't want a repeat of that foolishness again. If a ceremony like this creates the illusion that the Romans and Idomites are our friends and protectors, they'll think it's worth the effort."

I nodded. After King Herod passed away his lands were divided among his three sons, Archelaus, Antipas and Philip. Archelaus ruled Yehud and immediately earned the enmity of the Yehudim by violently crushing a half-hearted rebellion and massacring thousands of innocent men, women and children in retaliation. He then tried to assert direct control over the Temple and raised taxes to cover his enormous debts. Unable to quell the constant unrest, he was ousted by the Emperor Augustus, who put Yehud under the control of the governor of Assyria. Publius Sulpicius Quirinius now served in this role with Prefect Coponious serving as the day-to-day administrator. King Herod's son Philip was given control of the desert lands east of the Nahar al-Urdun. Antipas held nominal rule over Galil and the western lands.

As we passed through the Isiyim Gate, I doubted that any of the scowling guards who waved us through cared much about the history of our oft-conquered land. Nor would they know that this gate led to an area of the city that had spawned the Isiyim sect and had once been the epicenter of its spiritual life.

But those days had long passed. The only things the Isiyim who still lived here had in common with their brethren in Kumran were their linen cloaks and long, scraggly beards. There were few actual dwellings here. The inhabitants sat on the ground outside primitive lean-tos, mud huts and tents amid the scattered remnants of buildings that had probably been destroyed by the Bavel centuries ago. They stared into space, completely oblivious to the flies that swarmed their faces and the rats that nibbled at their clothing. The air was thick with the stench of sweat and human waste. I could see now why so many of them had abandoned the city to make a new home in the wilderness.

I sighed with relief when we left its squalor and continued along the road toward King Herod's old palace. It had been built on a platform in the northwest corner of the upper level of the city. There were two buildings, each with hundreds of rooms, surrounding a central garden lined with lemon trees and olive groves and a network of ponds and canals. Rising above the northern side were three gigantic towers.

King Herod himself had rarely stayed there, preferring to live in the many other palaces he had built in Yehud. When the Romans formally took over Yerushalayim they annexed the palace and now used it a government office and as lodgings for its petty bureaucrats.

Ironically, few Yehudim ever had the chance to venture beyond the imposing stone walls that surrounded the palace. The same monarch who had spent a vast fortune rebuilding the Temple had a strong aversion to fraternizing with his subjects. Was it because he was afraid of assassination, or because being in the presence of the children of Yisroel reminded him that his family had been forced to convert to our faith and his tenuous hold on power was due solely to his willingness to be a vassal of the Romans?

Commander Shaul and I were among the few commoners who had actually visited the palace and seen the old king in person. It was after our regiment had won a great battle against some enemy in the north whose name I could no longer remember. We entered Yerushalayim bearing tribute, which we placed in the center of the great central plaza as the king gazed down upon us from the minaret of the tallest tower. For me, the sight of all this majesty was overwhelming. But what had impressed me most were the huge marble blocks out of which the towers had been constructed, each one larger than a man. It was said they had all been fitted together perfectly without mortar and that not even a herd of elephants could dislodge them.

We left the cart at the palace gate and were escorted by a Roman guard to the main courtyard. It was no less impressive today than it had been during my first visit. The main difference was the unsettling presence of numerous statues of naked men and women occupying prominent places in the gardens and ponds. And the seemingly endless stream of guards and toga-clad officials who bustled about like ants. It drove home the point that, bit by bit, the Romans were chipping away the Yehudi identity of this ancient city.

We were taken to the central plaza where we joined a group of 34 other men ranging in age from 30 to 70. Commander Shaul and I recognized several former members of our regiment. I hadn't seen any of them in more than a decade. They must have been as shocked at the sight of my graying hair and wrinkled skin as I was with theirs.

An old hunchback ambled over to us and waved his cane at our faces. "Ah, if it isn't my old squad leader Shaul and his trusty manservant."

Commander Shaul stepped in front of me to prevent me from answering this insult. He needn't have worried. I would never harm a cripple.

"It is good to see you, Yediah," said the commander.

"Likewise," the old man replied, flashing a grin of toothless gums. "It appears that the years have been kind to you."

"Baruch ha-Shem," Commander Shaul replied.

"Alas, I haven't been so blessed. As you can see, I never fully recovered from my battle wound. You remember, don't you?"

Commander Shaul nodded uncomfortably. One day our squad was conducting a routine patrol in the hills surrounding Yericho. As we were entering a narrow pass we were ambushed by bandits. We killed all of them, but Yediah had taken a spear in his lower back. We brought him back to our camp, where he lingered on the edge of death for three days. For two weeks he could not move his legs. Eventually, he recovered but he could no longer stand up straight. Now useless as a soldier, he was discharged and sent home. I was surprised he had lived this long.

"So, what have you been doing all this time?" asked Commander Shaul.

"When I returned home to Yaffa I discovered that no one wanted to hire a cripple, and my discharge pay wasn't enough to keep my wife in fancy clothes and jewels. So she divorced me and married the tailor she had been seeing while I was fighting the Arabs with you. Since the only thing I was good for was begging, I came here to Yerushalayim, where I've been shaking a bowl outside the Temple gates ever since. I'm hoping fat Antipas will be giving us money today. Business hasn't been since so good lately."

Commander Shaul reached into his pocket and brought out a handful of shekels, which he held out to Yediah. The old man snatched them and wandered off.

"Not even a thank you," I said.

"He doesn't need to show gratitude. He lost everything because of me."

"He was a soldier, like all of us. He knew the risks. I took an arrow in the knee and I don't hold that against you."

"Yes, but you were wounded in a real battle. He was injured by bandits because I didn't anticipate their attack. I was lax in my duty and he suffered for it."

I was surprised at his candor, because I had felt the same way back then. We had been told that there were no enemy soldiers in the vicinity so Shaul hadn't ordered us to wield weapons and shields. We were essentially defenseless when we were ambushed. It was one of the commander's few mistakes but it had been costly. In all these years I had never spoken to him about it. Seeing Yediah again had clearly rekindled his feelings of guilt.

Was it any wonder that most of us had few fond memories of our service? All those years and lives lost, and for what? To keep an imposter in power long enough to hand over our ancient homeland to the Romans? No wonder so many in Yehud were yearning for a Messiah to free us all.

The unlikelihood of such deliverance occurring anytime soon was driven home by the sight of a dozen Roman guards emerging from the palace, followed by a thin man with short gray hair dressed in a toga.

"That's Prefect Coponious," Commander Shaul whispered.

The guards formed a circle around us, leaving the Prefect standing by himself. He eyed us with disdain.

Several minutes later, ten of King Antipas' courtiers emerged, dressed in flowing white cloaks laced with threads of blue. To my surprise, they were followed, at a respectable distance, by Reb Lemuel.

What is he doing here? I wondered. As a member of the Sanhedrin, Reb Lemuel represented Bethlehem whenever the Romans needed well-connected Yehudim to do their dirty work for them, such as collecting taxes and turning in rabble-rousers for the Romans to crucify at their convenience. But I never knew he had this much influence.

Finally, King Antipas emerged, dressed in a fine white robe adorned with blue and green gemstones. On his head he wore an intricately decorated keffiyeh. I was surprised that he was walking. His father had always been transported in a lectica borne by slaves.

The king was a huge man, at least six feet tall and as round as a gourd. A patchy beard couldn't hide the acne scars on his moon-shaped face and his skin was as pale as sheep's wool. This was a man who rarely ventured outdoors and embraced a sedentary lifestyle.

I could hear the wheezing in his voice as he slowly ambled toward us, accompanied by his chamberlain and two heavily armed Roman guards. Apparently, he didn't trust his own guards for protection, and with good reason. Twice in the past year members of his household staff had tried to poison him. It was rumored that he had mounted their severed heads on poles in his courtyard as a warning to future would-be assassins.

He stopped a short distance from the edge of the circle that surrounded us. The chamberlain stepped forward and, in a nasal voice with a noticeable lisp, announced, "On this, the anniversary of the Battle of Teytma, His Majesty King Antipas welcomes the brave soldiers of Yehud who had the honor of fighting in the army of His Majesty's father against the barbarians who sought to conquer the Holy Land."

He placed particular emphasis on the word *barbarian,* a word the Romans used to describe their enemies. It came from the Latin word for "beard," reflecting their view that men with facial hair were uncivilized savages. This included the Yehudim, even though our kingdom had been established more than five hundred years before the first Romans stepped foot on our shores.

The chamberlain continued. "Today, His Majesty will reward you for your service by giving all non-officers the Award of Valor."

The Romans herded us into a single line, hands at their hilts in case anyone harbored thoughts of regicide. A courtier carrying a small chest approached the chamberlain and they and the king moved to one end of the line.

Turning to Commander Shaul, I asked, "Why are you being honored? You were a squad leader."

"That's not an officer's rank," he replied. "Only Idomites were allowed to serve as officers."

"You mean the ones who sat in their tents drinking wine and playing dice while we Yehudi rabble did all the killing and dying?"

"Yes. Now be quiet!" Commander Shaul hissed, looking around to make sure no one heard.

I stole a glance and saw the chamberlain place what looked like a necklace over a veteran's head.

"We came all this way for a medal?"

"Shhh!"

When the king's entourage reached me, I bowed my head and closed my eyes. I felt something rough brush against my neck. I opened my eyes and looked down at an oval silver medallion attached to a leather chain.

On one side of the medallion was an etching of a vine. On the other side, a pomegranate.

You weren't supposed to look directly at royalty, but I broke protocol and glanced at the king and noticed the same two symbols embroidered on his keffiyeh. Suddenly, all sense left me and I said, "The symbols on this medal are very intriguing, Your Majesty."

The king, who was clearly not expecting this kind of effrontery, nearly jumped out of his skin. Commander Shaul look startled. From across the plaza

I could see Reb Lemuel's eyes widening. Only Prefect Coponious seemed oblivious to my egregious violation of royal etiquette.

The king pulled the chamberlain aside and spoke into his ear. The chamberlain nodded and replied, "His Majesty is surprised that a veteran of his father's army is not aware that the pomegranate and the vine are the symbols of his reign."

Bowing, I said, "May His Majesty forgive me for being old and ignorant, but I don't remember His Majesty's father, blessed be his memory, using such symbols."

The other veterans began to back away from me, staring at the ground as if to say, *Who is this man? Wasn't in my squad. Never saw him before in my life.* I was tempting fate, but I could barely suppress my anger.

The chamberlain nodded. "That is correct. His Majesty introduced these symbols at the start of his own reign. Because you are from the rural village of Bethlehem your ignorance is understandable."

"Yes, we tend to be a bit behind the times on such things," I agreed.

The chamberlain huddled in conversation with the king for a moment and then asked, "What is your name, soldier?"

"I am Gidon ben Einan."

The king again whispered in the chamberlain's ear. He ran over to the Prefect and shouted, "Prefect Coponious, His Majesty the King demands the immediate arrest of this man!"

The Prefect looked up from a scroll he was reading and replied, in perfect Aramaic, "On what grounds?"

I was impressed. Most Romans never bothered to learn our language beyond its words for "wine" and "whore."

"For fomenting rebellion among the Yehudim."

The Prefect gazed at me with amusement. "This gimpy old man? He can barely walk."

I winced. That hurt, mostly because it was true.

"This Gidon ben Einan, who is employed as an enforcer of Yehudi Law, has been seen on many occasions championing the claims of a false messiah known as Yeshua ben Yosef."

The Prefect sighed and handed his scroll to an assistant. He then approached me and said, "Serious accusations have been made against you, Yehudi. How do you respond?"

"These accusations are untrue, honorable Prefect," I responded in Latin, much to his surprise. And much to the dismay of the king and his chamberlain, whose baffled expressions revealed their ignorance of the language spoken by their overlords.

Bowing my head, I continued, "First of all, Prefect, I am no longer employed as a law enforcer. Reb Lemuel, our town's magistrate, can verify this as he was the one who had me fired from the Bethlehem Town Watch. However, it is true that before I was let go I was investigating the theft of valuable items given to the infant Yeshua ben Yosef, who many in Bethlehem believe to be the Messiah as foretold by our Prophets. It is my contention that these gifts later ended up in the custody of another infant, Yochanan ben Nogah, who others in our small village also claim to be the Messiah."

Prefect Coponious smiled and replied, in Latin, "Infants, you say? Your saviors seem to be getting younger and younger these days."

It wasn't a particularly funny riposte, but I responded with far more laughter than it deserved. "Yes, Prefect, normally we try to wait until our messiahs are old enough to grow a beard, but we're an impatient people and always need to be arguing about something, whether it's the price of wheat or the person our God has chosen to be His Chosen One."

His smile disappeared. "What about you? Which of these infants do you favor?"

"I favor neither, Prefect. As an investigator, I shape my views based on evidence."

The Prefect gave me a quizzical look.

"You see, Prefect, neither of these infants has yet restored the kingdom of Yisroel to its former glory. As far as I'm concerned you can't really be proclaimed the Messiah until you've accomplished this. Of course, I realize that many people disagree with me on this point."

The Prefect chuckled. Inside, I felt relieved. The longer I amused him the less likely he'd order one of his guards to run me through with a sword. Or so I hoped.

"Then if you're not supporting either child, why does the king believe you are fomenting rebellion?"

Bowing my head, I replied, "This simple lowborn subject would never attempt to understand the exalted ruminations of royal minds, Prefect. Before I was fired from the Watch all I was trying to do was solve a theft. Oh, and to figure out who killed an old man who was the only witness."

The Prefect rubbed his chin. "If you were able to find those responsible for committing these crimes would this eliminate all this unrest I've been hearing about?"

"I'm sure it would, Prefect. In my experience I've found that capturing dangerous criminals is almost always a proven tonic for restoring the peace."

The Prefect nodded. He then stepped back and shouted, in Aramaic, "Can anyone here vouch for the character of this man?"

I held my breath. Had I gone too far? I looked around. The other soldiers stared at their feet. Reb Lemuel avoided my gaze. But was there a tiny smirk on his face?

Commander Shaul stepped forward. "I will vouch for him."

"And you are?" asked the Prefect.

"Commander Shaul ben Yoav of the Bethlehem Town Watch."

Pointing at me, the Prefect asked, "And how do you know this man?"

"He reports–used to report–to me."

"In your opinion is he fomenting rebellion in your town?"

Commander Shaul paused a minute to gather his words. "Gidon ben Einan is stubborn, argumentative, headstrong and occasionally exercises bad judgment. But he is also honest, law-abiding, objective, and a loyal servant of the Yehudim and a dedicated preserver of the peace. He would never do anything or align with anyone or any cause that would pose a threat to Yehud, the king, or the emperor."

Tears started welling in my eyes. I never knew that Shaul felt this way about me. He was going to get a new winter tunic for his birthday, even if had to shear the wool and weave it myself.

The Prefect stepped back. "And is there anyone here who has personally witnessed this man attempting to incite rebellion?"

I glanced at Reb Lemuel. I wouldn't have been surprised if he accused me of being the ringleader of the Kanai. But he kept his mouth shut.

The Prefect nodded. He stepped back and pronounced, in a loud voice that filled the plaza, "Then it is my decree in the name of Emperor Augustus that this man shall not be arrested. Furthermore, it is also the emperor's wish that he be restored to his former rank in the Bethlehem Town Watch to bring to justice those whose crimes have seeded this unrest."

I sneaked a glance at the king. He looked like a newly castrated eunuch. His lip trembled and his fat face seemed to sink into his multiple chins. I looked at Reb Lemuel and wished I had papyrus and a stick of charcoal to sketch his dumbfounded expression.

The Prefect stepped back. "And now, Your Majesty, I believe that you still have some awards to bestow, do you not?"

As the king and his entourage continued to hand out pendants, Commander Shaul leaned over and whispered, "You must learn to curb this death wish of yours."

I shrugged and replied, "I hope you haven't thrown away my sash and truncheon."

He nodded. "I've kept them in a chest at the Watch house, just in case."

"Thank you for standing up for me."

He sighed. "The Sanhedrin will make me pay for it later. Tell me, is there anywhere in Yehud where your presence doesn't raise havoc?"

I grinned. "I've heard there's a little village on the outskirts of Azzah, but that's only because I've never been there."

When the king was finished he led his entourage and Reb Lemuel back into the palace. As our little band of veterans was dispersing, Prefect Coponious called out my name.

"Uh oh," I murmured.

"Good luck," Commander Shaul replied.

Approaching the Roman in a humble manner, I meekly asked, in Latin, "Yes, Prefect?"

Motioning for me to follow him to the shade of a fig tree, he said, "Is it true that you ran into a raging inferno to rescue one of your messiahs?"

"Prefect, what I can say with all honesty is that I ran into a burning building to save the life of a baby."

"It's also said that you killed a snake that would have poisoned your other messiah."

"Again, Prefect, I was trying to prevent harm from coming to an infant."

He smiled. "You're getting quite a reputation for acts of heroism. There are some who call you 'the messiah's savior.'"

How does he know so much about me? I wondered, while replying, "I try not to make a habit of it, Prefect."

"Of course, we Romans consider the very idea of a messiah to be nothing more than superstitious nonsense buoyed by a conquered people's misplaced hope. Nonetheless, there are some who say that you Yehudim would all be better off had both of these infants perished."

"I hope never to encounter such men, Prefect, for among our people there is no greater sin than causing, permitting or wishing for the death of a child."

He laughed. "You truly are as flippant as your detractors claim, Senior Constable Gidon. And you seem to attract excitement like manure attracts flies. Fighting off bandits, saving messiahs, investigating grisly murders. When do you find the time to patrol the streets?"

"Trust me, Prefect. The job is rarely this exciting."

"Perhaps so," he said. "But since I admire your bravery and devotion to duty, let me warn you that you came very close to losing your life today."

Before I could respond, he leaned in and said, "Assassins were hired to kill you and your commander outside the Isiyim Gate. That's why I placed extra guards there."

For a moment I was speechless. "Who hired them?"

"Take one guess."

I glanced in the direction of the palace and whispered, "The *king*?"

He nodded. "Antipas has at least two spies in Bethlehem. Fortunately, I have several of my own among his courtiers and servants. He appears to be obsessed with killing the infant Yeshua and anyone he believes is protecting him. Including you."

I'm not protecting him, I thought. *If anything, the child protects me.*

"Why is the king so afraid of him, Prefect?"

The Prefect rolled his eyes. "I can't even attempt to understand your people's obsession with messiahs. It seems like every day a new one pops out from under a rock."

"We're a hopeful people, Prefect."

"This I don't mind. As long as you're not a rebellious people. We can't have another ruckus like we had when Antipas and his brothers were fighting for the throne. That's why Emperor Augustus took direct control of most of Yehud and gave the unimportant parts to Antipas and his brother Philip. It works out well this way. Each man has a little bit of power but not enough to make waves. But this stability could be shattered if Antipas conspires to pave the way for his own kin to become king of the Yehudim."

I gazed at him in confusion. "Prefect, I apologize if you're already aware of this, but according to Yehudi traditions no one from Herod's family can be the Messiah. They're Idomites who converted to our faith."

"Actually, there is one member of Herod's extended family who qualifies."

"Who?"

"The son of Nogah ben Zilpah."

He smiled at my reaction.

"Wait–how is Yochanan related to King Antipas?"

"Nogah is Antipas's second cousin. From a branch of the family that can trace their unbroken Yehudi lineage back to your King Dovid, I am told."

I rubbed my chin. "Yochanan was born in Bethlehem, a few days after Yeshua."

"And Antipas's people made sure he would be. They even paid for his lodging."

I nodded. Now it made sense how a goatherd could afford to live at the Bet Shafa.

"And, from what I hear, there are almost as many people who believe that the Doran is your messiah as those who favor the Notsrim."

Looking him in the eye, I asked, "And what do you believe, Prefect?"

He dismissed my question with the wave of a hand. "As I said, this is all nonsense. Of course, if I'm wrong, it will be many years before either child will be old enough to lead your people into rebellion. By then, I'll either be reassigned, retired or dead. I'm less concerned about the future than I am about the present. You Yehudim can go on arguing about your saviors all you want. As long as you do it peacefully. And I'm trusting you and your commander to make sure the peace is kept."

He patted me on the arm. "In the meantime, I suggest that you return home as soon as possible. I'm fairly certain that Antipas won't try to murder you here in the city, but you will have to rely on the protection of your own god on your journey back since I cannot spare any guards to accompany you. Good day, Senior Constable Gidon. And good luck."

After he left, I quickly grabbed Commander Shaul and found our cart.

"What did the Prefect want?" he asked.

"Shhh," I cautioned. "I'll tell you later."

As we left the city I looked around and said, "Keep your eyes open. And be ready for a fight." On the way home I recounted my discussion with the

Prefect, while constantly scanning the hills and road for signs of assailants. Commander Shaul wasn't aware that Yochanan was related to Antipas. I wondered: *Do the Doran's followers know? And would it make a difference if they did?*

Fortunately, no one attacked us and we reached Bethlehem late in the afternoon. Commander Shaul returned to the Watch house and I limped home as fast as I could.

My heart nearly stopped when I saw streaks of blood spattered on the doorstep. I rushed inside. The table and chairs had been overturned and there were bloodstains on the floor and walls.

White-hot anger overcame me. I pulled out my dagger and screamed, "I will kill, kill, kill all of you!"

Two strong hands grabbed me from behind and stripped me of my weapon. I spun around and began wildly striking hard flesh with my fists and feet.

"Gidon! Stop it! Stop it!" A familiar voice wrenched me from my berserker's rage. I turned around and gazed into the worried face of Reuven.

"Naomi!" I gasped, straining against an iron-like grip.

"She's fine!" Reuven assured me, urgently. "She's not harmed in any way. That's more than I can say for the other fellows." He gestured for his burly guard to let me go.

Grabbing Reuven's arm, I said, "What do you mean?"

Wincing in pain, he replied, "Come with me. It is not safe to talk here."

"Where is she?"

"We'll take you there."

He gently touched my elbow and guided me into the street.

"What happened?" I begged.

"Shhhh," he replied. "All will be revealed."

They brought me to the Watch house. Naomi was seated at the table, surrounded by Commander Shaul and my fellow watchmen. As I rushed to embrace her she shook her head. "No, Gidon! I am unclean!" It was only then that I noticed the streaks of blood on her hands and cloak.

I didn't care. I grabbed her and held her close. "I went home–I saw the blood–"

Commander Shaul stepped forward. "Senior Constable, an hour before you and I arrived back in town two men invaded your house."

I glanced at Junior Constable Amos, who had a cloth pressed to his head. "You were supposed to be guarding her."

"I was," he replied. "They jumped me from behind. One of them knocked me out." He lifted the cloth to reveal a large lump on his head clotted with dried blood.

Naomi continued. "They had come to kill you, my husband. But when they discovered you weren't there they tried to attack me."

She stopped and shook her head in horror.

"What?" I asked, "How did you–"

"I was hoping to fend them off with a candlestick, but when I went to grab one I found this in my hand instead."

On the table was a bloodied knife with a long curved blade and a handle made of olivewood. It looked familiar. Very familiar.

"I don't know how it got there but once I felt its handle in my grip a spirit took over my body. I don't remember anything that happened next. When I came to, the two men were dead, and I was covered in blood."

"Who were the assailants?" I asked Commander Shaul.

He hesitated. "They were…wearing the garments of Isiyim."

"And wielding their weapons, I suppose."

He nodded, pointing to two double-edged daggers on his desk.

"Where are the bodies?"

"With Itzchak ben Akiba. He is preparing them for burial."

"I must examine them."

Commander Shaul shook his head. "It's late. You're exhausted."

Ignoring him, I said, "Someone needs to collect our bedding and clothes. Naomi will stay here until—"

Reuven waved a hand. "Senior Constable, in my home I have a comfortable guest room with a down mattress large enough for two. You and your wife are welcome to stay with me for as long as you wish. My men will bring anything you need from your house."

Commander Shaul shook his head. "I cannot allow a known criminal to—"

Reuven raised his hand to interrupt. Pointing to his guard, he said, "Commander, do you see this man?"

"Yes."

"He accompanied you and Senior Constable Gidon on your journey to and from Yerushalayim."

"I didn't see him."

"You weren't supposed to. But he was very busy. On your return trip he prevented a hidden archer from striking you down."

"How do you know he was targeting us?" asked Commander Shaul.

"The man confessed, after considerable discomfort."

"Who hired him?"

"Alas, my guard was not able to coax this information from the bowman before he—accidentally—shot himself with his own arrows."

The commander pursed his lips. "I could have you both arrested for murder."

"Perhaps, but you would need evidence, such as a corpse and a weapon. The chances of you finding either are negligible."

Thinking this over, Commander Shaul turned to me. "If you wish to accept this man's offer of hospitality, I will not stand in your way."

Naomi stepped forward. "But I must refuse. I cannot defile your home with my impurity."

Bowing, Reuven said, "Dear lady, my attitude about such things is far more moderate than those of the Sedukim. But if you are concerned we can stop by the women's mikveh on the way. While you are there I can dispose of your defiled clothes and provide the attendant with replacements, if you have no objections to wearing the garments of my late wife."

Naomi nodded. "You are very kind." She turned to me. "Is this is acceptable, my husband?"

"Yes. Go with him. I'll join you later. But first, I must speak to you in private."

When we were out of earshot, I leaned in close and said, "I know that your father trained you how to fight with a knife. Are you certain that you don't remember what happened?"

She looked me straight in the eye and replied, "It must have been a spirit. For how could a mere *woman* ever defeat two armed men all by herself?"

I kissed her on the forehead and motioned for Reuven to escort her to his home. After they were gone, I grabbed Commander Shaul by the elbow and said, "Quickly. We must get to Itzchak before he buries the bodies."

He shook his head. "You need to be with your wife right now."

"Yes, I know I do. But the knife that killed her assailants belongs to Yosef. Somehow, Adonai transported it to her hand so she could defend herself. I owe it to her–and Him–to find out who they were."

"All right."

"I want to come with you," said Constable Elihu.

"Why?" I asked.

"My lies have caused enough damage. Maybe helping you uncover the truth will help to mend my corrupted soul."

Were I more of a cynic, I might have replied, "Or perhaps you're looking for another way to have your suspicions about Isiyim confirmed." But when I looked into his eyes, all I could sense was his sorrow and desire for redemption. Maybe somewhere inside this young fanatic a great watchman was waiting to emerge after all.

Bethlehem's mortuary was a large stone building that stood alone in a fenced-in plot of land on the northeast edge of town. Behind it was the cemetery. Technically, both buildings were located outside town limits, since the Torah forbade burials within a community. My parents and Naomi's father were buried there, in unmarked graves overgrown with weeds. Members of priestly families and the wealthy were laid to rest in a special area under large stones engraved with their Ivrit names.

Itzchak ben Akiba, the town's mortician, greeted us at the door. "The Bethlehem Watch. That's twice in one day. I am honored."

A middle-aged man with a long, unshorn beard and rotting teeth, he looked like a beggar, but he was actually a very wealthy man. If you wanted someone to remove your dead parents and children from your homes and inter them for eternity in accordance with ancient Yehudi burial rituals, Itzchak was your only choice. He was, however, a fair man. He charged more for burying the deceased of wealthy families and waived his costs for the poor.

"Are the two Isiyim still here?" Commander Shaul asked.

"Yes. I was just getting ready to prepare them for disposal." Itzchak also earned a portion of his living burying the bodies of felled criminals in several mass graves in an isolated corner of the cemetery.

"I need to see them," I replied, urgently.

Ushering us into a large room that reeked of decay, he led us to a table and pulled back a burial shroud to reveal two corpses. Both men were tall and thin. Keffiyehs covered their heads and faces and their white cloaks were torn and stained with blood. *My sweet Naomi did this?* I wondered.

I turned to Itzchak. "Please remove their clothes."

Itzchak looked horrified. "Oh, no, the Isiyim have strong prohibitions against revealing their bodies, even in death."

"They aren't Isiyim," I replied.

Itzchak looked to Commander Shaul for guidance.

I was losing patience. "We need to examine them thoroughly."

"Remove their clothes," the commander ordered.

Itzchak stepped back. "I cannot. But were you to overpower me, I would be unable to prevent you from doing so."

Commander Shaul gently pinned the old man's arms behind his back.

"Oh, help, help me, protect me from these defilers," Itzchak murmured, as I removed the cloaks. Underneath they wore only loincloths. There were deep gashes in their chests. Naomi—or the spirit that had possessed her—had done an admirable job. But there were no tattoos or other markings. I lifted their shoulders to examine their backs. They were bare as well.

I searched the pockets of their cloaks. Empty.

I felt a lump of despair in my stomach. Was it possible that Isiyim really did murder Uriel and later returned to kill my wife?

Another thought occurred to me. I removed the keffiyeh from one corpse and examined his neck. Nothing. But around the other man's neck was a thin leather chain. I slipped it over his head.

Attached to it was an oval bronze medallion. One side was an etching of a pomegranate. On the other, a vine. I reached into my pocket and pulled out the pendant I had pried from Uriel's lifeless hand. I held both out for my colleagues to see. They were identical.

"Cassandra said that one of Uriel's killers said, 'Den boró na to vro.'"

Commander Shaul gazed at the medallions. "Greek for 'I cannot find it.'"

Turning to Constable Elihu, I explained, "Uriel was clutching this in his hand when he died. He must have yanked it from one of their necks in his struggle. But the murderer didn't notice. He didn't know where it was, and, praise Adonai, decided not to search Uriel's body. The saltseller knew his murderers weren't Isiyim and, in his last act, held onto it as evidence."

Commander Elihu looked puzzled. "What do the symbols mean?"

"I will tell you later. Itzchak, I need to borrow this pendant for now, but will you be willing to swear, in a court of Law, that you saw me recover it from this body?"

"Of course," replied Itzchak.

"Thank you. And now I must examine one more thing." I really didn't want to do this but I owed it to both Uriel and Naomi. I flipped both corpses onto their backs and, suppressing the urge to gag, removed their loincloths.

Commander Shaul's eyes widened. Constable Elihu refused to look until the commander ordered him to. When he did he gasped. Even the mortician seemed surprised. "Itzchak, may I also ask you to delay disposing of the bodies until Commander Shaul authorizes you to do so?"

Wrinkling his nose, Itzchak said, "The corpses are already beginning to decay. The smell—"

"Please. Just for one day."

Itzchak looked at Commander Shaul, who signalled his approval and added, "And don't let anyone near them. I don't care if it's a priest, the king or Emperor Augustus himself. If they have a problem send them to me."

I stared at my old friend with newfound admiration. Were my stubborn, headstrong ways rubbing off on him?

Next, we climbed to the top of a nearby hill on the northwest outskirts of town. After searching through the brush and sand for a few minutes, Constable Elihu said, "Here!"

We joined him near a swath of flattened grapevines and two sets of deep parallel ruts that extended from the crest of the hill down to the Yericho road, which connected that ancient town to the Pilgrim's Highway.

"A wagon of some sort?" asked the young constable.

"Not your ordinary wagon," I replied. "Look how deep these tracks are. It was carrying something very heavy."

We followed the tracks to the top of the hill. They ended next to the remains of a campfire. I stood in the ashes and extended my arm. My fingers were pointing directly at the distant remains of the Bet Shafa.

After returning to the Watch house, Commander Shaul said, "I owe you an apology, Senior Constable. My own antipathy toward the Isiyim blinded me from considering that others may have been responsible for the saltseller's death."

I shrugged. "That's water under the bridge. What matters now is: Are you willing to testify that the two men who attacked my wife were very likely the same men who murdered Uriel ben Teman?"

"Yes."

"And you?" I asked Constable Elihu.

"Yes," he replied, with humility.

"Good," I said. "However, we don't know who they were and, more importantly, who ordered them to do so."

"What should we do next?" asked Commander Shaul.

"*You* shouldn't do anything," I replied. "The Prefect wants me to complete the investigation."

Slapping his forehead, Commander Shaul said, "I realize that with all the excitement going on I never officially swore you back into the Watch."

As he reached into a chest to retrieve my sash and truncheon, I waved a hand. "No. I'm not officially rejoining. Not just yet. There's something I must do first. Legally, I may be able to get away with it as a citizen, but not as a watchman. And the less you know the better."

He stared at me with uncertainty. "Do you swear that you won't violate any Laws?"

I nodded. "I promise I won't violate any Laws. But I may need to bend them very close to the breaking point."

CHAPTER 24

Conduct enough night patrols and you begin to recognize the gait of those who venture out after dark. The man approaching the alleyway was one of them. While most would move cautiously, nervously scanning their surroundings to spot thieves lurking in the darkness, this tall, thin figure strode with the swagger of a chieftain who believed he owned the streets and knew that no one would dare harm him.

So it must have come as a surprise when two weathered hands reached out and dragged him into an alley. When he tried to scream, one hand clamped over his mouth and the other held the point of a dagger to his neck.

"Shout again and I will cut your throat," I hissed. "But do not worry. I'm here to talk, not to kill."

Reb Lemuel was not a fighter. A life of wealth and privilege had made him weak and delicate. He offered no resistance when I guided him to a shed not far away from the mikveh where my wife had cleansed herself a few hours ago. Inside, an oil lamp cast a dim circle of light that illuminated a small table and two chairs. I closed the door. "Sit."

He didn't move.

I pointed the blade at his chest. "Sit!"

Eyes widening, he gingerly lowered himself into one chair. I sat down across from him. On the table was a jar of wine and two cups. "May I pour you some?"

He shook his head. "This is madness. Do you know what the Sanhedrin will do to you? You'll be arrested and stoned to death. Your property will be confiscated. Your wife will be cast out and I personally will make sure she is shunned like a leper in every town from here to Yaffa."

Pouring myself a cup of wine, I replied, "We are not here to discuss my future. We're here to discuss yours. Specifically, whether you will still have one after tonight."

Sheathing the dagger, I continued, "Let me inform you that this shed and this very good wine were provided by Reuven ben Peleg, and that one of his men is standing guard outside. No one may enter or leave unless I say so. Should you try to escape and by some miracle manage to evade my grasp he has been instructed to break your arms and legs. Do you understand me?"

"What do you want?" he snapped. I was impressed. Even now, he couldn't suppress his arrogance.

I took a sip of wine. "Many things, all of which we will get to in time. First, we are here to discuss the murder of Uriel ben Teman."

"Yes," he replied with a smirk. "You didn't believe me when I said that the Isiyim were responsible for his death."

"I didn't believe you then, nor do I believe you now." I placed the two pendants on the table. "Do you know what these are?"

He barely glanced at them. "No."

"Two men disguised as Isiyim tried to kill my wife this afternoon. One of them was wearing this pendant. The other one I found clenched in the lifeless hand of Uriel ben Teman. He apparently ripped it from the neck of his assailant."

"Or maybe it was the saltseller's own pendant and he was trying to prevent his Isiyim murderers from stealing it."

"No," I replied. "Look closely at the medallions. On one side is an image of a pomegranate. On the other, a vine. Do you recognize these symbols?"

He waited a moment before answering. "I have no knowledge or interest in the fashions of the Isiyim."

"I concede that point. However, I find it hard to believe that a man as learned as you wouldn't be aware of Idomite symbols."

His eyes narrowed. "Why would I know of such things?"

"Because they are emblems of King Antipas's reign." I placed my new veteran's pendant on the table next to the other two. "As you can see, the vine and the pomegranate are etched onto the medals the king gave to me, Commander Shaul and the other soldiers who served in his father's army.

These same symbols were also embroidered on the king's keffiyeh. You must have noticed this at the ceremony today."

He said nothing.

I leaned forward. "Why were you there, Reb Lemuel? You were never a soldier."

"As Bethlehem's magistrate it is my responsibility to represent our community at important events."

"There were veterans from many other towns and yet none of them sent their representatives. Not even Yerushalayim itself."

I sat back. "No. You were there for another reason. To conspire with Antipas to get rid of me."

"That's preposterous! You have an overinflated sense of self-importance."

"Really? Once King Antipas discovered who I was he tried to convince Prefect Coponious to arrest me."

"That's understandable. Your rebellious and heretical attempts to promote the false messiah had reached the king's attention. He must have wanted to remove the threat you represented."

"Perhaps, but there were more than thirty of us there. No one knew our names. We were just anonymous old men. Yet, the king's chamberlain knew I was from Bethlehem. How did he know that?"

I waited for Reb Lemuel to answer. When he didn't, I continued, "Here's what I think, Reb Lemuel. Someone tipped him off. Maybe it was one of the other veterans. But I think the most likely informant was the one man who had no reason to be there."

Dangling the pendants in front of him, I said, "You're one of Antipas's spies. Were I a truly suspicious man, I might believe that this whole ceremony was designed solely to draw me out to Yerushalayim where I could be arrested and publicly denounced in the presence of the Idomites, the Sanhedrin and the Romans. But neither you nor Antipas expected the Prefect to take my side, did you?"

Reb Lemuel laughed nervously. "Why create such an elaborate and expensive ruse? Had the king wanted you out of the way he could have had you assassinated."

"Oh, he tried that, too. Over the past few weeks there have been at least two attempts on my life that I know about. These pendants prove that he sent two of his men to murder my wife and me today. These men also matched the description of Uriel's assailants."

"Because they were wearing worthless trinkets they could have bought from a street vendor?" he snorted. "They were Isiyim. They wore Isiyim cloaks and used Isiyim weapons."

I pulled out my dagger and pointed the blade at his face. "Are you willing to stake your life on such a claim?"

His eyes widened, his swagger suddenly dissipating like a cloud of fog evaporating in the morning sun.

Touching the pendants, I said, "The men who murdered Uriel and tried to kill my wife were disguised as Isiyim because King Antipas wanted people to believe that the sect was behind the attacks. But Isiyim do not wear jewelry of any kind. And even if they did it would never bear the symbols of the Idomites, whom they despise."

I let him ponder this for a moment before delivering the knockout blow. "Last, and certainly not least, neither man was circumcised."

His mouth dropped open. "How did you–"

I waved a hand. "There's a reason I'm known as Yehud's most thorough crime investigator. Unlike some of my peers, I'm willing to get my hands dirty if it opens a path to the truth."

I took another sip of wine. "So, now that we have established that the men who tried to kill my wife are not Isiyim, or even Yehudi, who are they then?"

Before he could interrupt, I continued, "The Idomites are known for employing gentile mercenaries. There were several regiments of them in King Herod's army. King Antipas apparently now hires them as spies and assassins.

Of course, under their disguises he would expect his hirelings to wear the talismans of his reign as a sign of loyalty."

Reb Lemuel shrugged. "All right. I will concede that the men who attacked your wife were probably mercenaries. But they did not kill the saltseller. Constable Elihu captured the culprits on Vultures' Ridge. They confessed to the crime and would be awaiting execution if your inept commander hadn't allowed them to escape."

"You are lying."

"How dare you make such an accusation against your magistrate!" he snapped.

Waving the dagger again, I replied, "Do you see me wearing my sash of office right now? No, you don't. That's because I have not yet been sworn back into the Watch. I'm just an ordinary citizen right now. One who, by the way, has credible corroboration of your deception from an eyewitness."

"Really?" he scoffed. "Who is it? A beggar or one of your criminal friends? Whoever it is, he is most certainly a liar."

"Do you think that Constable Elihu would look kindly on such an accusation?"

That shut him up.

"He confessed everything. How you placed the two phony assassins in his custody and convinced him to fabricate a story about capturing them at Vultures' Ridge."

After a long pause, Reb Lemuel replied, "I admit I made up the story of their capture. The two Isiyim came to my house and surrendered. I convinced the constable to participate in the ruse so the Watch would be credited with their arrest."

"I find it hard to believe that Isiyim would surrender to a Sedukim."

"Nevertheless, I had no reason to believe that they weren't the saltseller's killers. They were wearing Isiyim cloaks streaked with blood and carried double-edged daggers. And they possessed pouches of salt."

Was there no end to this man's deceptions? "The two men you delivered to Constable Elihu were Greek actors. You hired them to play the role of Uriel's murderers. You gave them Isiyim garments and daggers and salt pouches you took from Uriel's home. They admitted this to Commander Shaul and me."

"That is completely different than what they told me!" he exclaimed. "I never laid eyes on them until they approached me. If they were actors disguised as Isiyim then it is to their credit that they were able to convince me that they killed the saltseller."

"Oh, you knew they were actors all right."

"What is your proof?"

"On the day of the fire that consumed the Bet Shafa, you said, 'Since the saltseller's murderers have probably returned to Assyria by now.'"

His lips began to tremble.

"Why Assyria, Reb Lemuel? There are no Isiyim communities there. But I know of two men who are from Tyre. Vasilis and Petros, two Greek actors. It was a slip of the tongue and I thought I was the only one who heard it. But Commander Shaul and my wife heard you say it as well. Either you hired those two actors yourself to play the role of Uriel's murderers or someone else hired them on your behalf."

Reb Lemuel stood up. "I demand to be released right now!"

"Whether I release you or not depends on how much longer you will continue spinning your endless web of deceit."

Racing for the door, he screamed, "Help me! Help me! I'm being held prisoner—"

I grabbed his arm and swung him back into the chair. He tried to rise again and I slapped his face. Hard.

He clasped his hand to his cheek and stared at me in disbelief. Assaulting a member of the Sanhedrin was a crime punishable by death.

"I may be an old man with a bad leg, but my muscles and reflexes are as sharp as ever. Remember that."

Leaning closer until our noses nearly touched, I said, "Reb Lemuel, I am normally a very patient man, but the attempt on my wife's life and your limitless arrogance are keeping me in a highly agitated state. If you try to escape again, or raise your voice above a whisper, then the next time I strike you I will use something far more capable of inflicting pain than my hand. Let me also add that from this moment on if you do not answer every single one of my questions truthfully and to my satisfaction, I will leave this room and let Reuven's guard take over this interrogation. You may remember him. Three months ago you sentenced him to one hundred lashes for stealing a handful of shriveled apricots from Avrum the fruit seller. He's been living as a beggar on the Pilgrim's Highway ever since, but Reuven hired him tonight for this occasion. If I let him in I doubt that nothing short of the direct intercession of Adonai Himself will prevent him from exacting his revenge. Of course, if you would like to test this possibility, feel free to lie to me again."

The last vestiges of resistance drained from his face. I almost felt sorry for him. One slap and a threat had turned his world upside down. Neither his position, his wealth or his connections could protect him now.

He reached for the empty cup. I filled it with wine. He downed it all in a single gulp. I refilled it. He drank half.

"Let us start from the very beginning. Who stole the chests from the Notsrim?"

He hesitated for a long time before answering. "King Antipas's agents."

"So, you knew all along that they had originally been given to Yeshua?"

"No. I didn't believe the chests existed at all until they showed up in Nogah's apartment. That convinced me that Yochanan was the rightful and only recipient of these gifts. But at the ceremony today one of the king's courtiers told me the truth. The agents stole the chests from the Notsrim's barn during the night and hid them until Nogah and his wife arrived. They then disguised themselves as princes and brought the chests to their apartment."

I found it hard to believe that he had only learned of this ruse today but since I would never be able to prove otherwise, I moved on.

"Who killed Uriel ben Teman?"

He blinked several times and then answered, "Two of King Antipas's mercenaries disguised as Isiyim."

"And the murder was your idea."

"No!" He finished the wine. I topped it up. "It was the king's idea. The saltseller was convincing too many people to support the Notsrim. The king wanted him silenced. I could have talked him out of it but I only learned of the plan after the saltseller was murdered."

I didn't believe this either but I also had to accept it at face value. "I can understand the reasoning behind the murder, but why disguise the assailants as Isiyim?" I knew the answer. But I wanted to hear it in his own words.

He obliged. "The king believes that the Isiyim are a threat to the Yehudim. He hoped that convincing everyone that they were responsible for the saltseller's death would motivate the Sanhedrin to ask the Romans to eliminate them."

"And you felt the same way."

He nodded.

"And the two men who were falsely arrested for Uriel's murder?"

He pursed his lips. "It is true that they are actors from Assyria."

"How did they become part of this conspiracy?"

"The king was getting worried that the Watch might find the real murderers. So I convinced him that if we staged an arrest it would persuade Commander Shaul to end the investigation. The king agreed and sent the two Greeks, who were staying with him in Metsada, to Bethlehem for a few days of rest."

I tapped the blade of the knife on the table. "Go on."

"One of my guards pretended to arrest them for drunken and lewd behavior and brought them to my home, where I offered to drop the charges if they agreed to play the role of the saltseller's killers."

"Where did you get the salt pouches from?"

"One of my guards took them from his house while it was being purified."

"Was it the king's idea for them to be 'captured' by the Watch?"

His face brightened slightly. "No, that was my idea. Constable Elihu was the natural choice for the job. He's a fellow Sedukim who also despises the Isiyim."

"He's also an honest man. I'm surprised he would agree to participate in this charade."

Reb Lemuel shook his head vigorously. The wine was clearly having an effect. "The funny thing is that the constable really did believe that the two actors were the saltseller's killers. His only lie was to claim that he captured them in the hills."

I refilled his cup and waited for him to take another gulp. Wine dribbled down his beard.

"The whole thing would have ended then and there if Commander Shaul had been able to stop you from continuing your own investigation."

"But he couldn't. That's why you ordered him to fire me."

"The king wanted you dead. But I tried to convince him that if you were removed from the Watch you would no longer pose a threat." He paused. "Obviously, I was mistaken."

About so many things, I thought. But it was time to move on.

"Who smuggled a ribbon viper into the infant Yeshua's cradle?"

He shrugged. "I don't know."

"Who hired bandits to attack the Watch when we were traveling to Yerushalayim with the Notsrim?"

"King Antipas's mercenaries, I presume. I wasn't informed of these plans."

"But you knew that Antipas wished to kill Yeshua, didn't you?"

"I knew that the king wanted the Notsrim to leave Bethlehem. I tried every means possible to convince them to go. For their own protection."

He waved the cup at me, sloshing wine all over the table. "But you watchmen didn't obey my order to evict them. I suppose that left the king no other choice."

"There is always another choice. And your duty, as magistrate, is to protect all law-abiding residents of Bethlehem, not just those you favor."

"And it was your job as a watchman, as well. Yet, you always seemed to cast your lot with the carpenter's son and his Isiyim supporters."

Seething, I replied, "May I remind you that I ran into a burning apartment building to save the life of Yochanan ben Nogah."

"Yes, and I'm sure the Isiyim who set the fire weren't happy that the true Messiah survived!"

"This is the third time you have falsely accused the Isiyim of crimes they didn't commit."

"Maybe not the other two, but of this one I am certain!" Reb Lemuel slurred. "The Isiyim support the claims of the Notsrim!"

I nodded. "That is true. And they also support the claims of the Dorans. The Isiyim believe that both Yeshua and Yochanan are the Messiahs predicted by the Prophets."

A tiny smile formed on his face. "You learned much in Kumran."

Now it was my turn to be surprised. "You knew!"

"Of course I did. One of my guards saw you hobbling along the Yam ha-Melah path. It wasn't likely you were going for a swim."

"But how do you know about–"

"Their ludicrous multiple-messiah theories?" he snorted. "I've spent years studying the beliefs of these heretics."

"Why?"

"You must learn everything you can about your enemies if you ever wish to conquer them."

I marveled at his resourcefulness. In another life he might have made a fine general, gathering intelligence and formulating battle strategies safely behind the lines while never having to lift a weapon.

"Whatever you think of their beliefs, the Isiyim wanted both infants to live. Since you know this, then you cannot possibly believe that they were responsible for the fire."

He waved a hand. "Fine. If it wasn't the Isiyim, it was the Notsrim's supporters who started it."

"I don't think so. Witnesses said they saw arrows falling from the sky. This means they must have been launched from a great height. Yet, the closest hill to the Bet Shafa is more than three hundred yards away. Even the strongest archer couldn't shoot an arrow that far."

I leaned forward. "But the Romans have a siege weapon. A large crossbow mounted to a wagon."

Reb Lemuel took another sip of wine. "So?"

"We found deep wagon ruts and the remains of a campfire at the top of the hill overlooking the Bet Shafa. I think they used it to shoot fire-tipped arrows at the apartment building. At night people would only see the flames, not the machine that fired them."

"Why would the Romans set the Bet Shafa on fire?"

"Because they wanted to get rid of Yochanan."

"Why?"

"Because he's kin to Antipas."

I waited for his reaction. The wine had loosened his emotions. Even in the dim light I could see the blush spread across his face.

"Who else knows?" I asked.

"Only I, the king and his courtiers," he replied. "Or so I thought. How did you find out?"

"Prefect Coponious told me. Until now I couldn't understand why he did. Or why he ordered me reinstated in the Watch. Now I do. He wanted me to prove that Antipas ordered the murder of Uriel and the attempted murders of Yeshua and his family."

"Why would a Roman bureaucrat care about the Notsrim?"

"He doesn't. But he would be concerned if a large faction of Yehudim swore their loyalty to a Messiah who was Antipas's cousin. The Prefect is committed to preventing another rebellion, especially one that might be spearheaded by the Idomites and their mercenaries."

"But if the Romans wanted to get rid of Yochanan, why go through such trouble to transport a machine here? They could easily send their own soldiers to kill him in broad daylight."

"Killing Yochanan would have made him a martyr, and that's the last thing Coponious would have wanted. Prefects are appointed to maintain order, not incite unrest. I don't think the Romans intended to start the fire. They just wanted to scare the Dorans into fleeing Bethlehem. Who doesn't fear mysterious balls of flame falling from the night sky? But I think that one of their arrows accidentally landed in one of the apartments and hit an oil lamp or a straw mattress."

"The Romans would want the Notsrim to flee as well," replied Reb Lemuel.

"That's probably true, but they're less of a threat since they're poor and Yeshua's followers are mostly common people. Besides, Prefect Coponious knew that Antipas was trying to murder Yeshua. If the king succeeded, half of this messiah problem would go away. The Prefect would only have to take care of the other half."

Reb Lemuel waved a hand. "All of this is conjecture. None of it can be proven."

"You've acknowledged that Antipas ordered his men to murder Uriel and admitted your complicity in his scheme to shift the blame to the Isiyim. And you've publicly declared your support for Yochanan. If I were the Prefect, I'd consider you as much of a threat to the Romans as the Dorans."

He gazed at me with bleary eyes. "I am a servant of Adonai and the Laws. He will protect me."

"You are a liar who conspired with the Idomites to favor one Messiah over the other. Do you truly believe that Adonai will save you when the Romans come to your door? If you're lucky, they will let you take your own life."

His head wobbled as he answered, "Sometimes a lie is justified if it's for the greater good. The Patriarch Yaakov pretended to be his brother Esav to receive the blessing of the first born son from his father Yitzchak."

"Are you comparing your actions to those of our ancestors?" I asked, in mock astonishment. "Do you truly believe that your fellow Sedukim would agree? Or your devoted followers like Constable Elihu?"

He laughed. "Constable Elihu is a stupid ewe who is all too willing to be led by the right kind of shepherd. A simpleton with a mind as malleable as clay."

"Really? Are you so sure about this?"

"Yes. He believes everything I say and does everything I ask."

I looked beyond Reb Lemuel's face into the darkness. "Is this so?"

There was a rustling behind us and then a tall, thin figure emerged from the shadows. "Not anymore."

Reb Lemuel tried to stand up. "You–you were spying on me!"

"No, he's serving as my scribe," I replied, slamming him back into his seat. "A witness to your confession."

Comrade Elihu held up several sheets of parchment filled with carefully scribed letters. "I've written everything in Ivrit, the language of the Laws."

"The Sanhedrin will never believe a *watchman's* words," Reb Lemuel scoffed.

"Yet they will believe the word of a fellow Sedukim, one who has proven his fealty time and time again," I replied. "He will even admit to his complicity in your deceptions, won't you, Constable?"

Constable Elihu nodded vigorously. "Yes. I have broken the Laws forbidding the bearing of false witness and will accept whatever punishment the Sanhedrin decides I deserve."

"That may be problematic if the Sanhedrin participated in this conspiracy."

"No!" Reb Lemuel slammed his fist on the table. "I acted alone, with the help of King Antipas's agents. The Sanhedrin was not involved in any way."

"So it was your idea to take the two Greeks to Yerushalayim and allow them to be put on trial and executed for a crime they didn't commit?" I asked.

"No. One of King Antipas's agents was going to accompany us. Somewhere along the way we would free the actors. The agent would injure me and we would later claim that the prisoners overcame us and escaped."

I glanced at Constable Elihu. Our theory about Reb Lemuel's plans for the actors' fate was mostly correct.

"Reb Lemuel, did it ever occur to you that Antipas would never allow the Greeks to live long enough to tell their tale?"

He reached for the cup. I moved it beyond his grasp. He pouted and replied, "What happened to them after they escaped was of no concern to me."

I turned to Constable Elihu. "Constable, as a man whose intricate knowledge of the Laws is far greater than mine, let me ask your opinion: Now that you have heard and documented Reb Lemuel's confession, what do you think we should do with him?"

He thought about this for several moments and then replied, "Senior Constable, if you were not in this room with me and if I was not a lawful man, I would be tempted to beat him to death with my bare hands."

Reb Lemuel nearly fell out of his chair in fear.

"But you can't right a terrible sin by committing another," the constable continued. "So I think we should arrest him and deliver him to Yerushalayim for judgment."

I nodded. "A very wise suggestion. However, we must look at the bigger picture. Putting Reb Lemuel on trial and exposing his conspiracy will only heighten tensions between the Sedukim and Isiyim, the Romans and Idomites, and the followers of Yeshua and Yochanan. Yehud is already a tinderbox waiting for a spark of unrest to stoke another rebellion that will only result in more bloodshed. Worst of all, since these crimes were committed in Bethlehem, the reprisals will start here. I, for one, have seen enough massacres for a lifetime. I do not wish to see our peaceful little village destroyed. Again."

Constable Elihu thought about this for a moment and then asked. "Then what should we do?"

"To cleanse the corruption we must remove it entirely. And quickly."

I pulled out my dagger and stared at Reb Lemuel for several minutes, letting him stew in terror. "Much as I would like to see you hang from a tree, Reb Lemuel, your silence is more valuable at this time. I am willing to keep everything that has been said in this room tonight a secret from the Sanhedrin, the Romans and the Idomites."

"Senior Constable, I cannot allow–" Constable Elihu interrupted.

I waved a hand. "Hear me out. Constable. Reb Lemuel, I will suppress public revelation of your crimes under five conditions."

Eyeing me suspiciously, Reb Lemuel asked, "What are they?"

"First, you will publicly disavow your advocacy of Yochanan been Nogah as the Messiah. This may put your relationship with Antipas at risk, but it will probably also keep Prefect Coponious away from your door."

He thought about it for a moment and then nodded. "I agree."

"Secondly, you will convince Nogah ben Zilpah to leave Bethlehem and return to Dor. If Yochanan is indeed the Messiah then Adonai will protect him. Therefore it doesn't matter where he grows up, as long as it's not in Bethlehem."

Reb Lemuel pointed a finger at me. "Yes, you'd like that, wouldn't you? Your Notsrim will have no competition."

"No," I replied. "I realize now that Yeshua and his family must leave as well. I will make sure of that."

He seemed surprised. "Easier said than done. I ordered the Watch to evict them weeks ago."

"And until today there was no reason for us to obey that order. But now I'm convinced that Bethlehem must be Messiah-free."

He rubbed his beard. "If both of the families leave then I agree."

"Good. Now for the third condition. The scholars' gifts rightfully belong to the Notsrim. However, I don't think they have any use for frankincense or myrrh. But they will require funds to start over in a different place. So, you will take half of the gold and bring it to Constable Elihu, who will deliver it to Yosef."

His eyes widened. "How will I convince the Dorans to let me take what they believe is rightfully theirs?"

"That's your problem. Tell them it's a tithe for the synagogue. Or tell them the truth. I'm sure you'll think of something."

He sighed. "Fine."

"Fourth, even though we agree not to bring this matter to the Sanhedrin, I will need to tell Commander Shaul. He deserves to know the full story behind the theft of the gifts and Uriel's death. It's for his own protection."

"But what if he arrests me?"

"Constable Elihu and I will do our best to convince him not to. In any case, the issue will be moot, in light of the fifth and final condition."

He frowned. "You are saving the most difficult one for last, I suppose."

I nodded. "Yes. You must retire from the Sanhedrin and leave Bethlehem forever. Furthermore, you must not move to Yerushalayim or any part of Yehud currently under the direct control of Rome or King Antipas."

His jaw dropped. "That's preposterous!"

"No it's not, since Naomi and I will do the same. I'm sure the king hasn't given up on trying to kill us. And who knows who else he'll go after once his kin have left town. All of our lives are in danger right now and that makes everyone in Bethlehem a target. To protect our community, we all must go."

"I can't leave!" cried Reb Lemuel. "I've lived here my whole life!"

"You never married, your parents are dead and your only remaining sister lives with her husband in Perea. Retire and join her there."

"I'm a magistrate! People depend on me for guidance in the Laws!"

"I would think that your recent actions have destroyed any credibility you may have had as a legal authority."

There was still some fight in him. "And how can I believe that your wife will willingly give up any possibility of seeing her son again?"

I shrugged. "We lost him to the Isiyim long ago."

He rubbed his beard. "There's one problem. How will I convince Nogah ben Zilpah to leave Bethlehem?"

I had to admit I was having the same concerns about Yosef. Yeshua's followers had given the poor carpenter a home and a thriving business. Now I would be asking him to start all over again. He couldn't return home to Notseret, which was still under the control of King Antipas. I doubt that the Idomite king would welcome his cousin's messianic rival into his territory.

I was beginning to despair of the entire idea when suddenly Comrade Elihu chimed in. "Makat bechrot!"

It took me a few seconds to translate the Ivrit phrase. "Kill the eldest sons?"

"The slaying of the first born!" said Constable Elihu, excitedly. "When we were slaves in Egypt, the Pharaoh threatened to kill our first-born sons. Instead, Adonai sent the Angel of Death to kill the first-born sons of the Egyptians."

"What does this have to do with—" asked Reb Lemuel.

"The Prophets and traditions say that the Messiah will be a first-born son, born in Bethlehem to a direct descendant of King Dovid. If you were King Antipas, how you would try to keep the Messiah from fulfilling his destiny? By killing all the eldest sons born in Bethlehem who claim King Dovid as an ancestor. We could warn the Notsrim that the king plans to kill Yeshua. That might convince them to leave."

Warming to the idea, I said, "Okay. But what about Nogah? Why will he believe that his cousin the king wants to kill Yochanan?"

"Murdering family members is an Idomite tradition," replied Reb Lemuel. "It's how they stay in power. King Herod himself executed his wife and three of his sons. Nogah must know that King Antipas wouldn't think twice about killing him and Yochanan if he believed they posed a threat."

With cautious optimism, I replied, "This could work, especially if I can convince Yeshua's followers of the danger. Reb Lemuel, you will convey this threat to Nogah and Yochanan's supporters."

I noticed the troubled expression on Constable Elihu's face. "Constable, do you have a problem with this plan?"

"Yet more lies," he sighed.

"Perhaps. But at least these will save lives rather than endanger them."

He nodded, slowly.

Turning to Reb Lemuel, I said, "Do you swear to Adonai, Elohim, El-Shaddai or whatever name you call our Creator that you will abide by the five conditions I have laid out to you?"

After a long minute, the magistrate replied, "Yes, I swear to Adonai."

"Commander Elihu, take Reb Lemuel back to his home and help him pack his belongings and accompany him to meet with the Dorans. Do not let him out of your sight until you are satisfied he has fulfilled all the promises he has made tonight, including leaving town. Oh, and one more thing."

I gave him a purple pouch. "These coins belong to Uriel's daughters. Please find a way to locate them and give them their inheritance."

The constable took the pouch and tapped Reb Lemuel on the shoulder. The magistrate rose unsteadily to his feet and followed him out the door. May Adonai forgive me, but I felt absolutely no mercy for the man.

After several minutes, I grabbed the parchments and extinguished the oil lamp. I left the shed and informed the guard he was free to go. As I was closing the door, a figure emerged from the shadows. "Did your interview end with satisfaction?"

"Nothing about this is satisfying in any way," I replied. "How is Naomi?"

"She has purified herself and now sleeps like the dead," said Reuven.

The relief I felt could have filled the entire alley. "Good. Thank you."

"It is my pleasure. So, what happens next, my friend?"

I took it for granted that he had held an ear to the wall of the shed during my interrogation. "First, I need to meet with Commander Shaul. Then I must awaken Naomi and take her home to pack our possessions. We must leave Bethlehem as soon as possible. But before we go I must sell my home to raise funds for our journey."

He rubbed his chin. "You should have no problem. It is a sturdy house blessed with fertile soil."

"Good. Will you pay me a fair price for it?"

He laughed. "I own plenty of properties in Bethlehem and elsewhere. Why should I purchase yours?"

"Because you'll be able to re-sell it at a tidy profit. And because of the other benefits."

"Such as?"

"Well, for one thing, you'll have one less watchman to worry about. It's unlikely that Commander Shaul will find a replacement for me anytime soon. And, more importantly, Reb Lemuel will be leaving Bethlehem as well. It will take a while for the Sanhedrin to appoint another magistrate. This will give you a lengthy window of time to conduct and expand your businesses with minimal legal harassment."

"My goodness. Your discussion with our learned legal authority has led to these auspicious tidings?" His sly grin confirmed that he had been eavesdropping. But we needed to play our little pantomime to its conclusion.

"Let's just say that Reb Lemuel and I agree that Bethlehem will be a safer place if we're both no longer here."

I told him about the plan to spread a rumor about the makat bechrot to convince Yosef and Nogah to leave.

He nodded. "If you wish, I can spread this rumor around town and expand the scope of King Antipas's death threat to include all census pilgrims who traveled here to claim to be descendants of King Dovid. This should convince most of them to leave."

I smirked and replied, "I sense that your motives aren't entirely altruistic."

He grinned. "They will all need provisions for their journeys home, which my outfitters will be only too happy to supply."

Waving a finger at him, I said, "If I hear that you're overcharging them, I'll come back and yank that gold tooth right out of your mouth."

"Perish the thought. I may even offer a discount as a demonstration of my civic duty." He grabbed my hand. "I shall miss you, Senior Constable. For a watchman, you had a very sensible view of where the eye of the Law should gaze, and when it should look the other way."

"Thank you. And, for a criminal, you've always acted righteously when it truly mattered."

He leaned in close and whispered, "So, where shall you go? No, wait, better that you not tell me, just in case the king's men or the Romans feel a need to question me. I'm not sure how well I would stand up to torture."

"Don't suffer on my account. Tell them I'm heading east, to Persia."

"Ahh," he tapped his nose. "Perhaps you can take a side trip to Bavel on the way and visit the tomb of my ancestors."

"If I have time. Now, how much will you pay me for my property?"

His offer was far more generous than I expected.

"Thank you. I'd like half of that in silver and the other half in supplies for our trip. I'll give you a list in an hour. Everything must be ready by sunrise."

"It shall be done."

"Good. And now we must part, as I have a long list of errands to complete, starting with convincing my wife that going into exile isn't such a bad thing."

With a chuckle, he replied, "I wish I could be there to witness this negotiation. The Prophet Moshe may have had an easier time persuading the Almighty not to destroy the children of Yisroel for worshipping the golden calf."

CHAPTER 25

The sun had barely risen above the hills and already I was sweating in my new gray cloak. I'm sure Naomi wasn't very comfortable in the beige burka that covered everything except her face.

We stood next to a caravan of five covered wagons lined up on the Hebron road just south of town. Each wagon was hitched to two mules. Behind us, a large group of townspeople was tearfully saying goodbye to Yosef, Miryam and the infant Yeshua, handing them loaves of bread, satchels of figs, olives and dates and jars of water and wine. Their wagon was heavy with furniture, bedding, and Yosef's tools. Ours, on the other hand, was relatively empty. Other than food and drink all we had taken from our house were our Kiddish cup and Shabbat candlesticks, several blankets, our cooking pots and utensils, two plates, four large amphorae of water and our clothes. I also dug out the chest of shekels from the pasture and, at the last minute, grabbed my army battle armor and half-eaten shield.

On our way here we had noticed many other hastily loaded carts and wagons heading out of town. Apparently, Reuven had been successful in spreading rumors of the makat bechrot. It was strange to see large expanses of bare ground that until recently had been crowded with tents and makeshift hovels. Bethlehem was returning to normal. For everyone else.

Squeezing Naomi's hand, I said, "I am truly sorry that it has come to this."

She smiled. "Do not worry, my husband. After what I did to those two men I could never live in that house again."

"If the Romans decide to get rid of the Idomites we may be able to return someday."

"I don't need to. Unlike you, I have no ancestral ties to this town. Or a son to give me comfort in my old age. I can live anywhere, as long as you are at my side."

I held her hand. "No man has ever had a more beautiful and supportive wife."

"That is true," she replied, squeezing my fingers.

The loud clearing of a throat alerted me to the presence of Yosef and Miryam. As usual, she was holding Yeshua. How much the infant had changed since I first gazed upon him nearly a month ago. His head was fully covered with curly brown hair, and his large brown eyes gazed at me with a mixture of curiosity and wisdom beyond his years.

"Excuse me, Senior Constable?" asked Yosef.

"I'm no longer a watchman. You can call me Gidon."

"Yes, well, I've been speaking with the Friends of the Messiah. They're questioning why we must leave Yehud."

I sighed. Unlike Naomi, it hadn't been easy convincing Yosef and Miryam to abandon their home. Fortunately, the news that Nogah ben Zilpah and his family had left town in the middle of the night eased their resistance. The large satchel of gold coins Constable Elihu had delivered earlier this morning also helped. But what I think finally convinced Yosef to leave were the three couples who agreed to accompany them. Reuven had used a portion of the money he had paid for my property to provide the mules and wagons, each of which was provisioned with food and water to last several weeks. One of his men delivered the rest of the money to me at sunrise. Judging by the heaviness of the bag, I assumed that Reuven had used some of his own fortune to build and stock our caravan. I tried to think of it less as charity and more as an investment in his future prosperity.

To Yosef, I said, "We have to travel as far as we can to avoid King Antipas's reach. You won't be safe anywhere in Yehud."

"Adonai's love for Yeshua will protect us," replied Miryam.

I sighed. The girl could be infuriating at times. Especially since she had been right every time so far. "Perhaps, but it would be better if we weren't so dependent on His protection. And if we settle anywhere in Yehud your presence will cause unrest that will draw the attention of the Romans, who need very few excuses to spill innocent blood. Where we are going there will be fewer Yehudim. I doubt your enemies will want to travel so far to find you."

For a moment it looked like Yosef was going to protest. But then, unless I was imagining things, I noticed Yeshua staring at him. His large head bobbed up and down.

Yosef sighed. "All right."

When he was out of earshot, I said to Naomi, "Did you see that? I think Yeshua somehow convinced Yosef to agree with me."

Expecting her to call me a fool, I was surprised when she replied, "You are a most persuasive man."

After Yosef and Miryam had completed their farewells, I motioned for them and their companions to take the reins and get ready to move out.

"Halt!"

I turned. Commander Shaul and Constables Elihu and Amos stepped out in front of me. Last night I had met with the commander to debrief him on my interrogation of Reb Lemuel and our mutual agreement to leave Bethlehem. To my surprise, it took little effort to convince him to refrain from mentioning any of this to the Sanhedrin. Perhaps he realized that with Reb Lemuel gone his life was about to become a lot easier.

He placed a hand on a mule and said, "Senior Constable, I have not given you permission to retire from the Watch and leave Bethlehem."

I dropped to the ground and approached him. "Since I was never officially sworn back into the Watch, I don't need it."

"That may be true, but once a watchman, always a watchman. And you may need this on your journey ahead." He reached into his pocket and held out my official Watch truncheon.

With mixed feelings I gazed at my trusty old weapon. "That is very kind, but I am armed with my sword and dagger and have several clubs and spears packed away in the wagon." I didn't mention that Naomi had Yosef's knife concealed in the folds of her burka.

"Take it anyway, in case you ever decide to become a watchman somewhere else."

Gingerly taking the truncheon, I said, "Thank you."

"Of course, you will need more than weapons to fend off evildoers. Constable Elihu?"

The young watchman handed me a heavy blanket. "Open it."

As I unwrapped it I was nearly blinded by a flash of light reflecting off hundreds of metal links. It was a brand new set of chain mail. Naomi gasped.

Commander Shaul smiled. "Dov the blacksmith crafted this for one of his Arab customers, but we persuaded him to let us purchase it for you instead."

For once, I was speechless. But since my fellow former watchmen continued to gaze at me expectantly I removed my father's battle armor and strapped myself into the new mail. It fit perfectly.

"I will wear this with honor," I said, trying to choke back tears.

They nodded. But that wasn't enough. These men weren't just my colleagues. They were also my brothers-in-arms. And brothers needed proper farewells.

Approaching Amos, I said, "Farewell, Junior Constable. You've proven your worth as a watchman these past few weeks, and I expect that stories of your future exploits will spread across the desert to my ears."

He grinned. "I slipped three bottles of the Yaffa wine you like into your wagon."

I laughed. "If you don't stay with the Watch, you may have a future as a politician."

We shook hands. I then turned to Elihu. His face betrayed a mix of emotions. "Constable Elihu, I know that you and I have had our differences. And I know it must not have been easy for you to confess your complicity in Reb Lemuel's scheme. That took a great deal of courage."

He nodded. "I offered to resign from the Watch. Commander Shaul wouldn't let me."

"With good reason. The Watch needs you more than ever, if only to remind the Sanhedrin that its job is to serve and protect all Yehudim, not just those who share their beliefs."

Pulling him aside, I whispered, "And you need to protect Commander Shaul. He's going to be under a great deal of scrutiny, and he will need to know that you are guarding his back. In turn, you will learn many things from him, as I have. This knowledge will come in handy when you take his place as commander one day."

Constable Elihu's eyes widened. "Me? I'm not fit to lead the Watch."

"Not now. But your promotion to senior constable will place you on that path."

"What—"

"Shhh! It's supposed to be a surprise. Commander Shaul and I discussed it last night. He agreed that someone needs to take my place in the ranks and that it was time for you to live up to your potential."

"But after what I did. Conspiring with Reb Lemuel—"

"A terrible mistake, yes. But one that hopefully has taught you something about the nature of sin and how even the most pious among us are not necessarily immune to its temptations. Remember this the next time you're thinking about arresting a drunk or a sloppy butcher."

He was about to say something, but stopped and extended his hand. I shook it and patted his arm. "Good man. One important quality of leadership is knowing when to speak up—and when to shut up."

Now it was time for my most difficult farewell. "Goodbye old friend."

Commander Shaul haltingly fingered his sash. "It has been an honor serving with you in times of war and peace. I still don't know exactly where you're going, but wherever you travel may Adonai clear the way for you."

Blinking back tears, I reached out and embraced him the way old soldiers always do, in a combination of strength and emotion conveying unspoken memories and secrets born of a lifetime of shared triumphs, failures and friendship whose bonds can never be unraveled by distance and time.

As I watched them go, I finally allowed the tears to flow. When my former comrades were out of sight I jumped onto the buckboard and cracked the whip. Our journey had begun.

We continued for several hours in a southeasterly direction along the dusty, winding road. Merchants and pilgrims passed us heading north toward Bethlehem. Under my new chain mail I was sweating as much as the mules, but I dared not risk removing it. Who knows what awaited us beyond the next curve?

At mid-day we sighted two distant minarets that marked the location of the tombs of the Patriarchs Avraham and Yitzchak. We were on the outskirts of Hebron. As we entered a narrow valley between two low hills, a group of shadowy figures emerged from the shelter of an outcropping and stood in the middle of the road a hundred yards away.

I signaled for our caravan to stop. As the figures approached, I turned to Naomi. "Get inside the wagon and don't come out until I tell you."

A second later her hand emerged, the handle of the knife clenched in her palm. "No. You need my help."

The confidence in her voice worried me. I knew all too well that once you overcame the horror and guilt of killing your first man it was so much easier to kill your second...and third. I added this to my growing list of justifications for leaving Yehud. But right now, I needed her skills. "All right."

We jumped to the ground. "Stay here and keep watch."

I ran back to the three wagons driven by Yeshua's followers. "Grab your weapons and prepare to defend yourselves!"

The three couples who accompanied us weren't fighters. But they knew the risks of joining our entourage and had stocked their wagons accordingly. Without hesitation, they grabbed pitchforks, carving knives and clubs and moved into position surrounding the wagon carrying the Notsrim.

Returning to Naomi, I said, "Well, at least Yeshua will be protected."

"And I will protect you," she replied.

"May Adonai protect us all," I added, unsheathing my sword as the strangers approached. There were ten of them. They wore fezzes and short tunics that exposed their bare legs and feet. Their weapon of choice was the shamshir, the curved sword favored by Persians.

Desert bandits, I guessed. Their strength was in their numbers, but they were not accustomed to fighting. They probably only attacked merchants and travelers who didn't employ professional guards. People they thought would buckle down and give them what they wanted.

I smiled. *How wrong they are.*

Pointing my sword at them, I yelled, "Do not step any closer!"

The leader, a tall man with a long black beard, shouted, "Should we quiver in fear of a caravan of tradesmen?"

I cursed myself for not being more vigilant. They had probably been observing us from the surrounding hills. Had they been armed with bows they could have picked us all off at any time.

"If it is money you want, I can give you two hundred shekels."

He laughed. "King Antipas will pay us five times that amount to deliver the Notsrim and a hundred more for the head of the famous warrior who protects them."

I groaned. I had hoped to avoid spilling more blood, my own most of all. How had Antipas's spies gotten word of our journey to him so quickly?

The bandits began to spread out. I could take on three at most. Naomi might be able to stop one more. That left six armed assailants facing off against a farmer, a weaver, a baker and their wives.

Naomi must have been reading my mind. Waving the blade of her knife, she said, "At least we have the Messiah on our side."

I laughed. "One of them, anyway." I then murmured, "Yeshua, now would be a very good time to prove once again that you're a Chosen One."

To this day, I'll never really know whether the infant heard me or not, but as soon as the words left my lips there arose a great swirl of wind that filled the air with sand and dust, making it impossible to see anything more than a few feet away.

The blade of a shamshir suddenly cut through the dust swirls. I parried it with my sword and then thrust forward, feeling it pierce through fabric and flesh. A moment later, the bandit leader fell to the ground in front of me.

"Naomi, are you all right?"

I heard a low-pitched wail followed by a thud as another bandit landed on his back to the left of me, his hand fruitlessly trying to stem the flow of blood from his throat.

Even though Naomi was only a few feet away I couldn't see her. But I could hear her. "I'm unharmed, my husband! Which cannot be said of the man who just tried to kill me—" Another scream of pain echoed through the air. "Or this one. Oh dear."

"Can you see the others?"

"No."

I reached through the swirling sands and grabbed her arm. "Come with me!"

We ran toward the wagons, fighting against swirling eddies that pushed us back. We heard more screams. A huge man suddenly lunged at me, his shamshir held high. I slapped it away with the flat slide of my sword and then swung the truncheon up to smash him in the jaw. *Shaul was right,* I thought as he fell to the ground.

Then, suddenly, the wind began to die down. We ran to Yosef's wagon. Three of his followers were still standing, their features obscured by the slowly dissipating dust clouds. Ten feet away I saw the shadowy outlines of three bandits splayed on the ground.

"Are you all right?" I shouted.

"Yes!" one yelled. "The Messiah saved us! He sent a great wind that stopped the men who would have murdered us!"

I looked around for my wife. "Naomi?"

From the other side of the wagon, I heard her shout, "I'm over here. Three more of the bandits are down. Everyone else is fine."

"What about the Notsrim?"

Miryam poked her head from under the tarp of their wagon. "We're unharmed. Adonai's love for Yeshua has protected us once again."

Is there anything more annoying than a smug teenage girl? I thought as I limped to the other side of the wagon. Yeshua's three other followers stood, holding their unbloodied weapons and staring at three more fallen bandits. *Did Yeshua do all this?* I wondered.

"Gidon!"

I turned in Naomi's direction. Four more figures emerged from a lingering dust cloud.

I groaned. *Do all the assassins in Yehud know we're here?*

Stepping forward, I yelled, "Take one step closer and you're dead men! We've got a Messiah and we're not afraid to use him!"

A dim figure, surrounded by dust, raised a hand and shouted something I couldn't hear.

I heard a loud cry. Naomi rushed past me. I tried to stop her and then lurched forward into the swirling dust. I blindly swung my sword with my right hand and the truncheon with my left and made contact with something hard.

"Hey!" shouted a familiar voice. "Is this any way to treat your own flesh and blood?"

Two hands grabbed my wrists. "Gidon! How could you strike your own son?"

The dust subsided. Naomi was standing in front of me. She let me go. Standing beside her was Binyamin, dressed in his usual linen cloak and keffiyeh.

I shook my head. *I should have known.* "Are you hurt?"

Binyamin unwound his keffiyeh and shook his hand. "Fortunately, you only hit my weapon." The broken remains of a club lay at his feet.

"Sorry," I replied. "Just for once it would be nice if you identified yourself before you joined a fight."

"I didn't have time," replied Binyamin. "We just got here."

"Before or after we were attacked?"

243

"After."

In the distance I saw a group of Isiyim staring down at the fallen bandits.

As if reading my mind, Binyamin replied. "Four of your assailants are dead. The others are unconscious. We'll bind them so they won't escape."

Naomi and I gazed at each other and silently agreed that he didn't need to know that she had killed two of them.

"How did you find us?"

"Our agents informed us that you would be leaving," he replied. "They heard rumors that you were traveling east."

Glancing at Naomi, he continued, "However, as the son of Gidon ben Einan, King Herod's wiliest soldier, I knew better."

I winced.

"I remembered the many stories you told of the deceptions and misdirections you and Shaul used to fool foes with superior numbers and weaponry. I convinced our leaders that Persia wasn't your destination."

"But we could have gone anywhere. How did you know we'd be here?"

"Because the Hebron road leads to the port town of Eilat, where ships can take you to Oxyrhynchus."

I smiled. "How did you guess?"

"It wasn't a guess, just a logical conclusion. Oxyrhynchus is a long way from Yehud. Antipas is reviled in Egypt, so it's doubtful he'll have many agents there. The small community of Yehudim who live there don't practice ritual sacrifices, don't make pilgrimages to the Temple and don't believe in messiahs, so it's doubtful that Yeshua's presence will cause unrest. Plus, Mother may still have kinfolk there who will be able to get you settled."

Naomi patted his cheek. "You always were an intelligent and perceptive child."

I looked around. Isiyim now seemed to be everywhere. "How many of you are here?"

"Twenty."

"Who's taking care of the cooking and the cleaning back home?"

He shrugged. "They'll manage."

"So many of you," I marveled. "I always thought you Isiyim only traveled in small groups."

"Normally this is so, but this situation called for added protection," replied a familiar voice. I turned to see a figure in a white burka emerge from behind the wagon. Only her eyes were visible.

Before I could speak, she grabbed Naomi's hand. "I am so pleased to meet the wife of the Moshiya and the mother of Binyamin, one of the Isiyim's most promising acolytes."

Naomi glanced at me, her eyes asking, *Who is this?*

"Naomi, this is the Nochmah."

My wife didn't seem very happy to meet her. "So you're the one who convinced Binyamin to abandon his family and become a cave-dwelling hermit?"

The old woman shook her head. "Me? No, I never met him in person until yesterday. But, collectively, yes, we Isiyim are notorious for wooing Yehudi sons from the comfortable bosoms of their families with our seductive promises of lifelong poverty, chastity, hunger and back-breaking toil. Isn't that so, Binyamin?"

My son smiled. "As you say, Nochmah."

"Why are you here?" I asked. "I thought they don't let you out of your sanctuary."

"On certain occasions I insist on freedom of movement," she replied. "Today, for example, I'm here to make sure that this caravan's leader is heading along the correct path."

Huffily, I answered, "I didn't realize I needed your approval—"

"Not you!" she hissed, waving an arm. She climbed onto Yosef's wagon. "Parents of Yeshua, show yourselves!"

Yosef and Miryam lifted the flap.

"Give the child to me," she commanded.

Later I decided that the Nochmah must have been practicing sorcery because without hesitation or suspicion Miryam handed Yeshua over to the old woman.

The Isiyim and Yeshua's entourage formed a circle and together we watched her rock the baby in her arms and press her ear to his lips. He gazed at her with his usual expression of calm and curiosity.

After several moments she handed Yeshua back to Miryam. "Thank you."

"Is that it?" I asked. "Aren't you going to bless him?"

She shook her head. "Only a rabbi or a priest can bestow blessings and I am neither. Besides, the child has already been blessed by Elohim."

"Then you just wanted to find out what a Messiah feels like?" I asked.

Looking both ways, she drew me aside so we could speak privately. "No, I held him so I could accurately augur his future."

I waited a moment before asking, "And?"

"The prophecies are mostly correct. While Yeshua will become a beloved rabbi, his life will be short and end in the painful and lonely throes of martyrdom."

"You got all this from holding him for a few minutes?"

She nodded. "Yes. He shared his thoughts with me. When he reaches adulthood he will establish a ministry. His teachings and miracles will create a loyal following throughout Yehud. But the Romans will arrest him for causing unrest and execute him by nailing him to a tree. His death will create a schism pitting the priests and Sedukim against his followers, many of whom will share his tragic fate. And—"

She paused.

"And what?"

"Yeshua's followers will not spread the Yehudi religion throughout the world. Instead, they will start a new faith based on his teachings and a belief that he is the divine son of Elohim. It will be embraced by millions of gentiles and eventually will become the official religion of the Romans. However, most Yehudim will disparage this new faith, only to find that they are falsely blamed for Yeshua's death. In retribution, many will be murdered and thousands more will flee to distant lands to avoid persecution."

I rubbed my chin. "Hmmm. That doesn't sound promising. What about Yochanan?"

"At an early age he will join the Kanai and spend most of his life leading raids against the Romans. When he is an old man his followers will proclaim him the Messiah. But instead of restoring the kingdom of Yisroel, he will lead a massive rebellion that will be violently suppressed."

"Yes, you told me this."

"But I know more now. Yochanan and his followers will make a last stand in the fortress at Metsada. They will hold out for a year against a Roman siege. But they will finally run out of food and water. Rather than submit to enslavement or execution, Yochanan and his followers will kill themselves."

She paused before continuing, "As punishment, the Romans will destroy the Temple and end the priesthood. Thousands of innocent Yehudim will be slaughtered. Thousands more will be enslaved. Most of those who are left will also leave Yehud. Before two centuries have passed, more Yehudim will live outside the Holy Land than within it."

I thought about this for a moment. "Wait a minute. You said you only augured Yeshua's future after you held him in your arms just now."

"Yes."

"Then how did you learn of Yochanan's fate?"

"The same way."

I stared at her suspiciously. "When did you meet him?"

"The morning of the fire at the Bet Shafa," she replied. "Apparently, you didn't notice me. This is understandable, given that you were busy saving his life at the time."

Only two days had passed since the fire, yet already my memories were fading. I could vaguely recall the flames, the smoke, my burning hand, people dousing me with water as I ran out of the building–

And then I remembered. "The woman in the burka who took Yochanan away from me."

She nodded. "Yes. I had come to Bethlehem the night before to meet Yochanan and his parents and hold the child in my arms. I only wish that something other than a fire provided the opportunity."

I rubbed my chin. The Isiyim would never have let her come alone. But I didn't remember seeing any men dressed in white linen cloaks and keffiyehs that day. Of course, they were very good at keeping out of sight.

"Your actions during the inferno confirmed your destiny as the Moshiya for both children," she added.

Suddenly, the enormity of what I had done filled me with resentment. "Some protector I am. If I had known that safeguarding these infants would lead to a future of misery for our people I might have been tempted to let both of them die."

She gently patted my arm. "I understand your remorse, but I know that you would never stand by and allow the innocent to perish. And if it will bring you some comfort, I now know what will happen if Yeshua and Yochanan do not both live to fulfill their destinies. The successors of Emperor Augustus will no longer tolerate our religion. The Romans will end the reign of the Idomites. Instead of destroying the Temple, the Romans will install their idols there and bribe and coerce the cowardly priests to conduct ritual sacrifices to their gods. They will invade Kumran and annihilate the Isiyim. They'll dissolve the Sanhedrin, close down the synagogues and outlaw the study of Torah. They'll forbid Yehudim who don't become idol-worshippers from owning property or businesses and won't permit them to emigrate. Trapped in an occupied land and believing that Elohim has forsaken them, most Yehudim will abandon our faith. Within four generations there will be fewer than a hundred Yehudim left in the world."

She let all of this sink in for a moment. "So you see the paradox here: Our survival as a people depends on the failure of Yeshua and Yochanan to fulfill the traditional role of the Messiah as the restorer of the kingdom of Yisroel. Only by totally destroying ancient, outdated institutions in Yehud while simultaneously exiling most of our people to distant lands can we ensure that our faith will survive."

"I would think that exile and isolation would make us lose our faith, rather than keep it."

"Ah, but remember that the children of Yisroel were foreign slaves in Egypt for four hundred years, yet during their captivity they cried out to Elohim, rather than the Egyptian gods, to deliver them from bondage. And when they wandered the desert for forty years, they always believed that the Holy One would one day lead them to the Promised Land."

I nodded. "Good point."

"And when the Bavel invaded Yehud, destroyed Yerushalayim and sent our people to exile in foreign lands, they never lost faith that Elohim would eventually let them return. We remember our Covenant most fervently when we are strangers among gentiles. You will see this when you meet the Yehudim of Oxyrhynchus. Many are descendants of those exiled by the Bavel. They're outnumbered a thousand to one by idol-worshippers, but their piety would make even the most stalwart Sedukim seem like apostates by comparison."

Gazing at Binyamin, who was still talking to Naomi, she continued, "Indeed, the Yehudim of Egypt are already showing us what the future of our people will be. With the Temple gone, pilgrimages and sacrifices will no longer be required, enabling Yehudim to settle in all four corners of the world. Synagogues will become the center of Yehudi worship and learning, and rabbis and scholars will replace priests as our spiritual leaders. Yehudim will have to rely on their own moral fortitude and righteousness, rather than outdated rituals, if they wish their names to be inscribed in the Sefer ha-Chaim –the Book of Life. This is the new Covenant Elohim will establish with us."

She placed a hand on my shoulder and said, "I am telling you these things to inspire you to complete your journey, rather than to cause distress. In any case, most of us standing here will be dead long before any of these events take place. So you need to focus on the here and now. On taking your wife and son and Yeshua's family to Egypt, to make sure they will be safe until Antipas is no longer a threat and they can one day return to Notseret."

As I stared into her eyes, I wished that she hadn't come here today. It was so simple when my only concern was to get us all to the sea, where we could board a ship to take us away from this troubled land. But now I felt that the fate of the Yehudim rested on my shoulders. What if more bandits awaited us on the road ahead? What if Antipas's own mercenaries came after us? What if–

"Wait a minute. You said my *son?*"

A moment later, I heard Naomi cry out in joy. "Gidon! Binyamin is coming with us!"

It wasn't even noon yet and already the day had enough surprises for two lifetimes. Turning to Binyamin, I asked, "You're leaving the Isiyim?"

"Only temporarily. Yeshua needs an experienced bodyguard to make sure he and his family arrive and are settled safely."

Bristling with indignation, I replied, "This caravan already has an experienced bodyguard." Gazing at Naomi, I added, "Two, actually."

He grinned. "But not an experienced young bodyguard."

To the Nochmah, I asked, "The Isiyim approve?"

"The rabbis were resistant at first. But I can be very persuasive."

Another thought occurred to me. "You said the Isiyim were protecting both Messiahs. But Nogah ben Zilpah and his family left Bethlehem last night."

She nodded. "Eight Isiyim are shadowing their caravan."

"Is Nogah aware of this?"

By the twinkle in her eyes I could tell she was grinning. "No. And, if their train is not accosted by fools–"

Or Romans, I thought.

"–He never will be."

I imagined a squad of bushy-haired men in white cloaks hiding in the hills as they watched over the wagon taking the Dorans home. I wondered what

King Antipas would think if he knew his kinfolk were traveling under the protection of his mortal enemies?

"Oh, there is one more thing," said the Nochmah. "It wasn't easy convincing the Isiyim to let so many of us take leave from our community at one time. So I offered to solve a problem they were unwilling to address themselves."

I knitted my brow. "Which is?"

"Me."

I turned to see a small thin woman dressed from head to toe in a white burka. Several locks of red hair flitted through her eye-slit.

"Cassandra?"

She nodded. "Yes. I hope you don't mind if I join you."

I glanced at Binyamin and then at the Nochmah. "But—"

"Cassandra can't stay with the Isiyim forever, and she has nowhere else to go. In Oxyrhynchus she can start a new life. Preferably not in her former profession, but that is, of course, up to her."

I glanced at Naomi, nervously. She stared at me with hard eyes. "This is she?"

I gulped. "Y-yes."

Naomi approached Cassandra. "I am Naomi, the wife of Gidon ben Einan. You are the gentile whore who witnessed the murder of Uriel ben Teman?"

Cassandra raised a finger. "Half Yehudi."

"And you dragged my son Binyamin into this mess?"

"Yes."

Turning to me, Naomi concluded, "And without her involvement you never would have met the Nochmah and learned of your appointed role as the Moshiya of Yeshua and Yochanan, leading to the events that have reunited us with our son?"

Nervously, I answered. "I suppose that is true."

Naomi placed her hands on Cassandra's shoulders. "Welcome."

I sighed in relief. Binyamin and the Nochmah seemed relieved as well. Then one of Yeshua's followers stepped forward. "Are we truly going to allow a whore to accompany us?" Pointing at Yeshua, he said, "What would the Messiah say?"

I looked around. I had killed two men today. Naomi had killed two more. Someone—or something—had incapacitated the others.

I placed a hand on the baby's head. "My guess is that if Yeshua could speak he would say, 'Only if you have lived a life fully free of sin are you entitled to condemn others.'"

A loud squeal emerged from the baby's lips. Looking down, I could swear he was smiling in agreement.

The Nochmah waved a hand and four Isiyim stepped forward. "And now, we must return home. We will take custody of the surviving assailants."

I raised an eyebrow.

"Don't worry. We will allow them to live. Perhaps not as comfortably as they're accustomed to, however. Farewell, Gidon ben Einan. Remember that the Holy One journeys with you."

I laughed. "I don't think He cares where I go. It's the child who is important."

"No. Today you all walk with Elohim. And may every step take you closer to Him."

I nodded. "Safe travels."

We watched the Isiyim and the bandits disappear into the hills. Naomi then stepped between Binyamin and me and grabbed our hands. "It is good for our family to be together again, even if it is only for a short time."

Binyamin patted his stomach. "Do you have anything to eat, Mother? I've had nothing but a handful of raisins today."

"We slaughtered our four lambs before leaving. We were going to save them for a celebratory feast once we arrived in Eilat." Naomi turned to me. "But after all we've been through today, perhaps we should have it earlier?"

I gazed at her and then at my son and Cassandra. And then at Yeshua, Yosef and Miryam. And then at the three couples who had given up everything to follow their Messiah into a future that, according to the Nochmah, would not turn out to be anything like they expected. If I told them that Yeshua would someday die at the hands of the Romans, would they turn around and go home? Perhaps. Or perhaps not.

Faith is a funny thing. After he crafted my battle armor, my father had it blessed by a priest in Yerushalayim to provide an added layer of protection. How many times had Adonai saved me from the thrust of a Nabataean's spear or a bandit's club? How many times had I filled graves with the corpses of foes and thanked Him for allowing me to survive? How could I have wooed and won a woman such as Naomi without the Holy One letting the love in her heart overcome the public stigma of marrying a man of lowborn birth?

Maybe the Nochmah was right. Maybe I truly was the Moshiya. If this were true, I was reasonably certain Adonai wouldn't abandon me now. And, to be honest, I could use a break from all the excitement.

I motioned for everyone to gather around me.

"We rest here, near the tombs of our ancestors Avraham and Yitzchak. After we bury the dead, we will have a mid-day meal. We will build a fire and roast our lambs, one of which we will offer in sacrifice to Adonai. I am hopeful that will He forgive us for not using a priest. We will then have a feast in His glory. After that, we will continue, all day and all night if necessary, until we reach the sea."

Gazing at Yeshua, I said, "I don't know what else awaits us. But I have a very strong feeling that the Almighty will guide us there safely."

As Binyamin, Yosef and I dug graves and Naomi and the other followers built a fire and set up a table with bread, olives, figs and wine, I thought about the Nochmah's predictions. Was it really true that both Yeshua and Yochanan were destined for violent deaths at the hands of our enemies? Would the Temple be destroyed? Would the Yehudim become a people living forever in exile?

And were these two Bethlehem-born infants truly aware of their tragic fates? If so, Yeshua at least seemed to be bearing his burden with calmness and dignity. I hoped Yochanan was as well.

The skeptic in me said that no one, not even the Prophets, could truly foretell the future. But maybe it was possible to nudge it along. In our caravan, and in another one many miles north of us.

However, as the Nochmah said, that was their future, not mine. Perhaps, generations from now, a scribe sitting at his desk in a synagogue far away from the reaches of the Roman empire would chronicle the lives of two infants who changed the history of our people. No one would remember the roles an old soldier, his wife and son, a whore, a community of cave-dwellers, a rural village, and a ragtag squad of watchmen played in this story. We weren't kings, Prophets or legendary warriors. We didn't part the sea, draw water from stone, blow down city walls with a ram's horn, slay giants with slingshots or vanquish mighty armies.

But if what we did today enabled our ancient people to survive into the far future, then, borrowing a word from a prayer traditionally chanted during Pesach when we told the story of the many miracles Adonai performed for the children of Yisroel as He led them from slavery out of Egypt, we could say "Dayenu:" It would be enough.

THE END

ABOUT THE AUTHOR

Jeffrey Briskin is a writer and marketing professional. He lives in the greater Boston area.

Learn more about the making of *Bethlehem Boys* at www.bethlehemboys.com.

Made in the USA
Monee, IL
08 July 2022

MEL RENFRO

Forever a Cowboy

To Sam.
Best Wishes

Mel ~
20 ~ Ren
HOF 96

9-10-2016